Ryan looked at his old friend. "You know what to do, J.B."

His hands up, the Armorer stepped into the line of fire. "Now, take it easy," he said to the tall, backlit figures just inside the cave entrance. "You know we can't hurt you. You don't have to prove anything more to us. We're giving up. See?"

Black figures approached with their laser rifles pointed at his head. One of them came within ten feet of him before it stopped. "Where are the others?" it asked.

"Yahhh!" J.B. bellowed at the top of his lungs.

Ryan echoed the yell as he swung out from behind the rock. The others yelled, too, as hard as they could, to keep from being deafened as the Smith & Wesson pump gun roared in the enclosed space. Orange flame from the muzzle blast licked the ceiling. Ryan racked and fired, racked and fired as fast as he could. On the third blast, there was a mighty groan from above, then in a cloud of dust, the ceiling of the entry chamber came crashing down.

Other titles in the Deathlands saga:

JAMES AXLER

DEATH LANDS®
Breakthrough

A GOLD EAGLE BOOK FROM
WORLDWIDE®

TORONTO • NEW YORK • LONDON
AMSTERDAM • PARIS • SYDNEY • HAMBURG
STOCKHOLM • ATHENS • TOKYO • MILAN
MADRID • WARSAW • BUDAPEST • AUCKLAND

First edition March 2002

ISBN 0-373-62567-7

BREAKTHROUGH

Copyright © 2002 by Worldwide Library.

Printed in U.S.A.

We first crush people to the earth, and then claim the right of trampling on them forever, because they are prostrate.

—Lydia Maria Child
1802–1880

THE DEATHLANDS SAGA

This world is their legacy, a world born in the violent nuclear spasm of 2001 that was the bitter outcome of a struggle for global dominance.

There is no real escape from this shockscape where life always hangs in the balance, vulnerable to newly demonic nature, barbarism, lawlessness.

But they are the warrior survivalists, and they endure—in the way of the lion, the hawk and the tiger, true to nature's heart despite its ruination.

Ryan Cawdor: The privileged son of an East Coast baron. Acquainted with betrayal from a tender age, he is a master of the hard realities.

Krysty Wroth: Harmony ville's own Titian-haired beauty, a woman with the strength of tempered steel. Her premonitions and Gaia powers have been fostered by her Mother Sonja.

J. B. Dix, the Armorer: Weapons master and Ryan's close ally, he, too, honed his skills traversing the Deathlands with the legendary Trader.

Doctor Theophilus Tanner: Torn from his family and a gentler life in 1896, Doc has been thrown into a future he couldn't have imagined.

Dr. Mildred Wyeth: Her father was killed by the Ku Klux Klan, but her fate is not much lighter. Restored from predark cryogenic suspension, she brings twentieth-century healing skills to a nightmare.

Jak Lauren: A true child of the wastelands, reared on adversity, loss and danger, the albino teenager is a fierce fighter and loyal friend.

Dean Cawdor: Ryan's young son by Sharona accepts the only world he knows, and yet he is the seedling bearing the promise of tomorrow.

In a world where all was lost, they are humanity's last hope....

Prologue

A chunk of burning plastic the size of a softball sailed past Dr. Huth's lowered head. Smaller objects, bits of concrete, shards of metal and rock, pelted his arms and legs as he struggled down the middle of the street under the terrible weight that lay upon his shoulders, a weight that bent his back to the breaking point and made his thighs tremble.

Seven levels below the surface of the planet, in the swirling smoke of open trash fires, a mob packed the crumbling sidewalks and spilled onto the potholed roadway. Their angry chant of "Die, whitecoat, die! Die, whitecoat, die!" echoed off the two-story-high, gridwork concrete ceiling and the wall-to-wall buildings that lined the gritty street. Like an earthquake, it rattled the No Response Zone's few surviving windowpanes.

This was Gloomtown, so named because neither the light of day nor the dark of night penetrated here. Mercury-vapor lamps caged in the soot-stained ceiling cast a perpetual sulfurous pall over its squalor and suffering. In Gloomtown there were no police. No emergency services. And there was no way out, alive or dead.

As Dr. Huth advanced along the mob's gauntlet, grinding out one shaky step after another, tears flowed down his cheeks. Everything he had ever done in his remarkable scientific career, he had done for them. Not for "them" individually, of course, or even for "them" as a social class, but "them" as in, for the survival of humanity.

The survival of Huth's species had become an issue shortly after the turn of the second millennium A.D., when the long-sputtering population bomb had finally gone thermonuclear. Now, less than a century later, the planet was supporting one hundred billion people, and the rationing of food to the multitudes had become the all-consuming task of science and the one-world government known as FIVE. Because of the shortage of available calories, economic, social and political control teetered on the verge of global collapse. Dr. Huth and the other top scientists of FIVE were like whitecoated little Dutch boys sticking their fingers in a massively leaking dike. Their desperate measures had produced unforeseen and disastrous consequences.

Several structural levels down, a few hundred yards directly below Dr. Huth's feet, was the border of the Slime Zone, a vast area of the megalopolis made uninhabitable by an invasion of agricultural bacteria, the result of a failed attempt to solve the food problem. In computer simulation, the genetically altered cyanobacteria had looked like a perfect answer to the crisis. They were fast breeding, required no maintenance and were an inexhaustible source of easily digestible protein. Outside FIVE's biotech laboratories, they had proved themselves all of that, and more.

Once actual cultivation began, despite the protective measures put in place, the tailored bacteria quickly escaped the confines of the deep-level slime farms and began to swallow up the lower sections of the megacity, block by block. All efforts to turn them back, and to reclaim lost territory, had failed. And the irony was, the protein-rich bacteria were no longer even harvested for fear of spreading the contamination.

Because of Gloomtown's proximity to the Slime Zone, its residents lived under constant threat of suffocation. When the bacterial spores were inhaled, they bloomed in the lungs, rapidly filling them with their wet weight. Only the condensation layer of the atmosphere, a band of land fog at Level Eight, kept the slime at bay. If the climate fluctuated so much as a few degrees, Gloomtown would be enveloped by floor-to-ceiling drapes of smothering green slunk.

The cyanobacteria weren't the only lethal whitecoat-created hazard Gloomtowners faced on a daily basis. Equally deadly was the carniphage, an escaped biotech mil weapon. When inhaled, it ate a person from the inside out, stripping flesh from bone. The carniphages remained dormant in rivers and lakes for most of their life cycle, but during their reproductive phase, clouds of them were carried on the wind, eating and killing every animal in their path.

When the megacity's warning sirens announced an impending bloom of carniphages, the people of Gloomtown packed themselves into windowless rooms and closets, and sealed the doors with rags and dirt. Those caught outside were found after the all-clear, their bones picked clean, plastic bags or trash cans pulled over their heads. On the upper levels of the city, for the convenience of FIVE's CEOs, its whitecoats, and its white-collar support staffs, there were ample, roomy, phage-proof shelters.

How the carniphages had gotten loose in the environment was still a mystery. Some claimed FIVE's Population Control Service had released them on purpose, to slow the growth of the unemployable class.

"FIVE" stood for the five global conglomerates who, after the big shakedowns of the nineties, had by treaty divided up the rights to exploit the remaining resources of the earth. Those four capital letters were stitched in crimson above the breast pocket of Dr. Huth's lab coat.

In the boardrooms of the globals, Huth was a very important man, considered a genius comparable to, if not surpassing, Newton, Einstein and Watson and Crick. As director of the Totality Concept, he had shifted the focus of its most advanced research program from time trawling—the dragging of objects or persons from the past or future to the present—to the creation of a passageway between parallel universes. Using Operation Chronos technology as a foundation, he had succeeded in establishing a corridor between nearly identical alternate existences, between his Earth and another, which had come to be known as Shadow World.

After sending robot drones, then a human exploration team through the passage, Dr. Huth had discovered that the event horizons of the twinned Earths had permanently diverged on January 20, 2001, when an all-out nuclear exchange had devastated Shadow World. Though its human population had been nearly wiped out, the catastrophe had left many of its natural resources intact. Which presented a simple, elegant solution to his own Earth's problems: colonize Shadow World, relieve the population pressure by moving selected, qualified people to the new resources. It was nothing less than a second chance for the human race.

Unappreciated in some quarters.

Under a hail of rocks and burning trash, the tall, lanky scientist strained to keep moving forward with his burden. Perhaps the Gloomtowners had correctly concluded that they wouldn't be invited to partake of Shadow World's salvation. Perhaps that was the reason for this horrible mistreatment. If so, it was typically selfish and shortsighted of them.

Then Huth caught a glimpse of a grimy video billboard suspended from the ceiling, and the live picture of himself that was being projected to the crowds. When he saw what he was towing through the streets, he froze in disbelief.

It was a guided missile more than one hundred feet long.

The startling image reminded him of a vid he'd seen as a graduate student. It had shown a single ant struggling to carry an impossibly huge beetle carcass back to the nest. That vid had to have been at least twenty-five years old when he'd viewed it; the last ant and beetle had long since departed this reality.

As Dr. Huth stood there immobilized, gasping for breath, some of the mob dipped into the latrine buckets they'd brought along and splattered him with handfuls of bloody excrement—evidence of yet another failure of science to solve the global food crisis.

The ingenious whitecoats of FIVE had genetically tailored a bacterium whose internal processes could turn igneous rock into something edible. But when the pseudo-fast-food product was consumed regularly, its mineral components built up in the human body, giving rise to a range of alarming physical symptoms, including bloody stools and psychopathic behavior. Despite the known side effects, FIVE dispensed Beefie Cheesies and Tater Cheesies by the truckload to placate the Gloomtowners. The discarded plastifoil wrappers swirled ankle deep around the feet of the mob.

A fresh hail of stones cut Dr. Huth's cheeks, forehead, and neck. He knew he had to keep moving or be stoned to death. His long legs quaking from the effort, he broke the missile's inertia, but managed just a few more steps before collapsing under the weight of the nose cone, which pinned him to the street, crushing the air from his lungs and making him pass out.

Merciful oblivion lasted only a heartbeat.

Dr. Huth awoke with a gasp, his burden gone. He flew upward in a metal mesh cage, his wrists shackled together with two feet of chain. Looking up from his manacles, he realized he hadn't completely escaped the missile. It now stood upright, its riveted skin gliding past him in a white blur as the elevator rose.

He also sensed he wasn't alone in the cage.

Dr. Huth whipped around, and in so doing came face-to-face with the human from the parallel world, the man he had ordered brought back to Earth for examination and interrogation. This was the same tall, rangy savage who had somehow managed to escape not just FIVE's custody, but its reality, as well, and in so doing had created untold havoc and destruction.

The one-eyed man stared back at him with malice. A scar from a knife slash, like a crudely drawn lightning bolt, divided his left brow and cheek above and below the black eye patch he wore. Black curling hair fell almost to his shoulders. A leather sheath strapped above his left boot carried a huge knife. In his right hand he held an equally massive chromed wrench.

Though he called himself Ryan Cawdor, FIVE's media consultants had renamed him "Shadow Man," and turned him into a symbol of hope for the starving masses. His birthplace on the parallel Earth was Deathlands, the heavily nuked, former United States of America.

"Why have you come back here?" Dr. Huth said. Behind Cawdor, a half-dozen children—filthy, hollow eyed, swollen bellied—clung like monkeys to the outside of the rising elevator cage. Huth ignored their bony little outstretched hands and demanded, "Where are you taking me?"

Shadow Man didn't answer either question. He held something inside his mouth, a round shape that bulged against the dark stubble of his cheek.

When the gantry elevator stopped, once again Dr. Huth faced the tip of the missile. He was relieved to see that there was no door in the side of the nose cone, and therefore no possible way he could be placed inside.

Shadow Man spun him, and with a forearm crushing against the front of his throat, pinned his back to the nose cone. Cawdor then grabbed the manacle chain and jerked it up, forcing Huth's arms above his head. Though the scientist struggled, the one-eyed man easily controlled him. Cawdor fitted a bolt through a chain link, threaded it into a matching hole in the nose cone and, using the chromed spanner, quickly torqued it down.

As Cawdor retreated a step, Dr. Huth bawled, "Why are you doing this to me?"

Shadow Man smiled and curled back his lips. Between his front teeth he held a human eyeball with a sky-blue iris. Its color and size perfectly matched his good right eye, as well it should have. Dr. Huth had had the eye genetically reconfigured to fit him, a replacement for the one Cawdor had lost to a knife slash years ago. The gift had been intended as an awe-inspiring demonstration of the biotechnological power of this reality, and of how cooperation with FIVE was rewarded.

When the scientist started to speak, Cawdor lunged forward, slamming a forearm back across his windpipe. Shadow Man took the severed eyeball from his own mouth and shoved it between Dr. Huth's teeth. His lips clamped shut by a callused palm, Huth could do nothing but whimper as the savage wound turns of duct tape around his head, sealing the eyeball inside.

While the scientist tried not to strangle on the mouthful, the monkey children rattled the cage's mesh, mocking his predicament by inflating their cheeks with air and bulging and crossing their eyes.

From the foot of the gantry, the rhythmic chanting of the Gloomtowners resumed. Shaking and pushing the structure, the mob rolled the gantry away from the missile. Huth's feet slipped off the edge of the platform's floor, and his full weight dropped onto his upraised wrists. His muffled shriek of pain was followed by a raucous cheer from below. As he dangled from the nose cone, as the gantry continued to retreat from the launch pad, the elevator started its rapid descent. Ryan Cawdor and the monkey children dropped from view, abandoning the scientist to his fate.

Which he now realized was a twenty-second-century version of crucifixion.

He was being punished for his contributions to a better way of life, to freedom from hunger and illness, the eternal banes of humankind. He had offered his world the salvation of science and in return...

A terrible rumbling came from below.

It grew louder and louder, and as it did, the vibration set his guts shimmying and made the trapped eyeball quiver between his tongue and the roof of his mouth. With a blast of flesh-melting heat, and the deafening bellow of wide-open rocket motors, the missile leaped upward. The jolt of liftoff caused the eye to slip back into his throat, blocking his airway. Huth had no choice; he gulped it down whole.

As the missile climbed and climbed, engines roaring, his body buffeted against the missile, his arms felt as if they were about to tear free of his shoulder sockets and the swallowed eye rolled around in the pit of his belly like a cannonball.

DR. HUTH AWAKENED on his hands and knees, retching. The violent spasms seemed to start from the soles of his feet, rippling through all the muscles of his body, building a terrible momentum that peaked as they reached his throat. He dry-heaved, over and over. Long strands of bile trailed from his lips into the powdery red dirt beneath his face.

When the convulsions finally subsided, he slumped onto his side. Disoriented and confused, Huth clung like a drowning man to his only clear memory. Moments ago, he had been in the Totality Concept's trans-reality laboratory. He had been there when the missile he had already sent across to Shadow World, a missile meant to put a recon satellite in orbit, had nosed instead back to his Earth, back through the shimmering lips of the passageway, its gigantic rocket motors thundering.

How that singular horror had come to pass, he had no way of knowing, but certainly the goal of firing the missile back through the corridor had been to destroy the connection between parallel worlds. Given the fuel capacity of the missile, and the fuel's volatility, there was every reason to expect the strategy had worked.

Huth had a much less distinct recollection of being sucked through the reality portal in the backwash from the rocket's exhaust, like a dry leaf caught in a whirlwind. That memory was jumbled with a nightmare of horrible punishment and death. Thinking about it made his mind wheel violently, so he forced himself to stop and pushed up on an elbow.

He was surrounded by an open space that stretched unbroken to the horizon in all directions. The sudden absence of physical boundaries, of human-scale walls and ceilings, filled him with heart-pounding panic, but he resisted the urge to bury his head under his arms.

Above him, the dome of the cloudless sky was still tinged with the rose-pink of dawn. The sparkling air felt strangely light in his lungs, and so dry it tickled inside his nostrils. He sat near the edge of a broad, flat table of rock the color of dried blood, elevated above the surrounding plain by several hundred feet.

The mobile missile gantry was nowhere in sight. Also missing were the five explorers who had preceded him through the passage. If this was Deathlands, and he had no reason to doubt that it wasn't, he had been deposited in a different spot, perhaps near the original landing site, perhaps not. Huth could only surmise that either the missile's full-power reentry into the passage or its subsequent explosion at the heart of the Totality Concept complex had distorted the shape of the reality corridor, shifting its terminus at this end.

Huth rose stiffly to his feet and took stock of himself. The left sleeve of his lab coat was fire-blackened from cuff to elbow, but he wasn't bleeding anywhere and he had no apparent broken bones. He patted his pocket and was relieved to find the instruments he'd slipped into it moments before the disaster. Both the microcomputer, which was the size of a playing card, and an equally small electron microscope seemed to have made the journey intact. The other scientific tool he'd brought along he carried locked away in his brain, and that was the Twenty-five Theories, which linked all human knowledge. With just these three artifacts, he was confident that he could reconstruct most of the advanced technology of his Earth.

Though the timing of the crossing had been accidental, Huth had been on the verge of departing his reality, with or without FIVE's approval. The most recent computer projections gave nine-to-one odds that the predicted mass die-off of humanity would occur within the next three months. Based on past experience with the CEOs, he couldn't be one hundred percent certain that they would let him use his own invention to escape. That decision had been taken out of FIVE's hands, and thanks to what he carried in his pocket and brain, Huth was in a position to become the most powerful man in the history of either Earth— as he saw it, a combination of Leonardo da Vinci, John D. Rockefeller and Joseph Stalin.

Huth stepped to the edge of the deeply rilled, red rock mesa. There were more mesas in the distance on the other side of a wide desert plain, and far behind those table rocks loomed a range of snowcapped mountains. Bisecting the plain were remnants of a prenukecaust highway, a ribbon-straight ghost of four-lane interstate. Lying across the old highway at odd intervals were great, tilted slabs—the fractured remains of fallen overpasses. At the horizon line to the northwest, the sun glared off something shiny. A body of water, perhaps. If the passageway's terminus hadn't shifted very far, it occurred to him that it might even be the remains of the Great Salt Lake.

As he continued to scan the landscape below, Huth saw white smoke rising in a thin column in the dead still air, indicating a human presence, if not a settlement of some sort, not more than ten miles away.

The scientist let out a whoop and celebrated his good fortune by dancing an ungainly jig. Then he carefully boulder hopped down a steep chute that led to the foot of the mesa, and once there, immediately headed across the plain for the ancient roadway.

Up close there wasn't much left of it.

Caustic rains had reduced the asphalt to sand, and had badly pocked the concrete layer beneath. Small, delicate white flowers with bright yellow centers grew here and there along the edge of the highway, sprouting from depressions where water and nutrients accumulated.

Huth picked one of the little daisies and gingerly nibbled at the white petals. Their explosive bitterness made him gasp. He spit them out with a curse, then groaned as the vile taste set him to dry-heaving again.

Pale and shaken, he trudged on toward the distant smoke plume. The only sounds were the scrape of his shoe soles on the asphalt sand and the wheeze of his breathing. The day's building heat made sweat ooze from his forehead. In the flat, shimmering distance lay the first of the dropped overpasses; he made slow but steady progress toward the jumble of concrete slabs.

When Huth first caught wind of the rank, feral odor, he didn't know what to make of it, except that it wasn't coming from him. As he continued walking, the smell got worse. Much worse. Only when the pack of robbers started popping up on either side of the ruined road did he understand the meaning of the noxious stench, and by then it was too late to run.

The dirt-caked, tangle-bearded bandits had been lying in wait in shallow hides they'd hacked into the desert hardpan. Their clothes consisted of countless layers of greasy rags; their boots were repaired with overlapping windings of strips cut from plastic bags. They carried battered black-powder shotguns and revolvers, rusting machetes and nail-studded wooden clubs.

As the robbers encircled him and closed in, the huge man who appeared to be the leader confronted him, toe to toe. He bore spiral-shaped brands on his cheeks and forehead. The angry welts of scar tissue looked like the tracks of some parasitic worm burrowing just under the skin. Below a mustache matted with dried saliva, Huth saw the snaggle stumps of yellow-brown teeth. The tip of the man's wide nose bore a sparse tuft of black bristle, half an inch long.

"Good morning to you," the scientist said, trying not to show his terror, and failing miserably. "I just arrived here from—"

Without warning, someone booted Huth in the buttocks so hard that his feet left the ground, so hard that his legs went numb and his knees buckled under him when he crash-landed. The bristle-nosed robber reached down and grabbed him by the collar, hauled him upright, then punched him straight in the face, breaking his nose and knocking him unconscious.

Huth came to with a moan as the big man kicked him in the ribs.

"What are these?" Bristle-nose demanded, holding a pair of small, flat objects in front of the scientist's bloodied face.

"No, please," Huth gasped, "those are my scientific instruments. Give them back. You can't operate them. They are of absolutely no use to you."

"He's bossin' me," Bristle-nose said to the others as he cocked back his massive fist. "This dimmie bastard's bossin' me...."

Huth saw another short, straight punch coming at him, but there was nothing he could do about it. At the impact, as his head snapped back, something cracked. A lance of white-hot pain shot through his upper jaw, and his mouth was suddenly littered with sharp shards. In a gob of fresh blood, he spit out the remains of his two upper front teeth.

While Huth thrashed and bled, Bristle-nose showed off his booty. "Looks like predark gear to me," he said. "Got to be worth a spoon or two of jolt over in Byram ville."

With that, the big robber turned and started off in the direction of the smoke. The other bandits quickly stripped off the unprotesting scientist's shoes and pants, leaving their victim his blood-sprayed and scorched lab coat and his tattered, gray-tinged under-wear and socks.

Huth waited a long time before he risked uncoiling from a fetal position in the dirt. And he didn't start walking again until the sun was high overhead. Hob-bling slowly toward the shade of the nearest fallen highway overpass, he looked like the survivor of a train wreck. Blood had dried purple black all down the front of his lab coat. He couldn't breathe through his swollen nose, and every time he sucked air through his mouth, electric needles of pain stabbed into the exposed nerves of his emptied tooth sockets.

As he stumbled along, he wept over the loss of his irreplaceable instruments, his permanent disfigure-ment and the unspeakable cruelty of fate. He was still sobbing when he reached the collapsed overpass. What he saw there put his suffering—and his predic-ament—in a new perspective.

At the foot of the largest block of concrete sat a line of sun-bleached human skeletons. He counted fourteen of them, all identically posed, their backs leaning against the block, elbows resting on raised kneecaps. Some were adults, some were small children, some still had isolated patches of hair on their massively caved-in skulls. A couple of feet above the row of drop-jaw grins, someone had chiseled three tall, spindly words into the eroded concrete.

Welkum Too Deflanz.

Chapter One

Fifteen days after a massive explosion destroyed the upper floors of the Totality Concept complex, Dredda Otis Trask stood naked and alone in a windowless stainless-steel room. The small, unfurnished chamber had two doors, both heavily gasketed and airtight. A warm wetness trickled down the insides of her thighs. Not blood, but the remnants of a clear surgical lubricant, melted by her body heat. The CEO of Omnico, one of the most powerful people on the planet, had just had her womb stripped of all its eggs.

In itself, there was nothing unusual about the procedure. On her world, the in-vitro-fertilized eggs of the executive class were routinely carried to term by surrogate mothers conscripted from the ranks of the white collars.

Nor was it strange that Dredda Otis Trask had chosen to have the extraction performed in the secure, private facilities of her own global conglomerate. But Omnico's CEO hadn't surrendered all her potential offspring to a test tube merely for the sake of convenience. Given the nature of the dangerous experimental treatment she was about to undertake, it was a necessary precaution.

Above Dredda's head on a wall bracket was a vidcam, its op light glowing ruby red. A team of faceless, nameless strangers was observing her through the fish-eye lens.

"Please stand beneath the ceiling nozzles," said a voice through the vidcam's speaker.

When Dredda stepped over the center-sloping floor's single drain, the shower spray commenced. The hot water that enveloped her was followed by foaming, pea-green jets of bactericide. After she had rinsed off the foam, vents along the base of the walls blasted her with heated air, drying her to the point of itchiness in a matter of seconds. As she raked her static-charged, auburn hair back behind her ears, an electronic lock snicked and the exit door popped outward a foot.

Through the tiny speaker, the voice said, "Please proceed to Level Three containment."

Dredda immediately moved into the well-lit, polished metal hallway, which was also windowless. She could have touched the ceiling with a raised hand, and the corridor was so narrow it wouldn't permit the full spread of her arms. The air hung heavy with a mist of disinfectant that stung the back of her throat. Auto-tracking vidcams mounted at intervals along the ceiling followed her barefoot progress to the next chamber, which was even smaller.

The bioengineering facility's hazard-containment system consisted of a series of concentric, hermetically sealed, metal enclosures. The more dangerous the biological materials, the smaller the enclosure in which they were stored. Level One's barrier, which took up an entire subfloor of the Omnico skyscraper, encompassed containment Levels Two through Four, Level Two encompassed Three and Four, and so on. Each of the interiors was reverse-pressurized so that if a seal failure occurred, external air would rush in, keeping contaminants from escaping to the next level.

When she entered the tiny room, the airtight door closed behind her. Sheets of tempered glass covered the walls, ceiling and floor; behind the glass were banks of five-foot-long light tubes. Yet another automated surveillance camera stood watch over her.

"Please put on the goggles hanging on the hook in front of you," the voice told her.

After Dredda donned the red-lensed eye protectors, there was a loud thunk, and the surrounding lights all came on at once. The intense ultraviolet bombardment lasted fifteen minutes, during which she was directed by the voice to assume various awkward positions that allowed the germ-killing radiation to reach otherwise hidden surfaces. When the bank of lights finally thunked off, she was told to pull on the pair of plastifoil slippers that waited for her by the exit door.

"You may now proceed to Level Four," the voice said.

The straight steel corridor leading to Level Four had a narrow, bunker-slit window along one wall. Through the three layers of thick glass, Dredda could see dozens of biotech workers in lemon-yellow hazard suits with oxygen canisters strapped to their backs. Because of the glare of the overhead lights off the hoods' visor plates, she couldn't see the workers' faces. And they seemed too preoccupied with their cluttered lab tables and banks of electronic machinery to notice her passing. The corridor ended in a circular bulkhead door, which stood slightly ajar.

The brightly lit Level Four operating suite was the tiniest of the nested defensive boxes—the most deadly and contagious microbial environment on the planet. The hollow steel cylinder was so narrow that the single bed it contained nearly spanned its diameter. On the walls opposite the sides and head of the bed were rows of triple-laminated glass portholes. Directly below the ob ports, from similar heavily gasketed circular openings, rubberized, liver-colored gauntlets hung down in pairs. Shelves packed with medical supplies and equipment ringed all but the foot of the bed.

At the sight of the cramped enclosure, Dredda experienced sudden difficulty in breathing. The observers noted her distress.

"Your anxiety is only natural," the voice said in a reassuring tone. "But it is best to continue without delay. Please climb onto the bed, and we will make you more comfortable as quickly as possible."

Dredda forced herself to crawl forward. The door automatically shut and sealed behind her. As she lay back on the bed, she saw movement through all of the portholes. Technicians in biohazard suits took up positions along the outside of the cylinder and proceeded to thrust their arms into the gauntlets, which allowed them to reach over the bed, more than halfway across her body. All those moving arms made the chamber seem even smaller. And no matter how hard she tried, she couldn't seem to fill more than the top third of her lungs.

To try to calm herself, the CEO focused on her own reflection in the curve of the ceiling. She strained to make out the details of her face, but the brushed metal turned her features into an unrecognizable blur—as if who and what she had been for her twenty-six years had already been erased.

Meanwhile, the pairs of gauntleted hands worked with practiced precision, strapping her down at the chest, waist and knees. Once she was tightly secured to the mattress, the anonymous fingers crawled over her, jabbing the needles for intravenous lines into her arms and inserting a catheter into her bladder. They applied a liquid adhesive to her skin and attached life-signs sensors and neuromuscular stimulators. Finally, gloved hands at the head of the chamber slipped an oxygen mask over her nose and mouth.

Dredda gulped at the hiss of oxygen, which was mixed with a quick-acting sedative gas. It also carried a massive dose of bioengineered virus. After that first deep breath, there was no question of going back. She gladly surrendered to the calm that settled over her.

You are a very brave girl.

Dredda felt hot blood rush to her face and neck. She recognized her father's voice. It hadn't come through the operating suite's intercom speaker; it didn't exist anywhere outside her mind. Regis Otis Trask, the former CEO of Omnico, had been dead for four years.

Whenever her father had said those words to her, and he'd had the opportunity to say them often, what he'd meant was that she was very brave for a girl. Brave considering that because of her sex, she possessed relatively limited physical and mental strength and endurance. Though she had long understood the reasons for her father's patronizing attitude, that had never made it any less painful or infuriating.

Dredda's personal abilities and achievements had very little to do with the power she currently wielded over the lives of tens of billions of human beings. She had inherited her father's position at the top of the conglomerate's executive hierarchy, and she had an army of highly capable, highly motivated defenders dedicated to keeping her there. For as long as she could remember, everyone she encountered had looked past her, or through her, and had seen only her father's awesome legacy.

But Dredda was very much the daughter of Regis Otis Trask. She shared his thirst for conquest and empire, and the need to burn her name deep into the pages of history, desires she could never satisfy as caretaker of a bureaucratic monolith on a dying planet.

For months, preparations had been under way for her unannounced, permanent departure to Shadow World. In secret, Omnico's top scientists had duplicated the Totality Concept's reality-jumping technology, and had managed to vastly improve upon it. The transfer of soldiers and matériel only awaited the successful completion of her Level Four treatment, which for security reasons had been postponed until the last possible moment.

Dredda had committed herself to the irreversible genetic procedure shortly after the CEOs' joint interrogation of the prisoner from Shadow World. The man called Ryan Cawdor had described his Earth as a place of chaos, of perpetual bloody turmoil. Social control did exist, but only in confined areas called baronies, and it was maintained by brute power.

Male power.

To cross over to Shadow World unprepared for that fact would have meant the surrender of everything Dredda had, of everything she had ever dreamed of.

Could Alexander the Great have succeeded if he had been a woman? Could Cortez? Or Napoleon? Her own Earth's history said no. In times of internal strife, during periods of conquest, males only respected other males, only feared other males. These were the lessons of Shadow World, as well. If Dredda failed to instill absolute terror in her adversaries on the parallel Earth, she knew her relatively small expeditionary force could not prevail.

And she not only had Shadow World males to contend with, but those in her own support units, as well. In a different reality, the old urges of one sex to dominate the other would surely resurface. The selective subordination and subjugation of females was bound to follow. Such an outcome was unacceptable to Dredda Otis Trask.

As her father had so often said, "Chains are meant for other people."

It might well have been the Trask family motto.

Dredda became aware of a ringing in her ears, the first sign of the spread of the genetically modified virus. Almost immediately, her body temperature began to rise, and as it climbed, the sedation was increased. Long before the infection's peak, she slipped quietly into a drug-induced coma. She didn't feel the plastic tube slide down her airway or hear the rhythmic hiss of the respirator begin.

The tailored virus carried a limited set of genetic instructions, which as it replicated, it transmitted to all her cells. These instructions permanently altered the chemistry of her body, reinitiating long dormant physical processes, reactivating the growth plates in the bones of her hips, legs, back, shoulders and arms. Under their new instructions, the targeted cells began rapid, controlled division. As her bones enlarged, cell layer by cell layer, they ached as if they had been shattered by sledgehammers; as they enlarged, the attached sinews, muscles and cartilage stretched to the splitting point. Nerve cells began multiplying in specific locations, as well, which only magnified the intensity of the skeletal pain. The transformation process was so agonizing that it required anesthetic narcosis—early test subjects who were fully conscious had died from the pain within a matter of hours.

Safe in a deep coma, Dredda felt nothing. She drifted in darkness while her body metamorphosed in its stainless-steel cocoon.

Inside and outside the chamber, the atmosphere was anything but tranquil. Biotech teams in three shifts saw to her considerable life-support needs around the clock. Her normal daily calorie intake was quadrupled, and she received constant electrical stimulation of new nerves and growing muscles.

Early on the morning of the ninth day, sedation was terminated. By 10:00 a.m. Dredda was breathing without a respirator. At 1:00 p.m. she opened her eyes. She was still securely strapped to the bed. Empty gauntlets hung flaccidly from the walls.

"How are you feeling?" said the voice through the intercom.

"I hurt," she said, her throat hoarse from the respirator tube. "I hurt everywhere."

"That is entirely normal, I assure you. We're going to release the restraints now. You need to start moving your arms and legs."

Technicians slipped into gauntlets on both sides of the chamber. Their gloved hands unfastened the straps, which slithered off her. When she sat up, she nearly bumped her head on the chamber's low ceiling.

"Please be careful," the voice warned. "You have grown four inches. You are now five feet eleven inches tall. You have gained sixty-three pounds."

Dredda looked down at herself. Even though she had known more or less what to expect from computer-morphed projections, she recoiled. Her breasts were still there, and the same size and shape, but they looked smaller, flatter because of the expansion of her chest in bone and muscle. The new muscle mass was smooth, quick, not corded or bulked up. Like her breasts, her hips had remained the same size, but they now looked narrow relative to the increased span of her shoulders.

She ran her fingertips over her lips and chin and was relieved to find no sprouting of coarse facial hair. Although her jaw seemed a little heavier, as did her cheekbones and brow, there was no other apparent external masculinization. She had changed into a very tall, very athletic looking female, the tallest, most athletic female the limitations of her existing genetics could produce. Of course, that was just the tip of the iceberg as far as the changes went.

Dredda flexed her right bicep and, despite a twinge of pain in her elbow, was momentarily transfixed by its unfamiliar bulge.

"Based on the previous experiments," the voice

told her, "your lean-muscle mass should continue to increase slightly for a more few days. The new neural connections are already complete, as is bone growth. You aren't going to get any taller.

"As you know, some experimental subjects, post-transformation, have displayed outbursts of extreme violence. We have only had combat simulations to work from, but it appears that spending long periods of time in a battlesuit under stress aggravates the problem. If you notice any loss of emotional control, you must start injecting yourself with antipsychotic drugs from the battlesuit medikits at once."

"What are their side effects?"

"Reduced reaction time and increased fatigue."

"But that would completely defeat the purpose of the procedure!" Dredda exploded.

The voice didn't respond.

"If I start dosing myself with these drugs, will I have to take them permanently?"

"I'm sorry, but that is impossible to predict," the whitecoat told her. "No one knows the long-term consequences of the genetic treatment you have been subjected to."

The slowly simmering anger that had always been part of Dredda's consciousness was now paired with an entirely different level of agitation, tangible like a hairy-legged insect buzzing, bouncing off the insides of her internal organs. Everything was taking way too long.

"Unseal the door," she said.

The airlock remained shut, and the faceless white-coat talked faster. As he spoke, his gauntleted hands made emphatic gestures above her head. "The viral agent we've used is extremely infectious and prone to rapid mutation and genetic recombination with other, potentially lethal life-forms. Understandably, we are very concerned about its containment. We strongly recommend that you spend another three days in Level Four quarantine to make sure it has all passed out of your system."

The other conglomerates that made up FIVE knew nothing of this lab's existence, nor were they aware of the genetic-engineering project that Dredda had made herself part of. All research connected to trans-reality and bioweapon technology was subject to the terms of FIVE's founding treaty—only to be pursued as a joint venture. If the alliance got wind of what she was up to, they would turn on Omnico and subject it to a combined military attack that would make her escape to Shadow World impossible.

Moving in a blur, Dredda grabbed one of the white-coat's gloved wrists. He tried to pull back, but she held him fast, and as she did, she applied pressure to the slender bones on the back of his hand with her thumb. "Delay of any kind is unacceptable," she told him.

"I understand your impatience—just do not rip the glove. You must not break the Level Four containment. If you relax for a moment, everything will be fine."

The other gauntlets rapidly emptied as biotech workers moved out of her reach.

"Let me out of here now."

"Please, listen to reason...."

There was no reason but hers, no need but hers. Under the ball of her thumb, the small bones snapped like dry twigs. A piercing scream burst through the intercom.

"Open the door!" she shouted. Her booming voice made the walls of the steel chamber vibrate.

Seconds later, the airlock door popped open and she was free.

Chapter Two

Ryan Cawdor stepped over an exposed tree root, slick, dark and as big as a human corpse sprawled across his path. A profusion of bare roots laced the winding trail and made the footing treacherous. The dim light didn't help matters, either. Though it was high noon, everything was cloaked in shadow, thanks to the dense canopy overhead and the seemingly endless groves of black-barked trees.

In all his travels, he had never seen this type of rad-mutated oak before. Its wood was like iron; hand axes bounced off of it, hardly making a dent. The bark and leaves were chem-rain resistant, as were the parasitic strangler vines that spiraled up trunks and limbs to reach the sunlight.

The forest's canopy had protected Ryan and his companions from the searing downpours they had endured since their last mat-trans jump, several days earlier. The intense storm activity of the past forty-eight hours had forced them to take shelter in a cave. From the safety of its entrance, they had winced at sizzling nearby lightning strikes and watched methane ice hail, as blue as robin's eggs and just as big, pound the earth. In scattered heaps, the chem ice had steamed for hours before it finally melted away.

If the local trees and vines had somehow adapted to survive the caustic rains, other types of foliage had not. There was no ground cover to speak of around the trunks, just slippery piles of fallen, blade-shaped leaves that rustled underfoot.

The passing storm front had left the air extremely hot and punishingly humid—it felt equatorial to Ryan. The weather was the only clue where he and the companions had materialized. The cloud cover and forest canopy had made it impossible for them to orient using the stars.

As he rounded a tight bend, he saw the group's pointman frozen like a bird dog fifty feet ahead. Ryan swung to hip height the scoped Steyr SSG-70 sniper rifle he carried. Jak Lauren, his pale skin and lank white hair almost luminous in the forest's half-light, held up a hand, indicating caution. Jak was a man of few words. Fiercely loyal, without an ounce of guile or deceit, he was a true wild child of Deathlands. Jak's weapon, a battle-scarred .357 Magnum Colt Python, remained in its holster. Whatever he'd found, there was no immediate danger.

"Cook fire," Jak said softly as Ryan stepped up, his albino eyes as red as rubies. He raised a hand to point downslope. "There…"

Ryan caught the faintest smell of woodsmoke, filtering up the winding trail through the forest. It was the first sign of another human presence since the mat-trans jump.

It smelled delicious.

For three days Ryan and his companions had been on starvation rations of mutie rattlesnake jerky and tepid water. The forest's lack of undergrowth meant there was no ground-dwelling large or small game for them to hunt. During the day, they had caught a few glimpses of little creatures darting about high in the branches, but the dense canopy made shooting at them a waste of ammo. And at night it was so black they couldn't see their own feet.

Though all their bellies rumbled, no one had complained.

A tall, skinny man, dressed in a dusty frock coat and tall boots, moved up the trail and closed ranks with Ryan and Jak.

Leaning on his silver-handled walking stick, Doc Tanner sniffed at the air, and said, "Dear friends, it would seem that Providence has seen fit to smile upon us once more." He inhaled again, savoring the aroma. "Somewhere below, the groaning board is piled high. Broiled flesh of some sort, I would venture."

Though Dr. Theophilus Algernon Tanner appeared to be a well-preserved sixty, chronologically he was four times that old. The Harvard-and-Oxford-educated man was the first human time traveler, albeit an unwilling one. He had been ripped from the loving embrace of his family in 1896, and drawn one hundred years into the future by the whitecoats of Operation Chronos. The twentieth-century scientists quickly tired of Tanner's ingratitude, truculence and general unpleasantness. Shortly before skydark, to rid themselves of the troublemaker, they had hurled him forward in time. In so doing, they had inadvertently saved him from the nukecaust that scoured away their civilization. Though Doc sometimes rambled in speech and broke into tears for no apparent reason, a consequence of his life's overload of trauma and tragedy, this day he was as sharp as the point of the steel blade hidden in his ebony stick.

A stocky black woman dressed in baggy camo BDU pants and a sleeveless gray T-shirt stepped up behind Tanner. Her hair hung down in beaded plaits. "Smells like somebody's had themselves a hearty breakfast," she said.

Dr. Mildred Wyeth had also time-traveled, but in a much different fashion than her Victorian colleague. After a life-threatening reaction to anesthetic, she had been cryogenically preserved just prior to the all-out U.S.-Russian nuclear exchange of January 20, 2001. She had slept in the land of the dead for a century, until revived by Ryan and the companions. Mildred's weapon of choice was a Czech ZKR 551 target pistol, the same gun she'd used to win a silver medal in the last-ever Olympic Games.

"Whatever it is, it's making my mouth water," said the boy following close on Mildred's heels. At age twelve, Ryan's son, Dean, was already growing tall and straight like his father.

"Dear child, the human nose is by no means an infallible instrument," Doc cautioned as the last two members of the group—a tall, red-haired woman, and the rear guard, a short, bespectacled man in a fedora—moved up the trail to join them. "What we Homo sapiens take for sweet succulence might well be the effluvium of some wayfarer not unlike ourselves. Someone whose grim misfortune was to be caught out in last night's chain lightning. That hell-struck sir or madam could be down there somewhere, quietly smoldering."

Dean made a disgusted face.

"Or it could be a trap," offered the leggy, green-eyed redhead. Because of the sweltering heat, Krysty

Wroth, Ryan's lover and soul mate, had taken off her long fur coat and tied the arms around her slender waist. The only visible effect of the radiation-induced mutations that skydark had inserted into Krysty's family tree was the prehensile ability of her long hair, which reacted to stress like a barometer. Her hair now hung in loose coils, indicating concern but not apprehension.

"Cook smoke could be the bait," agreed John Barrymore Dix, aka the Armorer. Ryan and J.B. shared a bond of blood that went back many years, to their wild and woolly days with the Trader, the legendary Deathlands entrepreneur and road warrior. J.B. rested the barrel of his well-worn Smith & Wesson M-4000 12-gauge pump gun on his shoulder and tipped his sweat-stained hat back on his head. "In a place like this," he said, pausing to thumb his wire-rimmed glasses up the bridge of his nose, "with no game to shoot, nothing growing to eat, a scent trail could draw victims from a long ways off."

Though Ryan respected J.B.'s and Krysty's trail savvy, he didn't consider an ambush likely. There had been no sign of stickies or cannies. No grisly heaps of red bones and bloody rags strewed about. Stickies and cannies, Deathlands most murderous, subhuman residents, hunted in packs, like wolves, seeking out norms—nonmutated humans—and muties alike, and failing that, they would prey on the weakest of their own kind. The condition of the path told Ryan there wasn't much foot traffic, certainly not enough to support the appetite of a large predator, or group of predators.

"Trap or no trap," he told the companions, "we've

got to follow the cook smoke, or we're going to starve in this bastard forest.'' He slung the Steyr and unholstered his SIG-Sauer P-226 pistol. ''Triple red, everybody,'' he said. ''Dean, middle of the file.''

The boy didn't protest his position in the column, but watched with undisguised envy as Doc drew a massive revolver from the front of his frock coat. The gold-engraved LeMat was a Civil War relic. It fired nine .44-caliber lead balls through a six-and-one-half-inch top barrel. A second, shorter, big-bore barrel hung beneath the first, chambered for a single scattergun load of ''blue whistlers''—odd bits of scrap metal and glass that added up to close-range mayhem. Dean left his own weapon, a 9 mm Browning Hi-Power, buckled down in its holster. He was under standing orders from his father not to draw the weapon unless they came under direct attack, and not to shoot unless he had a clear lane of fire.

With Ryan in the lead, the companions headed downslope. If anything, as they descended the winding trail, the canopy became more dense, and the air more humid. As Ryan rounded a turn, harsh sunlight backlit the groves of oaks ahead. Through the trees came the sounds of high-pitched, chattering speech and the rustle of movement. The one-eyed man dropped the blaster's safety and pushed on.

No command to the rear was necessary.

The companions reacted as one, spacing out along the path as they continued to advance. They dropped to their bellies and crawled the last few feet to the edge of the forest.

The clearing before them bordered on a sluggishly moving green river fifty yards wide. The activity was down by the water's edge. A group of three dozen people, men, women and children, all with straight black hair and skin the color of cinnamon bark, were tending thick, hand-braided ropes that stretched back from the river almost to the trees. The children were naked; the men and women wore short kilts.

Inbreeding was common in Deathlands's isolated, primitive communities. Noting the uniform distribution of low foreheads and underslung jaws, Ryan decided that these folks had been at it for a very long time.

Back from the river's muddy bank, nestled in the protection of the ironwood canopy, stood a ragged row of translucent yellow shacks made of tanned hide or skin that was stretched and tied over curving supports that looked like gigantic rib bones. Cooking pits lined with red hot coals had been dug in the soft earth. Whatever food had been roasted over them earlier had already been polished off.

Jak tersely summed up the cinnamon people's armament. "No blasters, just knives."

Ryan nodded. Their weaponry consisted of bows and arrows, spears, knives and short swords. And the edged weapons weren't made of metal, or even flint. To Ryan the blades looked like bone. Serrated bone. Given the twentieth-century firepower he and the companions carried, the villagers presented no real threat.

The breeze shifted suddenly, swirling along the bank. Cook fire odors were overpowered by a terrific stench.

"Smells like dead fish," Dean choked. "Tons of dead fish."

"Ugh, I just lost my appetite," Mildred said.

"Don't trouble yourself over that, my dear," Doc stated pleasantly. "If past is prologue, it will return to you shortly, and tenfold..."

At one time, Ryan would have expected the black woman to go ballistic over the snide remark. Not because she was the least bit sensitive about her weight, which was appropriate for her body type, but because of the outrageous presumption that being a woman, she should have been sensitive about her weight. Mildred had learned to fight fire with fire when it came to dealing with the bony old codger's needling.

"And how's the tapeworm doing today, Doc?" Mildred asked back sweetly.

Ryan pushed to his feet. "Come on, let's introduce ourselves," he said. "Stay alert. Watch the flanks."

The companions emerged from the forest, fanning out with weapons up and ready. The river people were startled at first, but they said nothing. None of them made a move to approach or to retreat from the armed intruders. After a moment or two of standoff, the villagers surprised Ryan and the others by pointedly turning their backs on them, and refocusing their attention on the murky river and their braided ropes, each of which was strong enough to tow a war wagon.

When Ryan advanced and opened his mouth to speak, a man wearing a translucent fish-skin vest held up a hand for silence. There was a warning in his extremely close-set black eyes. He pointed at the river, which silt and algae had turned the color of pea soup. Stretched across its width were floats made of clusters of blue plastic antifreeze jugs, tied together by their handles. The villagers had a fishing net out.

Dean stepped over to the bank for a better look. As quick as a cat, the boy jumped back from the river's edge.

Ryan swung up his 9 mm blaster in a two-handed grip. Over its sights, twenty feet from shore, he saw a swirl, like water sheeting over a great boulder just under surface. Then a five-foot-long bone blade, like a dirty yellow, two-handed broadsword, slashed up through the surface. It gleamed for an instant, then disappeared beneath the murky flow. Ryan held his fire, as did J.B., who had his scattergun hip-braced and ready to roar.

"Fireblast!" the Armorer sputtered. "What the hell was that?"

"Shades of King Arthur and the Lady in the Lake!" Doc exclaimed.

"King who?" J.B. said.

Ignoring the question, Doc went on, "In this case, Excalibur appears sadly the worse for wear."

Before the companions could unpuzzle Tanner's remarks, the strings of blue net floats jerked violently, then skittered across the water like a flock of leg-snared waterfowl. One by one, the clusters of anti-freeze jugs glugged under the surface...and stayed there, trembling in the current.

Whatever it was, it was caught fast.

The villagers leaped to their ropes and pulled them taut, their bare feet sliding in the mud. Only when the creature swam up to the surface and began to thrash midriver, rolling and wrapping itself in the fishnet, did Ryan realize how big it was. The brown-backed fish was easily thirty feet long. Its great tail slapped at the water as it momentarily turned belly up.

Before the river beast could get its bearings, the villagers began to draw in the net. Men, women and children hauled for all they were worth, their legs and backs straining. As they retreated from the waterline with the net in tow, they made the great fish roll over and over, further entangling itself.

The gargantuan mutated catfish flopped onto its belly on the edge of the bank, showering mud in all directions. Its mouth gaped. The gigantic lips looked plump and rubbery and almost human, as did the pale tongue. Its eyes, which were set far apart on a broad, flat skull wider than a man was tall, radiated a terrible fury. The ventral and dorsal fins were extended through the mesh, as were their cruel serrated spines. The cruelest of all stood atop its back like a hellship's mast.

Unable to pull the fish any farther onto shore, the villagers secured the free ends of their ropes around the tree trunks at the edge of the clearing. One of the men cautiously approached the animal. He walked stiffly, his head lowered, shoulders slumped, obviously very much afraid. Behind him, a pair of village women began to wail and cry and tear at their own hair.

"I don't like the looks of this," J.B. said out of the corner of his mouth. "Why don't they stop that guy? What the blazes is going on?"

"A chillin'," Jak said.

Ryan sensed it, too. Not just danger, but death.

The ropes groaned as the great fish lunged against the net. With a crack like a pistol shot, the line at its head parted in the middle, one end sailing high into the trees. Before the man standing beside the beast could retreat, it had him. Whipping its head sideways, the fish sank the point of a ventral spine into his chest, then it rolled on top of him. With impacts that shook the ground, it flopped, using its tremendous weight to pound the man and the impaling spine into the soft mud.

The screaming villagers grabbed the loose end of rope and drew it tight, then they angled the other lines until the fish was once again pinned flat on its belly.

Too late.

Skewered on the spine was a muddy, bloody rag doll, the head lolling backward on a broken neck. Three men carefully slid the body off the bone broad sword and laid it down gently on the bank a safe distance away. A handful of villagers, including the wailing women, knelt beside the corpse, sobbing. With cupped hands they dripped river water on the body, tenderly washing the mud and blood from the face and chest.

"Ugly way to croak," Jak spit.

"Let's make sure nobody else gets nailed by that rad blasted thing," Ryan said.

The companions quickly formed a firing squad beside the fish's head. But before they could shoot, the man in the fish-skin vest jumped in front of the raised muzzles, waving his hands. "No, no!" he shouted at them. "No lead! The metal will put a curse on the meat."

With that, the village leader scrambled onto the fish's head, using the net's mesh for hand and footholds. He was joined by another man who carried an ironwood club and a three-foot-long bone sword. The leader took the sword and knelt down, feeling around on the fish's forehead with his fingertips.

"What's he doing?" Dean asked.

"He's looking for the seam in the skull," Ryan replied. "A weak spot in the bone."

The village leader found what he was searching for. He positioned the sword point against the skull, dropped his hands below the skin-wrapped grip and nodded to the second man, who raised the club and struck the pommel of the sword a mighty blow. The impact echoed sharply off the riverbank's trees, and the serrated blade sank in a foot.

The great fish didn't seem to notice.

But when the man dealt it a second blow, driving the sword in another foot, the animal went berserk, humping up and heaving its body against the net, its long, fleshy whiskers curling and cracking like bull-whips. The man struck again with the club before the fish could throw them off. On the third whack, the blade slipped in to the hilt, the mutie catfish's eyes went dead, and its entire length began to quiver.

The villagers sent up a cheer and began preparations for the butchering. After untangling the net, several of the strongest men pried open its jaws, propping them wide apart with an ironwood stake sharpened at both ends. One of the men crawled inside the yawning mouth. Using the tip of his knife, he cut the lining of the throat away from the surrounding bone and muscle, and then disappeared into the dark cavity of its body. After a few minutes passed, he stepped out of the mouth, covered in blood and pulling the free end of the throat lining behind him.

The other villagers joined in and they began dragging the guts out of the catfish, five feet at a time. As they gave the empty, pale gray tube of muscle the heave-ho, it stretched down to the size of a man's arm. On the third pull, the tube caught on the far side of the stake. Redoubling their efforts, the villagers managed to free it.

The cause of the hang-up popped out onto the mud.

Inside the opaque gut lining was a blue-dark bulge easily as long as a man.

"Is it a person?" Dean asked, awed. "It looks like a person!"

The village leader immediately stopped the proceedings and using a borrowed sword, hacked through the gut tube in a single swipe. Covered in slime, a hairless, earless, mottled blue head peeped out. Its gaping jaws were lined with rows of needlelike teeth, its beady eyes had been turned the color of milk by the fish's corrosive digestive juices.

"Mutie eel," Jak pronounced, matter-of-factly. "Big un."

The eel's jaws snapped shut like a bear trap.

It was blind, but it sure wasn't dead.

The headman could have easily lopped off its head, but he just stared at it, sword at his side. The eel, sensing freedom, shot out of the fish's gut, frantically sidewinding for the defenseless women and children clustered on the bank. The women and children could have scattered to safety, but they didn't. They stood there. Waiting.

Whether the eel intended them harm or just wanted back in the river, Krysty reacted at once. Stepping between the onrushing animal and the innocents, she raised and fired her Model 640 Smith & Wesson. The

.38-caliber slug hit the eel square in the head, knocking it down, but not out. It writhed in the mud, toothy jaws snapping. Krysty gingerly pinned the thick neck to the ground with her boot heel, leaving the tail end free to slap and churn. Kneeling down, she held the muzzle of the revolver against the side of its head and snapped the cap. The coup de grâce cratered the eel's skull and sent a plume of blood, brains and bone fragments splashing into the river.

As Krysty straightened, the women and children encircled her, making cooing noises as they stroked the arms and hem of her fur coat.

"It's okay, really, it's okay," she told them, carefully holding the blaster out of their reach. They wouldn't be put off. They continued stroking the furry coat sleeves and cooing at her.

When things finally settled down, Ryan and the others retired to the shade of the forest's edge to watch the rest of the butchering. The village men skinned back the hide at the tail and started hacking out great, foot-thick slabs of pale pink flesh. These were passed to the women, who skewered them on ironwood sticks and began char-roasting them over the open fires. The sweet aroma of blackened catfish set the companions' empty bellies to gurgling.

After a few minutes, the headman walked over to where they sat. He carried an uncapped antifreeze jug, which he handed to Ryan. The one-eyed man sniffed the spout. "Whew!" he said. "That's powerful stuff."

"It's brewed from the fruit of the strangler vine," the village leader told him. "Drink and enjoy yourselves. After she has been served, the feast will begin.''

"Who's 'she'?" Krysty asked.

"Sirena," the leader said. "She told us of your coming, of the great fish, of Chambo's death on its spine and the eel alive in its gut. Sirena sees all, and knows all.''

"A doomie!" Dean exclaimed.

None of the others said a word. Ryan knew they were all thinking the same thing.

Bullshit.

Though doomies actually existed in Deathlands, the genuine article was as rare as a thirteen-year-old virgin. Real doomies were a unique race of humans, possibly mutated, possibly not. Each individual was gifted to a varying degree with the second sight, the ability to see past and future events. Usually, however, the folks claiming to have the doomie sight turned out to be con artists or coldheart chillers.

The companions watched as a floppy-breasted young woman carried a smoking hunk of fish past them on a carved bone platter. Escorted by the village leader, she disappeared into a hut at the end of the line.

Doc took the antifreeze jug from Ryan and tried a long swallow.

"By the Three Kennedys!" he croaked, wiping his streaming eyes and nose. "A ferment drawn straight from Satan's piss pot!"

"That good, huh?" J.B. said, accepting the jug.

"Go easy," Ryan warned.

After a single gasp-and-shiver-producing gulp, J.B.

handed the joy juice to Krysty, who whiffed it, made a face and passed it on to Jak without tasting.

In contrast to the companions' restraint, the male villagers hit their blue jugs hard, and the effects were immediate. Joined by their headman, they started singing, waving their arms and stamping their feet in the mud. Their tuneless song was as repetitive as it was nerve grating. And they directed it, and the accompanying rhythmic hip gyrations, toward their guests.

"We are rulers of the forest and the river," they howled. "We chill the great beasts with their own bones. Our powerful and manly seed will live forever."

"Now there's a comforting thought," Mildred muttered to herself.

At that point, another woman stepped forward and laid down a heaping platter of cooked fish before them. The companions used their bare hands to tear into the char-crusted and still scorching-hot meat.

"Tastes like free-range snake," J.B. remarked around a full mouth. He paused to extract a thin fibrous strand from between his teeth. "A hell of a lot more parasites, though," he said, flicking the three-inch serpentine of unchewable tissue into the forest.

The dinner bell ended the village men's caterwauling. They took seats in the shade across from the companions and started to eat. The women and children sat behind them.

Partway through the feast, one of the men gave the leader a nudge, indicating the young woman waving at him from the doorway of the far hut. The headman, who had washed down the fish course with numerous gulps of strangler wine, rose unsteadily to his feet, and said, "Sirena has been fed. You will pay your respects to her, now."

Ryan nodded. "It would be our pleasure."

The village leader ushered them into the tiny hut that was occupied by a withered old woman. She sat in an inverted catfish skull, a rocking chair hollowed out and packed with an excelsior of dried vine fibers. Over her skinny shoulders, she wore a fish skin cape with a tall, spiky fishbone collar. In her hand she held a long bone pipe, which gave off the pungently sweet smell of herbal tobacco. Even in the dim light filtering through the translucent yellow walls and the haze of smoke, Ryan could see that Sirena's pupils and irises were the color of milk. Like the eel's.

Dean was struck by this, as well, and whispered to his father, "Was she swallowed by a fish, or was she born blind?"

"If you've got a question, young man," Sirena said in a gravelly voice, "best ask me direct."

"Okay," Dean said. "You get eaten by a fish?"

A hoarse, cackling laugh burst from the old woman's throat. "Eaten and spit right back on the bank," she said. "See these beauty marks it gave me?" Skeletal fingers traced down both sides of her face, pointing out the stripes of pink-white discoloration where the flesh had been etched away. Her scalp had hairless patches of the same color. "Right off, folks around here took my coming out of that fish alive as a sign and a wonderment. And it was a bigger wonderment than anyone dreamed. Inside that fish's belly I lost normal sight, but I gained the doomie sight. Or mebbe I had it all along, and never knew until my eyes got melted away.''

The blind woman sniffed at the air like a rabbit, homing in on the exact location of Ryan's son.

"I've had visions about you, young man," Sirena said to Dean. "You and your six fine friends. Come sit here, and I'll tell you all about them...." She spread her thin legs and patted her sagging lap.

Dean wrinkled his nose. "Not bastard likely," he said, crossing his arms over his still narrow boy's chest.

"If you've got something to say to us," Ryan told her, "let's hear it."

"There's doubt in your voice," she said. "Looking for proof, are we? Well, how about I tell you something you already know? Your names? Your mothers' names? Their mothers' names?"

"Madam," Doc said, "if you could, as you suggest, pronounce the names of all our maternal grandmothers, it would certainly be evidence in your favor."

The old woman dismissed her own idea with a wave of her hand. "Nah, the back sight is too easy," she said. "And it proves nothing. There's other ways I could've found out the names. I didn't, but that's beside the point. It's the foresight, the telling of what's to come, that's the real test of doomie power. How about this for proof? There's a new kind of human being prowling the Deathlands. Not mutie spawned. These folks come from elsewhen."

"You mean elsewhere?" Ryan said.

Sirena turned her head, following the sound of his voice. "No, Master Cawdor, I mean what I said, else*when*. Another stretch of time in another place altogether. Our time and place and this other one started out identical, as alike a pair of fish eggs, but oh how different they grew. Nightmare different. These new people are a cross between us and a cockroach."

Expressions of surprise flickered over the companions' faces.

"My, my, it's gotten mighty quiet all of a sudden," Sirena said, returning to her pipe.

In the hut's golden gloom, Ryan watched her rock and blow smoke for a minute, then said, "That's the past, dead and buried. You said you were going to tell us the future."

The old woman chuckled. "It *is* the future. *Your* future, Master Half-Blind. I don't create it. I can't change it. I only see it with these...." With the tip of the pipe stem, she indicated the pale, hard-cooked eggs that were her eyes.

"Evidence, madam," Doc interjected, emphasizing the point by rapping the hut's dirt floor with his walking stick. "We require substantial and convincing evidence of your claims."

"Oh, I'll give you all the evidence you need," Sirena replied. "There's a brand-new star in the sky. Hasn't been a new star like that in more than a hundred years."

Ryan didn't get her drift, right off. He wasn't alone. The companions exchanged impatient looks. "We wouldn't know anything about that," he said. "We haven't seen the night sky for almost two weeks now."

"Well, you'll all see it tonight, over the river," the blind woman told him. "It's not a proper star, mind you. It doesn't twinkle like it should. And it sails from one side of the horizon to the other in the span of twenty heartbeats. This star was planted in the heavens by a roaring, flaming spear taller than the tallest tree in the forest.''

Mildred leaned close to Ryan and whispered, ''She means a goddamn guided missile. It's not a star she's talking about. It's a recon satellite!''

The one-eyed man had already figured that out. If what the old woman said was true, then he and the companions had failed to permanently close the passageway between realities.

''Master Cawdor,'' the doomie said, ''the cockroaches are already here, they are many, and there will be hell to pay.''

''If you really can see into the future,'' Ryan said, leaning close to her, ''then explain it to us in detail.''

Sirena shook her head. ''Even if I went over it minute by minute, it wouldn't help you. Preparations are a waste of precious time. I've lived with the doomie sight since I was your boy's age, and I know this for a certain fact—no one can change the course of what will be. My advice to all of you is to enjoy each passing moment as if it were your last.''

''In other words,'' Mildred said, ''we're going to suffer and die, but be sure and have a nice day. That's all she's going to tell us? Why are we listening to this hogwash?''

''I heartily agree,'' Doc said. ''Might I suggest that our 'passing moments' might be more enjoyably spent away from the confines of this cramped and stinking hovel.''

''You got that right, Doc,'' J.B. agreed.

As they began filing from the hut, Sirena called out, "Wait, young Cawdor! Before you go, I have a gift for you."

From under the translucent cape, she produced a slim six-inch bone dagger in a skin sheath.

Dean immediately glanced at his father, who indicated his permission with a curt nod of his head. The boy approached the old woman and took the dagger from her. There was no cross guard or pommel. The handle was wrapped with strips of scratchy fish skin. Unsheathing the blade, he carefully tested its serrated edge on the back of his thumbnail. "Demon sharp!" he said.

"It's made from the tip of a catfish dorsal spine," Sirena said. "It will fit nicely into the top of your right boot."

Dean tried it. The blade and sheath disappeared completely. "I can hardly feel it's there," he said. "Thanks."

Sirena reached out and seized his wrist in a grip that was amazingly strong. "I could have told you your future," she said, "and your children's future, too, if you'd just sat on my lap."

"Mebbe you could," the boy said, jerking his hand away. "And mebbe I don't want to know that bad."

As Ryan and Dean left the hut, waves of the doomie's shrill, hoarse laughter crashed against their backs.

IT WAS NEARLY midnight when Ryan saw it, in the tree break over the dark river. The single point of bright light appeared in the west, above the blackness of the canopy, and swept across the starry field of sky. He and the others watched the satellite arc overhead and vanish in the east.

"Fireblast!" Ryan's curse echoed off the surrounding forest.

"Couldn't it be something else?" Dean asked him. "Something real old...from before skydark?"

"It isn't old, son. All the space junk fell to earth and burned up a long time ago. It has to be new. The fish hag spoke the truth. People from the other Earth had to have put it up there. No one else could have done it."

"We should've chilled those four bastards," J.B. said. "Should've buried them along with all their fancy chilling gear."

Ryan grimaced. J.B. was talking about the turncoats, the members of the first scouting expedition to cross over from the parallel Earth. With success within their grasp, the warrior-whitecoats had decided not just to abandon, but to sabotage their primary mission, which was to lay the groundwork for the invasion and conquest of Deathlands by the armies of FIVE. Instead of firing the guided missile they had trucked with them into the sky, they launched it through the reality portal in the hope of sealing the gateway forever. That done, the alternate world conquistadors went native. They stripped off the segmented black battlesuits that made them immune to blasterfire, and they dumped the tribarreled laser rifles that cut through plate steel like so much tissue paper. Ryan and the others helped them dismantle their gyroplane and they buried it deep in a sandy arroyo along with the rest of their gear.

"Colonel Gabhart and the others might not have had anything to do with this," Mildred said.

"They could've changed their minds about bringing the armies across, too," J.B. countered. "Mebbe they had blood relatives starving to death on the other side. Blood being thicker than water, they decided to reopen the passageway and save them."

"However it happened," Krysty said, "they're here. The question is, what are we going to do about it?"

All eyes turned to Ryan.

He was the only one who had seen the other world. And though he'd tried to describe its bleakness and horror to his friends, mere words couldn't do it justice. They stuck in his throat like slivers of glass.

The nukecaust that had laid waste to Deathlands was an accident, an instantaneous, one-time event, but the alternate end to history that Ryan had witnessed was the final outcome of a civilization that had attacked nature as if it were a sworn enemy. There was nothing left on the parallel Earth but human beings and the avalanche of disasters their science had brought to life. They were indeed like two-legged cockroaches: indomitable breeders, surviving at all costs, consuming and destroying every living thing and every resource within their reach.

In his mind, Ryan could see gleaming, hard-shelled black armies pouring through the parted lips of the reality corridor. Armies carrying weapons and technology that nothing in Deathlands could match. Armies so vast that even without advanced weapons they could defeat any force the people of Deathlands could field against them.

Running away only postponed the inevitable. With an eye in the sky endlessly circling and searching their world, there was no safe place to hide. Fate had left Ryan and his companions one choice, and it was bad.

"We've got to go back to Moonboy ville," Ryan said. "We've got to find a way to fight the bastards and drive them out for good."

There was silence along the riverbank.

To enter battle with a slight possibility of victory was one thing; to walk willingly into the spinning blades of a meatgrinder was another. Ryan thought about the village man who had death-marched himself to meet the catfish's impaling spine. Sirena had told the poor bastard his fate, and he had surrendered to it. Just as they were about to do. There was an important difference, of course.

Ryan listened to the gurgle of the life-giving river and felt the embrace of the dense forest that loomed on all sides. Overhead, the blanket of stars twinkled as his world slowly turned.

The difference was, they wouldn't die for nothing. And they wouldn't die alone.

Chapter Three

A rag securely tied over his nose and mouth, Dr. Huth stopped hacking at the hardpan with the blade of his shovel. The sound of a distant car horn faded in and out, intermittently muffled by the gusts of hot wind that scoured the desert plain.

Abandoning the shovel, Huth climbed the side of Byram ville's defensive berm for a look. As he scaled the mound of dirt, his feet slipped around inside the oversize jogging shoes he wore despite the plastic bags he'd wadded up in their toe boxes. His polyester pants were as stiff as cardboard. Not because they were new—their rigidity came from the black blood that starched the lap, thighs and shins. The pants were cinched tight around his waist with a length of frayed electrical cord.

To earn a dead man's trousers and shoes, Huth had dug latrines barefoot and in his underpants for three days.

He was still digging latrines.

A mile away, a wag emerged from the dust devils that spun across the ruined interstate. It continued to honk as it approached the lone opening in the ville's mounded perimeter wall. The vehicle, originally a small school bus, was painted in garish pink, green, yellow, red, a chaos of spray-can squiggles and overlayed abstract shapes. Even the sides of the tires and wheels were painted.

Belching black smoke from its exhaust, the wag stopped at the security checkpoint, which consisted of a breach in the berm that was partially blocked by a heap of junked vehicles. The all-volunteer sec force emerged from behind that rusting barrier, shouting instructions as they aimed their handful of centerfire blasters at the driver. The bus's side door opened at once, and the sec men climbed inside to make sure it didn't conceal armed killers trying to loot the compound. The ville's sec men never robbed or extorted wayfarers themselves. Robbery and extortion were left to the twenty-four-hour gaudy house and the seven-days-a-week swap meet.

The hellpit of Byram ville, whose smoke plume Huth had first seen from atop the red mesa, had grown up around a predark truck stop. At the center of the enclosure were the remains of a service station, restaurant and minimart. The great steel awnings that had once shielded the rows of junked fuel pumps from the sun had been torn off by skydark's two-hundred-mile-per-hour shock wave. The original roof of the one-story structure had likewise vanished, the plate-glass windows turned to twinkling fairy dust. Roof and windows had been crudely repaired with sheets of metal stripped from the abandoned and overturned semitrailers that littered the huge parking area. These aging artifacts of long-dead interstate commerce were the very heart and soul of the place. Byram ville's upper crust lived inside the trailers and conducted their businesses out of them. The poorer residents kept house in the rusting hulks of passenger cars. The lowest of the low—Huth, included—slept curled up on the ground like mongrel dogs, in the lee of their economic betters.

Unless someone had died during the night, there were forty-five full-time residents of Byram ville. The locals survived by trading with travelers, taking whatever the newcomers had of value in exchange for jolt or juice or sex, or food or drinking water, or temporary protection from what lay outside the defensive perimeter. Though Interstate 15 was primarily a walking road, occasionally a wag would pass through, bearing trade goods and news from other parts of Deathlands.

After clearing the entry checkpoint, the bus driver parked alongside the ville's central structure and leaned on his horn for a good thirty seconds. Heads poked out of semis and car bodies and the ruined restaurant and minimart. Seeing what had arrived, people came running.

Carrying his shovel, Huth joined the crowd that surrounded the strangely decorated wag. The driver stood in the bus's doorway, grinning. He was a big man, easily 350 pounds and six foot two. He wore a squashed canvas fedora, which sat like a pancake on the back of his huge head, and faded bib-front denim jeans. "Come one, come all!" he yelled. "Gather 'round, everybody!"

As the crowd closed in, the driver used the metal ladder bolted to the bus's side to climb to the roof. Once there, he did a sort of flamenco dance, his arms curved gracefully over his head, his laceless logger boots hammering on the sheet steel.

Huth noticed the way the sun gleamed off his right

hand, which was the color of old ivory and obviously artificial.

"Come on and bring your cups!" the driver shouted. "I got free joy juice for everybody! I got free slip and slide, too!"

He stamped on the roof of the bus. "Wake up, you lazy sluts!" he bellowed. "Get up here and show your stuff!"

A frowzy female head appeared in one of the bus's rear windows, hair like a great lopsided wad of pink cotton wool. A second woman popped up beside the first, her face powdered white and her cheeks rouged a feverish red. The third occupant was male. Dense black facial stubble had grown through his many layers of Pan-Cake makeup.

This unwholesome trio exited the bus and started up the ladder to the roof. They were dressed in matching outfits: a white string T-shirt and stiletto-heeled leather boots. None of them wore anything below the waist. Their well-worn genitalia had the ruddy brown color of smoked meat; their buttocks and thighs were badly bruised. The pink-haired slut carried a battery-powered boom box, which she passed up to the driver.

The big man propped the boom box on his shoulder and hit the power switch. Predark music blared from the speakers at ear-blistering volume. There were lyrics to the song, hard to catch at first, something about partying like it was the year 1999.

The three whores began dancing, and the driver did a few turns himself before setting the boom box on the roof.

"Got your cups?" he called to the crowd over the rhythmic racket. "Well, goddammit, go get 'em!"

As most of the folks rushed off, the driver descended the ladder and ducked inside the bus's doorway. When he reappeared, he had a gray insulated plastic mug in his good, left hand.

Huth was standing close enough to get a look at the prosthesis at the end of his other arm. It wasn't carved of ivory, or any other natural material. Every finely sculpted finger had two articulated joints, the thumb had one, plus the knuckles, and there was a small knurled knob on the back of the wrist. As he watched, the big man tightened down the knob, which made the fingers and thumb contract in a deathgrip around the mug's handle.

Mug in fist, the driver danced some more; he was very light on his feet for a man of his size. After a minute or two, he stopped and pulled the end of a length of plastic hose out a side window. When he opened the metal clamp on its tip, a clear fluid sprayed into his waiting tankard.

"We are gonna have so damned much fun!" he shouted to the cloudless sky.

Then he called up to the whores, "Dance, you sexy devils! Show these good folks what you can do!"

The trio began bucking their pelvises and rotating their hips with more enthusiasm.

"For those of you who don't know me," he told the crowd, "I'm Big Mike. Also known as Mike the Drunkard." He tipped back the mug and began to swallow, his Adam's apple bobbing. He didn't stop until he'd emptied it.

"Ya-hoooie!" he said. "Everybody belly up! Come on, now, don't be shy. It's fill-'em-up time!"

Huth, who had no cup, was shoved, elbowed and punched out of the way by those who did.

The boom box on the roof stopped playing for a second, then the same song started over again automatically.

Mike the Drunkard used his real hand to backslap and goose the spectators as he topped off their containers. And the whole while he jabbered at them. "Ooh, are we going to par-tay!" he said. "Get this bus a-rocking in no time." He made a lewd crotch thrust at his own drained mug before refilling it.

In short order, Big Mike had everybody around the bus drinking, dancing and laughing. Everybody but Huth, who stood at the edge of the crowd, leaning dejectedly on the handle of his shovel.

When Mike scrambled back up to the roof of the bus, he turned down the volume on the boom box. The song started over for the fifth time. By now, all the people knew the words of the chorus and shouted along. To them, 1999 meant predark. Happy days. Times of plenty, of relative order and safety. A golden age.

"Right about now," Big Mike said to them, "you're probably asking yourselves, where does this big old sexy magic man come from? And where did he get all the chiller joy juice he's giving away?"

"Tell us!" someone yelled back.

"Yeah," another person chimed in, "tell us!"

"The answer to both questions is Slake City," Mike said.

It took a few seconds for this information to sink

in. Gradually, the residents of Byram ville stopped dancing. They stood like statues beside the bus, glaring at the big man.

Mike raised his good hand. "Now, I know you've heard it's a wasteland over there. But that's a rumor started by some of the people who are already there. They're greedy bastards. They want to keep all the sweet stuff for themselves."

"That's Baron Jolt's turf," said a man standing up front, "and as far as I'm concerned, that raping, chilling bastard can have it."

"Everybody knows Slake City's nothing but a nuke slag heap!" another man said. "The background radiation turns you into a pile of pus and sores inside of a month."

"Nah-nah," Mike said, shaking his head. "That's how it used to be. Not anymore. The place is all cleaned up. It's safe as mother's milk. And Baron Jolt is long gone. We got real jobs there, now. It's fat, I'm telling you, just like before skydark. People are eating regular, getting drunk regular, living out of the chem rains in clean shacks with good shithouses. Slake City is starting over again, and the folks who get in on the ground floor are going to have the edge. Have a chance to get baron-rich. That's why I'm here. Slake City needs folks like you. Enterprising, right-thinking folks who know an opportunity when they see one."

While the crowd considered this, Mike the Drunkard clambered from the roof and quickly refilled all the empty cups.

It was then that Huth took note of the massive bracelet around the bus driver's left wrist. Dull silver in color, its surface was filigreed with solid-state circuitry. The sight of the ornament made Huth's mouth drop. Pulse pounding, he fought to get a closer look, though it meant absorbing numerous blows to his head, back and arms.

"How did you lose your right hand?" Huth called out.

"Got it caught up the wrong ass," Mike said.

Everybody laughed. Everybody but Huth.

The former chief whitecoat of FIVE, now latrine engineer, used the handle of his shovel like a lance, clearing a path to the front of the crowd. He held up the pocket of his lab coat to the big man. "Do you know what this means?" he asked.

Big Mike squinted down at the four letters stitched in red. "Can't read too good," he confessed.

Huth reached out and tapped the metallic wristband. "I came from the same place as that."

Big Mike stared at Huth's gap teeth, his dirt-caked face, his unspeakable pants and dismissed him with a "Yeah, right…"

"I know what it's used for," Huth went on, frantic to get his point across. "You've got bands just like it around your ankles, too, don't you?"

The big man's eyes narrowed. "So…?"

"Did it hurt much when they lopped off your hand?"

Mike the Drunkard seized Huth by the collar and dragged him and his shovel up the steps into the bus. Inside, it smelled like a cross between a distillery and a bear pit. The rear seats had been removed to make room on the floor for a pile of badly stained mattresses. A half-dozen fifty-five-gallon metal drums of joy juice were securely strapped to the floor. The drums were all stenciled with Baron Jolt.

Huth endured a brutal shaking, then the big man held him close and growled into his face, "How do you know about my hand? Who the fuck are you?"

"I crossed over ahead of the people who did that to you," Huth said. "My coming to this world was an accident. I was lost in the wilderness and then I ended up in this place, in very sorry circumstances. My name is Dr. Huth. I am somewhat famous where I come from. Maybe the others talked about me? Or mentioned my name in passing?"

"Nope," Mike said.

"One thing's for certain," Huth continued, "you have become their puppet. Those laser cuffs can turn you into a victim in a hurry. Without hands and feet you'd be a big lump of warm, helpless meat that any-one could play nasty with. How much chain did they give you? Fifty miles? A hundred miles? Go one step farther, break the transmitter's signal, and zap! All fall down."

"You better not queer my pitch here," Mike warned, poking Huth hard in the chest with a huge finger. "I got a quota to make."

"Take me back with you. Take me back to my people."

Mike gave him a dubious look.

"That's all I want. Really."

The big man's eyes glittered. "No problem," he said. "You can ride with me all the way to Slake City."

Overjoyed, Huth started to throw his shovel out a window.

"No, keep that," Mike told him. "It'll come in handy later. I got to go outside now. I got to make my closing pitch before these triple stupes start to sober up." He dug under a seat and removed a big yellow plastic tub. He patted the tight-fitting lid and said, "The deal clincher."

Huth remained inside the bus while Big Mike stepped out and addressed the crowd. "I'm looking for a few good folks who aren't a-scared of rumors," he said. "And I'm willing to sweeten the pie a little. I know you've all got a taste for what's in here." He opened the tub and showed them the heap of white crystalline powder it contained. "This is the real thing, people. One hundred percent pure jolt. It'll make you feel ten feet tall. And you'll screw my pretty sluts like a pack of slag heap weasels. Don't push, now. One at a time, now. Come and get it."

Using a battered teaspoon, he laid a heaping dose of powder on every outstretched palm. Though some people licked it, most of them snorted it. The powerful drug took hold quickly, with alarming effect. It made eyes bug out and sweaty faces grimace spastically. To quench their suddenly raging thirsts, the revelers guzzled more free joy juice, and they all fell into a slow-spinning, half-speed dance.

At a signal from Mike, the music abruptly stopped and the three whores climbed down from the roof with the boom box. They entered the bus and walked past Huth, heading straight for the pile of mattresses in the back.

"Come on, people," Mike urged, gesturing toward the bus's entrance. "The real fun is starting. Slip and slide. Slip...and...slide."

As stoned as they were, most of the Byram ville folks didn't fall for his spiel, but they were in no shape to try to stop the few who did. Four men between the ages of twenty and thirty, and a heavyset, thirtyish woman mounted the bus's steps. As the woman passed Huth and turned down the aisle for the rear, she jerked her black sleeveless T-shirt over her head and tossed it aside. Her huge soft breasts swayed pendulously as she struggled with the zipper on the front of her dusty BDU pants.

"Hey, it's okay if you don't want to come with me now," Mike assured the rest of the crowd. "I'll be back by here in a week or two. Give you all some time to think it over. Maybe I'll even bring back your friends for a visit. You can hear firsthand what you're missing."

With that, he climbed back in the bus, started it up and U-turned for the checkpoint. Huth took a seat up front, right behind the driver, as far away from the goings-on in the back as he could get.

After they had cleared the gate, Mike double-clutched and shifted the bus into high gear. "How about some driving music?" he said over his shoulder. He poked the boom box, which sat perched on the dash. The 1999 song started up again at top volume, canceling out the grunting, whimpering racket from the rear.

Big Mike, clearly feeling the effects of all the joy juice he'd drunk, threw back his head and falsetto-screeched along with the vocalist.

For his part, Huth was content to bob his head and

tap out the now-familiar beat with the toe of his size-13 jogging shoe. He watched the flat, parched landscape roll past the grimy window, toothlessly grinning while tears streamed down his face.

Chapter Four

Dredda Otis Trask deepened the tint of her helmet visor to shield her eyes against Slake City's blinding, panoramic glare. From the history of her own Earth, she knew that there had once been a vast body of water in this place, the last remnant of an ancient inland sea. In Shadow World's reality, on a late January day more than a century past, Great Salt Lake had been vaporized by a multiwarhead nuclear strike. And a fraction of an instant later, the sands of the exposed lake bed and the shattered metropolis of Salt Lake City were melted together, fused into a boiling, hundred-square-mile sea of thermoglass. As the infernal heat was sucked up into the atmosphere, towering waves of glass solidified in a nightmare snapshot, their peaks capped with a foam of rusting, fire-blackened litter. Massive, shock-blast-tossed fragments—skyscraper I-beams, sections of railroad track and metal utility poles—stuck up from the wave troughs like the masts of a drowned navy.

It was a place long dead, but it was neither silent nor still.

Between howling gusts of wind, the external microphones of Dredda's battlesuit picked up what sounded like the scattered, desperate cries of abandoned infants. There were no lost babies out there. The phenomenon had to do with the nukeglass's structural weaknesses, which were caused by mineral impurities, and by the pulverized debris and air bubbles it contained. Extreme changes in day-night temperatures caused hairline cracks to appear in the matrix, and as the splits spread and ran, they made the shrill, disturbing sounds.

Occasionally, there were much louder noises. As the fine cracks branched out, they became networks of fissures that eventually crashed down the roofs of hidden hollow spots. Some of these collapsed air pockets were the size of amphitheaters.

Dredda focused her attention on a distant column of human figures moving away from her, over the gray-green surface. The group of freshly captured slaves walked a road that ended at Ground Zero, some eight miles away from Slake City. A pair of huge black vehicles dogged the rear of the file, herding the work crew replacements.

Building a road across the nukeglass that could support heavy vehicle traffic had been dangerous work. Even with side-scanning sonar to point out the larger crevasses and voids, sudden cave-ins were frequent and nearly always fatal to the natives. The broken chunks had razor sharp edges and often weighed hundreds of pounds. Trying to pull trapped slaves from the cave-ins had turned out to be wasted effort: the shifting sections of thermoglass either sliced them to rags, or chopped them into pieces.

In the week that it had taken to complete road construction, Dredda had sacrificed half of the Shadow World work force she had pressed into service. Most of the slaves were young men who had been mining their meager living from the dead city. They used crude hand tools to hack holes in the surface and crawled into the hollow places in search of undamaged, pre-Armageddon odds and ends, which they then traded. As a rule, these independent scroungers only worked the outer edges of the nukeglass, where the lingering radiation was the weakest. Even so, after a few years of digging, most had developed angry sores and large, visible tumors.

At Ground Zero, tissue destruction proceeded much more briskly. After a few days in that high-dose radioactive environment, weeping blisters appeared on unshielded hands, faces and feet. Based on the rad exposure alone, the working life span of a slave was no more than two weeks. Because of other dangers related to large-scale mining in thermoglass, actual survival time was half of that. From Dredda's point of view, this wasn't entirely a negative: there was no need to feed slaves who were only going to live a week.

Her own survival, and ultimately the conquest of Shadow World, depended on the exploitation of local energy sources. The recon satellite's first mission, postlaunch, had been to pinpoint the nearest, hottest nuke zone, a place that could provide the suitable raw material for her reprocessing units. The energy reprocessors utilized strains of genetically engineered bacteria that feasted on irradiated inorganic matter and secreted useable nuclear fuel. Every critical component of Dredda's invasion force, from gyroplanes to battlesuits, was powered by this recycled material.

The skirmish Dredda had planned for this day would easily gobble up one-third of the precious little fuel that had been harvested from Slake City so far, but she had no choice in the matter. To stabilize the energy stockpile in the short term, she had to expand her mining operation, and to do that, given the life expectancy of her workers, she needed a much larger labor pool.

Behind her, eight huge landships waited, their nuke turbines humming at idle. Gleaming black and windowless, with smooth, aerodynamic contours, the 6×6s were the core of her ground force, able to traverse at high speed the most difficult terrain thanks to their seven-foot-diameter wheels, each with its own independent drive train and suspension.

As Dredda turned for her flagship, its right front door rose up like the wing of a great bird. Sunlight washed over the high-backed copilot seat, over a ceiling tangled with exposed conduit, wiring harnesses and gray Kevlar pipe. A fine film of desert dust coated the gangway's steps.

Sitting in the other cockpit's other chair, behind the steering yoke, was Mero. Her pale blue eyes gleamed through her battlesuit's transparent visor; her close-cropped blond curls were partially hidden by a red skullcap. Like all the officers of Dredda's invasion force, Mero was the product of Level Four genetic engineering. The experimental procedure had made her face less round, and her chin more square and prominent. The look of supreme confidence in her eyes, an expression that four tours with the dreaded Population Control Service hadn't dimmed, was now reinforced by additional bone structure and dense layers of muscle.

Dredda understood exactly what Mero was feeling at that moment. Excitement. Impatience. And an intense curiosity about the future. The two women, indeed all the Level Four females, shared a bond that went deeper than their rank or sex, or the war upon Shadow World they were about to wage. They were all sister changelings, birthed in the same stainless-steel womb, explorers of a new universe without, and an equally mysterious and promising one within.

This visceral connection, this transgenic sisterhood was something Dredda hadn't expected to feel so deeply, and it caught her unprepared. As much as the sense of belonging pleased her, it also unsettled her. She had never experienced anything quite like it before. Not even with her own father.

Looking between the cockpit seats to the rear of the vehicle, Dredda checked the rest of her crew. The male troops were strapped cross chest into twelve shock-mounted jump seats set between I-beams along the walls of the cargo bay. From the uniformly smug expressions behind their visors, they no longer had any fear of the enemy. During the slave raids on Slake City scrounger camps, they had absorbed barrages of fire from a variety of primitive combustion-powered rifles, shotguns and pistols. Their battlesuits had deflected every projectile with ease. Their own battle gear, tribarreled laser rifles and phage-foam back tanks, was netted, rattle proofed and lashed down to the middle of the cargo deck.

When Dredda sat down in the copilot seat, it immediately adjusted itself, inflating and deflating to match the curves and overlapping plates of her battlesuit. The windshield in front of her was dead black. When the wing door hissed down and locked shut, the only available light came from the instrument panel. It bathed the wag's interior in hellish red.

Dredda coupled her battlesuit to the dashboard umbilical and opaqued her visor. Immediately, the instrument lights and blacked-out windows vanished, as did the entire outer skin of the vehicle. Suddenly, Dredda was sitting alone, in the open air, five feet above the ground. Each crew member found him-or herself likewise isolated from the others and suspended in space. This illusion was produced by the hull's optical scanning system, which filtered out unnecessary detail and projected a three-dimensional image of the external environment directly onto the interior surface of the helmet visors.

Keying her battlesuit com link to the driver, Dredda said, "Start the mission clock."

Mero throttled up the turbines. As the hum grew louder, the chair in which Dredda sat began to move. It accelerated rapidly, until it was flying over the ground. To her right, the details of the Slake City massif stretched and blurred. G-force drove her deep into the contour seat, but there was no accompanying sensation of air pressure—it was the only flaw in the elaborate computer simulation. If she had really been strapped unprotected to a rocket-powered chair, the wind would have been a tangible, buffeting force against the front of her body.

Ahead, she could make out the lake-bed landing zone, and the six black gyroplanes on standby there. Dredda keyed the com link again and gave the order, "Airborne units proceed to the staging area."

The VTO/L attack aircraft immediately lifted off

and swung toward the mountains to the southwest, strung out in a quarter-mile skirmish line.

Dredda and her chair continued due west, rushing across the flat plane of pale dirt, leaving Slake City behind. The other wags ran on either side of her in loose, flying-V formation. Their speed over ground was 140 miles per hour. Dredda felt some vibration in the pit of her stomach and her feet, but it was disconnected from the images inside her visor, which moved only when she turned her head.

The formation slowed to make the turn south at old Iosepa Road. The undivided pavement had vanished long ago, but the roadbed was still there, covered by drifts of sand, salt and dust. It ran straight as a laser pulse for twenty miles.

As they approached the slight bend in the road where the predark hamlet of Iosepa had been, Dredda ordered the vehicles cloaked. This was accomplished by reducing the side-to-side distance between the wags to a few feet and then electrostatically charging the hulls, which redirected most of the dust cloud they were raising aft, and made it jet forward from under their front bumpers, creating a roiling, onrushing wall of dirt that preceded and entirely enveloped them.

Inside her visor, Dredda could see nothing but swirling beige.

Mero and the other sisters were driving blind at identical high speeds, maintaining tight formation over broken ground using battlesuit-sat link intel and helmet simulacra for steering. Dredda switched her visor screen to monitor what they were viewing.

Along the sides of the green-on-green field were a dozen inset windows with numbers rapidly scrolling

up or down. There were complex nuke-turbine function and tank-temperature indicators. Other windows
displayed the vehicle's true course over ground, in
latitude and longitude, and its true speed over ground.
There were flashing proximity warnings about the vehicles on either side, in feet. The distance to the target
was shown in yards, and falling rapidly. In the center
of the screen were eight wag-shaped, lime-green blips
in a sideways row. Beneath the shifting blips, a
shades-of-green, satellite-generated contour map of
the terrain unrolled wildly.

Only one of the blips on Mero's screen ran inside
a set of parallel lines—these boundaries indicated her
vehicle's computer-assigned course. The paired lines
were constantly moving as the computer adjusted for
the deflection of the irregular terrain, and driver error
and deflection in the seven other vehicles. As Mero
kept the blip within the course boundaries, her decision time was measured in fractions of a second. Al-
lowable, real-world error before catastrophe was measured in inches.

Dredda switched screens again, calling up the bio-
metric readouts of her wag squad. Her heart rate and
Mero's were holding steady at forty-five beats per
minute; the men's were four times that, and their
blood pressures were spiking. She quickly scanned
each trooper's current video input. None of them was
observing the driver's screen; they were either beiged-
out or off-line, presumably staring at the red gloom
of the cargo bay. Dredda tried to imagine how Mero's
screen would look to them.

Pure chaos.

An information and threat overload.

A helter-skelter fright ride, their lives in the hands of a gene-spliced maniac.

Dredda couldn't see their eyes, but it amused her to think they were all shut tight.

The Level Four procedure that she and her officers had endured had changed more than their external physiques, their fat metabolism and resting heart rates. It had expanded and fine-tuned their biological systems to match the extreme limits of the battlesuit's cyber-capabilities; something the male physiology, gene-doctored or not, could never achieve. Their increased numbers of neurons allowed them to intake and process information a hundred times faster than the men.

As Dredda understood the science, there were built-in bioengineering limits to each of the sexes, based on the amount of body space and chemistry devoted to their differing reproductive functions. In the case of the females, much more of their capacity—hormonally, metabolically, neurologically—was taken up by these duties. If the biochemical obligations of motherhood were removed, there was room for the system to change and grow. On the other hand, men's reproductive functions took up very little of their bodies' overall capacity, so removing it had no effect on potential growth. Evolutionarily speaking, the male of the species was already maxed out.

When Dredda uplinked her visor to the infrared image of the target compound, she saw human forms running. Now that the dust cloud was visible to them, the Shadow Worlders were taking up defensive positions inside the fenced perimeter. On their part, it had to be a precaution. They didn't know what the approaching cloud meant, and they weren't taking any chances. The important thing was, they weren't abandoning the compound in droves. Because they controlled the high ground from well-positioned defensive hardsites, with lots of conventional weapons, they believed they were invulnerable. The function of the dust cloak was to maintain this illusion as long as possible—slaves were more profitable caught in large bunches.

Dredda panned back for a broader infrared view of the kill zone. The exhaust ports of the heavily armed gyroplanes registered as six bright spots sweeping around the western flank of Mount Deseret, closing on the compound from the north. It was time for the ground units to uncloak, and she snapped out the order.

As the wags burst through the face of the electrostatic dust cloud, the compound's twelve-foot-high, wire perimeter fence appeared out of nothing, directly in front of them. Beyond it was the broad parking lot, and on the other side of it, the main complex that snuggled up against the foot of the mountain. The eight landships hit the fence at the same instant, flattening it and twisting it under their huge wheels. As they roared onto the parking lot, a fusillade of hostile fire zinged at them from all sides. The clatter of the gunshots and the ping-whine of bullets deflecting off her wag's EM shield was so loud it forced Dredda to turn down the audio in her battlesuit.

When she activated the wag's weapons pods, which were located on either side of the roof, two joysticks popped out of dashboard in front of her. As her gauntleted hands closed on the no-slip grips, a ring and crosshair sight appeared in the center of her helmet visor. Her targets, human-shaped figures in lime green, scattered to either side as the wag continued to rumble up the slope. Dredda flipped off the grip safeties with her thumbs.

Each of the joysticks operated its own cannon pod. As she moved her hands apart, the lone crosshair ring blurred, divided and became two. She simultaneously tracked a pair of men running in opposite directions. One was scrambling out of a foxhole hacked in the asphalt on her left; the other high-kicked to the right as he abandoned a sandbagged, burned-out hulk of a vehicle. When the computer target locks engaged, the sprinting figures turned red and she jiggled the firing buttons.

Green lances of light stabbed through both runners. Neither completed another step.

Foxhole Man fell in four pieces, sliced cleanly through the chest and both arms above the elbow by a single burst of pure energy. His transected parts landed in a jumbled heap. The other man took the laser slash at waist height. The emerald light separated his torso from everything below his hips. It was a grievous mortal wound, but not immediately so. Though the man had been chopped in half, there was no blood—the laser sliced and cauterized at the same time. Rearing up from the pavement with undamaged arms, he seemed to recognize the severed legs under his chin as his own. His mouth opened wide in a scream that Dredda couldn't hear. Frantically clawing, he tried to drag himself away.

He was all in red.

The target lock had him.

She tapped the right firing button again and sawed him neatly lengthwise, from the top of his head to his torso stump. The smoking halves of him flopped apart, like a cleaver-struck apple.

All around, the gunners in the other wags were likewise selecting individual running targets and chopping them to pieces. Dredda's visor compensated for the interlacing, intense bursts of light. In the real world, those flashes of green were blinding. They cooked the very air, as they cooked human flesh and bone. The attack was intended to produce maximum terror, and it was having the desired effect. Instead of holding their ground, the Shadow Worlders were already starting to fall back, allowing themselves to be herded toward the main building.

Her body in perfect sync with the wag's fire-control system, Dredda unleashed a furious two-handed attack. Tickling the firing buttons, she struck red targets not with one pulse, but with twenty, sectioning the human forms in as many pieces. To her, it seemed as if the running figures were moving in slow motion. To the troopers in the jump seats behind her, it was just the opposite. Everything was free spooling at triple speed, and the pulses of laser cannon weren't pulses at all, but sustained blasts. They watched sprinting targets in a 360-degree radius of their wag disintegrate like blades of grass before a grass trimmer. Maybe four highly trained troopers manning the vehicle's weapons pods could have had the same effect. Four men at the peak of their prime.

Maybe.

As the wags roared up the grade, Dredda called off the slaughter. Because the lives of the opposition had value, the idea was to kill as few as possible, but to do it in a way that demoralized and absolutely terrified the survivors. That part of the mission was accomplished. The enemy was in full-scale retreat. She and the other gunners began firing over the heads of the withdrawing forces, driving them across the parking lot and into the main complex.

As the wags closed on the three-story building's entrance, the squadron of gyroplanes swept in and like huge black hornets hovered above the roof. They sent intermittent beams of emerald green light spearing down through its walls and into the forces now trapped inside.

Mero stopped the wag in front of the complex's double doorway, beneath the big crumbling marquee. Thick black smoke was already starting to coil out of the upper-story windows.

Dredda unfastened herself from the wag umbilical and released her seat harness. She felt an incredible elation as she pushed out of her chair. Triumph was far too weak a word to describe the sensation. This, she thought, had to have been what it was like for Cortez and his men. Armed with advanced technology, facing a primitive and ignorant populace, with a world of uncountable treasure that lay waiting at their feet. And they didn't even have to bend and scoop it up themselves. That's what subject peoples were all about.

As Dredda moved to the rear, the male troopers stood at attention on either side of the cargo bay. For the first time, they had seen what their officers could do inside a battlesuit. She studied each of their faces in turn. Some had sober, distant expressions. Others wore frozen grins. There was fear in all their eyes. The fear of her. Of her kind. Their weakness irritated her, and she had to stifle the urge to smack them to their knees. If Dredda could have arranged it, she would have only brought sisters to the new reality, but there hadn't been time to complete the necessary transformations.

After the troopers peeled back the netting from the weaponry, she picked up a tribarreled laser rifle, checked its power pack, and then stepped onto the wag's rear platform. As the back door lowered, she was the first to charge out, followed by Mero.

Automatic-weapons fire chattered and muzzles flashed at them from the building's lower-story windows. Deflected by their battlesuits' EM pulses, the sudden downpour of bullets veered wide, sparking off the already pitted concrete of the sidewalk.

Dredda ducked under the overhang of the marquee, but not before she took a second to look up at it. Incredibly, its century-old black plastic lettering was still mostly intact. It said Mount Des ret C sino Resort. Fri./S t. Only. Direct f om Sparks, NV—Tony, Orlando, and Don.''

Chapter Five

A severed human head tumbled down the grand staircase, bounced over the banister and landed at the feet of Baron Charlie Doyal. Wide with surprise, the dead eyes stared up at him. Its neck stump was a clean, band saw slice and absolutely bloodless. The throat's shock-contracted tendons had been fused with the spinal column, which meant the jaws would remain clenched like that, the teeth bared, until the flesh rotted from the bone.

Baron Doyal made no attempt to kick aside the hideous thing.

The ground-floor lobby of the Mount Deseret Casino Resort was a scrap heap of similar horrors.

And worse—some of the scraps could still crawl.

The air inside the building vibrated with earsplitting whistles, the piercing tones accompanied pencil-thin beams of emerald light that slashed through the vaulted ceiling, three stories above, angling down, drawing lines of crackling flame along the faded, red-patterned velvet wallpaper. The light beams were unstoppable. They cleaved everything they touched: metal, concrete and, of course, humanity.

Yelling at the tops of their lungs, the baron's mutilated bodyguards dragged themselves back from the edge of the flashing buzz saw, clawing their way over the bright, razor-sharp fragments of the casino's dropped and shattered twenty-foot-wide crystal chandelier.

Doyal couldn't hear their cries over his own. A passing flicker of the green light had turned the little and ring fingers of his left hand into greasy, scorched stubs. He hadn't lost a single drop of blood, but the hand had gone rigid. It had puffed up, purple to the wrist, the surviving fingers as stiff and fat as little sausages. Excruciating pain throbbed all the way to his shoulder socket.

His weapon of choice, an autoloading 10-gauge shotgun with a sawed-off barrel and buttstock and a pistol-grip forestock, dangled in his good right hand, its magazine emptied. The Ithaca Magnum Roadblocker could blow a hole in a man big enough to stick an arm through, but in this battle its high-brass, double-aught buckshot loads had proved worthless, as had torrents of .223-, .308- and .45-caliber centerfire slugs.

The attackers seemed immune to all alloys of lead.

Only ten minutes had passed since the lookouts stationed on the lowest slopes of Mount Deseret, directly above the casino, had sounded an alarm. They had spotted a low dust cloud coming from the north, across the arid waste at the northernmost end of Skull Valley. The rolling wall of beige dirt had looked like the front edge of an approaching wind storm, but the sky was cloudless and the air was perfectly still. As the cloud rapidly closed on them, Doyal had put the compound on full alert. His sec men ran to take up their positions inside the wire-fenced perimeter, at machine gun nests and mortar emplacements.

When the cloud was within twenty yards of the

main gate, it had suddenly lifted and dispersed, exposing eight onrushing wags. Wags the likes of which none of them had ever seen. The gleaming black vehicles each had six enormous, churning, lug-treaded wheels. They had no windows or ob slits; except for what looked like rotating weapon pods on the roofs and sides, their outer surfaces were perfectly smooth. The heavy wags rammed, flattened and rolled over the hurricane fence as if it were nothing.

An instant after the fence came down, an even more astonishing thing happened. A half-dozen, shiny black flying machines swept low around the base of the mountain, clustered in tight attack formation.

Flying machines hadn't been seen in that part of Deathlands since skydark.

Understandably, Baron Doyal was caught unprepared. He had fortified and stocked the casino compound to hold off a ground siege of many months. But this was no siege. This was a rout.

When concentrated machine-gun, small-arms and mortar fire had no effect on the oncoming vehicles and aircraft, when the beams of light began to slice and drop sec men with uncanny accuracy, the only course left was a full retreat. Doyal and his troops scrambled to the cover of the casino building.

Which, as it turned out, was no cover at all.

As he squinted through the swirling smoke and dust, Doyal dimly saw two-legged black monsters marching through the entrance. Tall, with big, round heads, and limbs and torsos segmented like insects, they advanced in a straight line, ignoring the flurries of bullets that zinged at them. Their longblasters returned fire with narrow beams of whistling emerald light.

Unable to defend themselves, the baron's sec men were surrendering en masse, throwing aside their useless weapons and themselves belly down on the rubble.

"We can't stay here!" Doyal's second in command shouted at him.

The baron turned toward the man crouched on his right. Capo Waslick's right eye was nearly swollen shut, his cheek grossly bloated and as shiny as a balloon. The ear on that side of his face had vanished, replaced by an angry scorch.

"We've got to get out now!" Waslick said, and shoved him so hard that he dropped the shotgun.

Moving on rubbery knees, the baron hurried over the unspeakable carnage of the lobby, past the mingled pieces of the living and the dead, through an archway that led toward the kitchens at the rear of the building.

The escape tunnel was hidden behind a massive floor-to-ceiling pantry shelf. Its secret door was balanced to open at a touch, even when the shelf was loaded with goods. The underground corridor beyond had been built in the predark days, by the casino's original, Native American owners.

Eleven-thousand-foot Mount Deseret had shielded this small corner of the Skull Valley Indian Reservation from the brunt of the three-warhead airburst that had turned Salt Lake City into a hardened glob of thermoglass and the Great Salt Lake into a cloud of superheated vapor, which had flash-cooked every living thing between the predark cities of Ogden and Provo.

The native peoples of the Skull Valley reservation had vanished in the same blinding instant as the Great Salt Lake. Their shapes were still visible on a few of the exposed boulders, permanently burned into the rock by an initial energy pulse brighter than ten thousand suns. The only artifacts of their culture that had survived doomsday were the concrete pads scattered over the valley floor, pads that had once underlayed shoddy, government-provided housing and, of course, the Mount Deseret Casino Resort.

When the tremendous weight of water was suddenly lifted from the lake basin to the north, it set violent geologic forces in motion. For decades afterward, strong earthquakes shook the area. The shifting of plates of subsurface rock caused pure springs to bubble up from the slopes of Mount Deseret. The Slake City side of the mountain remained barren, its soil poisoned by radiation, but the more protected Skull Valley side soon supported lush stands of trees and wide meadows.

Sixty years after skydark, the first resettlers moved into the resort complex. Before long, a small community had grown up around the sweetwater stream formed by the confluence of nukecaust-created springs. With uncontaminated water and land at their disposal, the settlers began cultivating crops for profit. They used remnants of Highways 80 and 15 to build their trade routes.

Charlie Doyal was neither farmer nor merchant. His talents lay in his unique "people skills." He had moved into Skull Valley at the head of a band of heavily armed, no-mercy blackhearts. With brutality and intimidation, he had quickly turned the disorganized squatters into his agricultural slaves and crowned himself baron. After taking over the outlets for beans and corn that the farmers had established, Doyal changed the nature of the business. Instead of selling corn for food, he boiled it down for its sugar, which he used to distill a highly alcoholic beverage. In Deathlands, where any escape from the hardship and terror of daily life was greatly prized, his joy juice was a high-demand, high-profit item.

Over the years, Doyal also perfected his own version of jolt. He started by cultivating opium poppies, then traded the black-tar heroin he manufactured for a stockpile of predark pharmaceutical and industrial chemicals—the makings of crystal methedrine. His jolt recipe was a superaddictive combination of narcotic and stimulant, with a little Mindburst mushroom thrown in for its hallucinatory effects. The rad-mutated fungus was one of the few living things that thrived inside the thermoglass monolith. The success of this product had earned Doyal the nickname of "Baron Jolt."

To service and expand his operation, he maintained a fleet of gas-and diesel-powered vehicles, which weren't cheap to maintain. The distribution of the goods and collection of the profits required a standing army of sec men. Minutes ago, it was one of the largest and most far-reaching enterprises in Deathlands.

Now it was history.

In the feeble, flickering torchlight of the concrete tunnel, Baron Doyal ran for his life. He ran past seeping walls lined with barrels and crates, his suddenly useless cache of arms, ammunition, joy juice and jolt. Capo Waslick was right behind him. At the mountain end of the corridor, a steel ladder led up through a vertical tunnel hacked into the rock. It was a long climb in darkness to the sealed hatch at the top of the shaft. Doyal turned the small locking wheel, shoved the hatch open and scrambled out into the bright sunshine, followed by his second in command.

Five hundred feet below their position, the black flying machines hovered above the casino, spitting shrieking bolts of green light. The aircraft had twin rotors, a large one on top of the fuselage, and a slightly smaller one spinning perpendicular to it, at the tail.

Waslick nudged the baron, pointing out the two sec men slinking along the back side of one of the outbuildings. Both carried fully extended, olive-green rocket launchers. Reaching the building's corner, they shouldered the LAWs, stepped out and fired upward at nearly point-blank range. The pair of rockets got within ten feet of their stationary targets, then abruptly veered off, corkscrewing away, and exploding harmlessly out in the green-and-pink poppy fields of Skull Valley.

One of the gyroplanes immediately broke off its attack on the casino, banked in a tight circle and swooped down. The unsuccessful rocketeers dumped the spent LAW tubes and took to their heels, back the way they'd come.

They didn't get far.

As the flying machine swept over them, a black net dropped from its belly, scooping them up, then dragging them along the ground. Meanwhile, another of the gyroplanes stopped firing and abruptly climbed, heading straight for the baron and his second in command.

"They've seen us!" Waslick cried.

There was no cover among the low boulders. Doyal turned and dashed up the narrow mountain trail. Before he'd climbed seventy feet, a dark shadow passed over him, followed by a gust of wind and a fall of stinging mist. When Doyal looked up, he saw the glittering spray jetting from a nozzle at the rear of the aircraft. As he ran on, he covered his nose and mouth with his good hand and tried not to breathe.

It didn't make any difference.

After a few steps, he became tanglefooted. Then his legs gave way beneath him and he hit the ground, hard. He lay there fully conscious, heart thudding in panic, but unable to move his arms or legs, or raise his head. The flying machine returned, its propwash whipping his back as it slowly descended. A mechanical claw reached down and caught Doyal by the ankle. It jerked him up and deposited him in the waiting net. Moments later, both he and Capo Waslick were unceremoniously dumped in the middle of the casino parking lot.

It took twenty minutes for Doyal to recover the full use of his limbs. By that time, all of the surviving sec men and agri-slaves had been rounded up, either by gyroplane or ground forces, and deposited in the parking lot. Close to one hundred captives sat crosslegged on the ground. Most of them kept their eyes downcast, afraid to look at the inhuman black figures that surrounded them.

Though Doyal was afraid, too, more afraid than he

had ever been in his life, he had to see—and under-stand—what had brought down his hard-won enter-prise.

Almost all of the attackers were over six feet tall. Their outer covering, which he had first taken for a mutie insect shell, on closer inspection looked more like some kind of synthetic full-body armor. The black material was segmented to allow free move-ment of arms, legs and torso; the hands were pro-tected by gauntlets made of the same stuff, the feet by overlapping plates. The smoke-colored, wrap-around visors on the fronts of their helmets concealed their faces from view. There was no way to tell whether they were norm or mutie. Their massive-looking longblasters were a bullpup design, with a single claw-toothed flash-hider over the muzzles of the three barrels. The weapons either weren't heavy, or these creatures were superstrong.

Doyal estimated there were at least seventy-five of the bastards. More than enough, considering their fire-power and defenses. As terrifying as the light weap-ons were, it was their defensives that shook his mind to its core. Experience told him that bullets couldn't be deflected without first striking a solid object, nor could LAW rockets for that matter. What he had seen with his own eyes made no sense.

As he sat there, trying to puzzle it out and failing, two more enormous black wags rolled up to the park-ing area. They towered over the attack vehicles. Their single trailers were longer than a triple semi, and their tractors were the size of earthmovers. The combined weight of the two trucks cracked the ancient pave-ment like a thin glaze of ice. As soon as the vehicles had stopped, some of the black creatures rushed over and began unrolling long hoses from them, which they then coupled to the parked wags and aircraft. Doyal concluded they were being refueled.

Without any apparent signal, the rest of the creatures began separating the captives into two groups at blasterpoint. A pair of them loomed over Doyal, looking closely at his injured hand for a moment before walking on. The slaves and sec men who had lost a leg or an arm, or who had been blinded or severely brain damaged, about thirty in all, were brutally dragged away from the others, to the far side of the parking lot. They didn't go quietly. There was a lot of screaming; some of it from the pain caused by rough treatment, most of it from their abject terror.

When the prisoners had been divided, one of the creatures stepped between the two groups. It stopped in the middle of the parking lot and a disembodied, electronic-sounding voice boomed forth, "I want obedience. If I don't get it…" It made a sweeping gesture toward the wounded.

At the signal, four of the black monsters with tanks strapped to their backs unclipped the nozzles on their hips and strode through the injured, squirting a creamy yellow foam over them.

The effect was horrific. The yellow foam dissolved both flesh and bone on contact. As it was heaped upon the feebly struggling wounded, it melted them like guttering brown candles, into so much sticky goo. When the foam stopped bubbling and shrank away, all that was left of thirty human beings was a slowly spreading wet spot on the asphalt.

"You will perform hard labor for me," the monster

in charge told the stunned captives. "If you meet your individual daily quotas, you will be given water. If you don't, you will go without. If you fail to meet your work quotas three days in a row, you will be foamed."

Sec men and agri-slaves knew a death sentence when they heard one. They began to weep and moan.

"Where is the baron of this place?" the creature demanded. "Is he still alive?"

Doyal's stomach dropped. He had been hoping to blend in with the others, to avoid being singled out for some special punishment. He prayed that the others would say that he was dead.

All around him, his former supporters and friends somehow found the strength to raise their arms and point in his direction. He bared his teeth at them like an animal.

The talking monster loomed over him. "Stand!" it commanded.

Charlie Doyal rose shakily to his feet. He could see his own reflection in the surface of the opaque visor, his gray hair in wild disarray, eyes already pleading for mercy.

The electronic voice boomed again. "Laser cuff this one first."

Two creatures grabbed him. A third attached dull silver bands to his wrists and ankles. Then they let him go.

Doyal stared uncomprehendingly at the ornaments. They weren't connected to each other. They didn't limit his movement like manacles. What they were supposed to do, or prevent him from doing, he couldn't imagine.

"Can you run, Baron?" the monster said.

Doyal looked up at visor. He nodded. "I can run."

"If you make it past the fence, off the parking lot before I can zap you with this," the creature said, patting the side of its laser weapon, "I will let you live. Otherwise you will die where you stand. Do you understand?"

"Yes," Doyal said.

The monster then addressed the other captives, "This is a lesson meant for all of you. Watch closely." To the baron, it said, "Feel free to start whenever you're ready."

Doyal had butterflies in his stomach and the muscles in his legs were locked tight. He couldn't do anything about the butterflies, but he stretched his thighs, first one, then the other, all the while looking over his shoulder at the monster. He had no doubt that clearing the parking lot was his one and only chance to survive.

As he turned away, preparing to make his sprint, the creature lowered its weapon, pointing its muzzle at the ground. The weapon stayed down as Doyal took off running. Arms pumping, legs driving, he dashed as fast as he could for the line of monsters that stood between him and the downed fence. As he approached them, the monsters stepped aside to let him pass. Doyal immediately began zigzagging, figuring that their leader had its weapon up and a clear line of fire.

His legs started to give out fifty feet from the crushed fence. At every stride he thought surely he would be hit. Wheezing from the effort, Doyal threw himself across the finish line. He stumbled over the mesh and turned to face the parking lot. Still backing away, he had enough energy to thrust his balled right fist into the air. A gesture of victory.

Cut short.

His legs buckled under him and his right hand sailed away from his wrist, arcing back toward the parking lot. The baron sat down hard on his backside. At first, he didn't understand what had happened. His brain couldn't make sense of what his eyes were seeing. The silver cuffs lay on the dirt beside him, along with both of his severed feet and one of his severed hands. Awful truth and awful agony struck in the same instant.

The monster in charge turned its back on Doyal's shrill screams and snarled an order to its subordinates. "Now that they understand how short the leash is, cuff them all."

Chapter Six

Ryan Cawdor awoke in pitch darkness, gasping for breath. The air reeked of ammonia. It burned like cold fire inside his nose, his throat, all the way to the bottom of his lungs. Though he couldn't see anything, he sensed he was in an enclosed, crowded space.

Sitting up, Ryan fumbled at his belt for the rubberized grip of a battery-powered flashlight. When he turned it on and played the bright circle of light over his surroundings, it revealed a confusing world of green-on-green. Slick, convoluted drapes hung like baffles from the high ceiling and trailed down to the floor, blending into the landscape of erratic folds and rounded humps.

It was quiet.

So quiet Ryan could hear the pounding of his own heart.

He knew exactly where he was. Somehow he'd materialized in the Slime Zone of the parallel Earth, a whitecoat-created no-man's-land deep beneath the surface. With every breath he was sucking in spores of genetically modified cyanobacteria. Unless he found a way out and quickly, the microscopic organisms would fill his lungs like wet cement and suffocate him.

He used his free hand to push up from the ground. As he did, his fingers slid off a solid object hidden beneath countless layers of bacterial membrane. Whatever was hidden, it shifted under his weight. It shifted, then slowly twisted back. Automatically, he swept the flash beam over it.

And to his horror saw the dead face of Krysty Wroth.

Her pale white cheeks, which his touch had cleared of slime, were smeared with streaks of green-black. Trickles of the same color oozed from her nostrils, and out from between her bloodless parted lips. Her prehensile red hair lay dark, matted and still.

His beautiful Krysty was wrapped in a living shroud.

Ryan coughed and the pain, like an icy dagger, twisted deep in his lungs. Overcome by the lack of oxygen, by the wet weight of the spores already blooming inside of him, he felt the urge to lie down beside his lover, to close his good right eye and join her in death. As powerful as the urge was, he couldn't make himself do it.

With a groan, Ryan hurled himself away from her corpse. The instinct for survival was something he'd been born with, something that the intense violence of his life had only served to hone. It wouldn't be denied. As he ran, he slogged knee deep through heaps of the out-of-control agricultural bacteria. A maze of hanging folds blocked his view on all sides, heavy, membranous curtains that fell upon his head and shoulders as he furiously batted them out of his path. Ryan didn't know which way was out. He didn't know if there *was* an out. With no landmarks to guide him, he could only choose a likely direction and try to stay on course.

He had thrashed and slogged no more than twenty feet when his boot heel hit something buried and he lost his balance. He went down on his hands and knees, plunging into the slunk up to his armpits. Somehow he held onto the flashlight. As he jerked himself out, a thick coating of slime fell away from yet another face, directly in front of him.

It was Dean.

It can't be, Ryan told himself, reaching out and gently touching the cold forehead with his fingertips. It can't be....

But it was.

Ryan shoved off the encasing slime and drew the limp body into his arms. He dropped the flashlight and it rolled away. He let it go. It didn't matter anymore.

Nothing mattered anymore.

The future was gone.

Rocking back and forth, Ryan cradled his dead son. Each breath was more difficult than the last. After two or three minutes, he began coughing up dark, bitter fluid and little clots of fibrous matter. Pain skewered his chest, and the spreading chill in his hands and feet matched the cold that squeezed around his failing heart.

RYAN JERKED as he suddenly regained consciousness. Waves of nausea slammed him, his throat opened, and it was all he could do not to splatter himself as he projectile vomited. Minutes later, when the sickness finally passed, he found himself curled on the floor of a mat-trans chamber. Its armaglass walls were bright yellow with gold flecks, and cottony wisps of jump mist still clung to the ceiling. Krysty, Dean and Mildred were out cold on the floor beside him. They hadn't even begun to stir. He checked Dean's breathing to make sure the boy was all right. Jak, J.B., and Doc were awake, but not yet recovered from the ordeal of rematerialization. In separate corners of the chamber, they retched on all fours, like dogs.

His head swimming, Ryan struggled to his feet.

Traveling via the mat-trans gateways was never pleasant, but it was the only quick way for the companions to move from place to place. More than a century ago, the nukecaust had destroyed the rail lines and the shipping and airline fleets. They had never been rebuilt. Without constant repair, the interstate highway system had mostly turned to sand. The network of secret mat-trans gateways, high-tech artifacts of the military industrial complex, was blast protected, self-powered, computer controlled and automatic—you got in, you closed the door and you were transported to another gateway chamber somewhere else.

No one knew what the long-term health consequences of using the system might be. But short term, there was both physical and psychological discomfort, and they were directly connected. As Doc had explained it once, the gateways reduced human consciousness and physicality to a stream of electrical charges. During the mat-trans deconstruction process, all the buffers, the self-protective partitions of the brain fell away.

Which meant that things surfaced in jump dreams. Ugly things the conscious mind refused to face.

The companions rarely discussed the details of

their dreams, other than to say, "Whew, that was a bad one!" These were private horrors better left to private contemplation, or even better still, plain forgotten. None of them had ever shared the fear that they each felt, that one of these times they wouldn't wake up. That they would get stuck between gateways, existing only as streams of charged particles, forever trapped in their own worst nightmare.

There was nothing subtle about the meaning of Ryan's jump dream. His unconscious and conscious minds were on the same page: he not only faced his own death, but the death of hope for his world. All that he loved, all that he valued, was on the verge of being smothered.

Ryan started to feel queasy again—the smell of vomit, the smell of the smoked catfish they carried in their day packs and the sharpish, unpleasant odor of mat-trans by-product chemicals was getting to him. He stepped carefully over Krysty's legs and found the chamber's exit door.

Outside was a rectangular floor of poured concrete surrounded by rough-hewned red rock walls and a very high rock ceiling. In the light of a caged electric bulb over the door of the chamber, he could see the spiral metal staircase leading up. Ryan checked his weapons, adjusted his pack, then climbed the stairs. At the top was another level of cave and more concrete floor, which narrowed at its far end and led him through switchbacked walls of rock.

As he rounded a turn, bright sunlight from the cave's opening stabbed into his eye. He let his vision adjust before he stepped out. In front of him, the bone-dry Utah desert stretched off in all directions; behind him was a towering red mesa.

Though the creators of this gateway had tried to match the bedrock around the artificial entrance they had constructed, they hadn't figured on the effects of the chem rain, which had aged the synthetic and natural materials differently. Jak Lauren had been the first to notice the strange discoloration in the rock formation. When he had checked it more closely, he had found the man-made cave.

Ryan sat down inside the shade of the entry and waited there for the others, grateful for a few moments alone to think. He figured that the companions' best chance of winning the fight, and perhaps their only chance, was to find a way to confront the enemy from the parallel Earth head-on, and the sooner the better. If the invaders were distracted or confused by the strange new environment, they might make tactical mistakes, and therefore be vulnerable. It was a long shot, and he knew it. From what Ryan had seen, both on this world and its near twin, the opposition was whitecoat-efficient and bastard ruthless. If the invaders had already gotten used to their new home, there would be no escape for those who resisted.

For the thousandth time, Ryan asked himself whether he should send Dean away with Krysty or Jak. Or with both. That way the boy could avoid what was looking more and more like a suicide mission, and perhaps enjoy whatever remaining life fate offered him.

It seemed a simple, straightforward decision, but it wasn't.

Ryan knew Dean's heart as well as he knew his

own. Dean wanted more than anything to prove his worth to the group, to be valued as his own person by his father and the others, all of whom he hero-worshiped. Under the circumstances, Ryan knew his son would take being sent away as the ultimate rejection, the most terrible event in his life. It was like telling him, "Boy, you aren't fit company to die with, so go off and die by yourself."

For a father who loved his son, that was the ultimate lie.

In the end, Ryan concluded that it wasn't his place to force his son to go or to stay. When the time came that the decision couldn't be put off, he would offer Dean a man's choice: die now, fighting at your father's side. Or die later, without him.

RYAN AND THE COMPANIONS arrived at the rim of Moonboy ville's box canyon early in the morning of their third day of march. Shouldering his Steyr, he used its telescopic sight to scan downrange. The sun was angled behind him so flare off the front lens wouldn't give away his position.

Before Armageddon, Moonboy had been a bedroom community of Salt Lake City; now it was a shamble of huts, lean-tos and rubblized lots where a development of upscale, three-story tract homes had once stood. Four of the ville's original streetlight poles still stood more or less upright, their gutted sockets trailing pigtails of severed power cord. The poles cast long, crooked shadows over the jumbled roofs of rusting corrugated metal.

Moonboy had once prided itself as being a "pure norm" ville. Which meant that in the vicinity it was always open season on muties, or suspected muties, who happened to wander by. It was the kind of place that accumulated human trash like the corner of a back alley. Hopeless marginals—over-the-hill black-hearts, inbred droolers, assorted triple stupes—swirled randomly around Deathlands for years only to wind up in this or some similar blind-canyon graveyard. With their backs to the wall, literally, at the end of the road, literally, they could tell lies in the shade and safely rot.

Or so they had thought.

Unfortunately for them, the first expeditionary force from the parallel universe had made Earthfall smack in the middle of the ville's main street. The drunken residents had mistaken their black battlesuits for some kind of mutie insect shells, and had opened fire in a wild but ineffectual free-for-all. After easily subduing Moonboy's inhabitants, Colonel Gabhart and his crew examined the survivors for brain viruses and for invisible but inheritable mutation-caused disorders. Ironically, they found that all the "pure norms" were incurably diseased.

A quick survey of the landscape told Ryan that no one had moved into the vacant huts since he and the companions had been there last. That didn't surprise him much. Even in broad daylight, Moonboy ville had a bad feel to it. It wasn't just deserted; it was tainted, spoiled. And if there were no visible signs of life below, there were still plenty of visible signs of death. Since Ryan knew what to look for, he could find them even at a distance of six hundred yards. They were nestled in protected places where the chem rain couldn't wash them away—under the collapsed roofs of lean-tos, inside the doorways of hammered-down hovels.

And if a passing would-be squatter didn't realize what the oblong brown blotches in the dirt signified, one whiff of the sick-sweet stench that hung over Moonboy like an evil fog would be clue enough.

Because Colonel Gabhart was afraid of contagious diseases spreading to his crew, he had used carni-phage foam on the dead and the dying to sterilize the place. Ryan had witnessed the foam in action. He could still remember the way the cannie had squealed as he tried to drag himself out from under the mounds of ravening microorganisms, as muscle and bone dissolved into a brown liquid that apparently even wild animals wouldn't touch.

The pervasive odor of decay had forced Gabhart and the rest of his team to make their permanent camp a good distance from the site of the massacre, on the farthest edge of the faint gridwork of the development's streets. That was where Ryan and the others had left them.

The camp was still there, but nobody was home.

"It looks like our friends have already moved on," Ryan said, lowering the rifle.

"Question is," J.B. said, "where did they go?"

"And did they go willingly?" Krysty added.

"No way of figuring that out from up here," Ryan said. "If we check the arroyo, we can see if they dug up the gyroplane and chilling gear. That would tell us something."

"Walk across canyon no good," Jak said, his red eyes glittering. He raised an arm and pointed around the top of the rim. "Hides for shooters along summit. Go down there we're in bastard cross fire."

"He's right," Mildred said. "Once we're in the middle of the canyon floor we've got nowhere to run. All the enemy has to do is seal off the mouth and start pushing us back. We'll end up pinned against the canyon's rear wall, facing a firing squad."

Ryan eyeballed the expanse of unprotected ground below. He couldn't argue with what Jak and Mildred had said. The trouble was, they had run out of completely risk-free options. "I'm going to go check the arroyo," he said, shouldering his scoped longblaster's sling. "Anybody wants to stay here, that's okay."

Whether they wanted to or not, none of the others stayed behind.

It was midmorning by the time they had descended the rim and safely crossed the canyon. The burial spot was in a dry creek bed that followed the sweeping S-curve of the canyon wall. From a long way off, they could make out the hatching of black scorch marks on the rock face. As they got closer, they could see the deep cuts in its surface, as well.

"By the Three Kennedys!" Doc exclaimed when the arroyo finally came into view.

The creek bed looked as if it had been systematically dynamited. It was an obstacle course of scattered mounds and deep pits of discolored dirt. The chaparral and sagebrush that had lined the dry channel was uprooted and fire blackened.

"Some of the gear's been dug up, that's for sure," J.B. offered.

"Not get far, though," Jak said. He bent and picked up a half-buried piece of black armored material, the end of which was shredded into a fan of stiff fibers.

"That's part of a gyroplane's main rotor," Ryan stated.

"More pieces of it are scattered all over the place, but they're a lot smaller than that," Mildred said. "Looks to me like it absorbed a direct hit from a missile."

"Another gyroplane landed and took off over here," Krysty said. She pointed at deep parallel marks made by an aircraft's skids. "And look at these wheel marks...."

Ryan knelt beside the tire prints. They were a yard wide and sank eighteen inches into the dirt.

"Big suckers," J.B. remarked as he looked over Ryan's shoulder. "I make it three wags. And from the boot prints all around, twenty-five or so ground troops."

Ryan nodded. The jury was still out on whether Gabhart and the others had left as recruits or as prisoners. "Spread out and let's see what else we can find," he said.

They fanned out along the edge of the disturbed area and then set off in a search line across the creek bed's unnatural ups and downs. It quickly became clear that all of the other-world battle gear had been recovered, but not by whom or why. Then Dean let out a shout.

When Ryan and the others joined the boy, he was standing on the edge of a blast crater. He stared down at a black-gauntleted hand and arm sticking out of the sand.

Mildred nudged it with her boot and it toppled

over. It was severed at the elbow. She picked it up by the wrist.

They all gathered around for a better look at the stump end of the grisly relic. The battlesuit material had been sliced through cleanly.

"That's a laser cut," J.B. said.

"An Achilles' heel!" Doc exclaimed. "It would appear that our foes can be harmed by their own terrible weapons. Their armor isn't invincible, after all."

"Something else there," Jak said. With that, he hopped into the bottom of the pit. When he climbed out, he was carrying the lower half of a battlesuit helmet. It had been cut twice crosswise by a laser beam, once at the neck where it joined the suit's collar, and again just below the point where the wearer's nose would have been. The upper part of the helmet, the visor and the wearer's skull were missing, perhaps carried off by some animal.

"Found this at the bottom, too," the albino said. He showed them a red brimless cap with the word FIVE stitched on the front.

Mildred took the cap from Jak and examined it more closely. The inside was caked with dried blood. "This was Ockerman's," she said, referring to Gabhart's systems engineer. "It looks like at least one of our friends didn't go back to the dark side."

"Where's the rest of him, though?" Dean asked.

"Let's keep looking," Ryan said.

They never did find Ockerman's body, or his head, for that matter, but a few minutes later they came across another corpse. It, too, was missing numerous parts.

Pedro Hylander had been the biologist on Gabhart's expeditionary team. His armless, legless, battlesuit-clad torso sat propped up against some boulders at the base of the canyon wall. He was without a helmet, and the vultures had been at him. They had emptied his eye sockets and torn off his lips and cheeks. Fat black flies crawled over his ruined face. Ryan could tell that the poor bastard had been alive when the birds got to him. Blood had crusted all down his chin and neck and the battlesuit's chest plate. His heart was still pumping when the vultures ripped out his tongue.

"They could've chilled him clean if they'd wanted to," J.B. said. "They messed him up like that and let him die slow for a reason."

"Could have been payback because Gabhart's team went renegade, or because they fought back when they were found," Mildred suggested.

Ryan stepped over to the cliff to examine the score marks on the rock face more closely. Up to this point, he had only seen the laser weapons cut through thin material—wood, steel, bone. From the shallow gouges in the sandstone, it appeared there were limits to the penetrating power of the laser weapons. The beams removed a few inches of rock at a time, but couldn't cut through more than that in a single swipe.

His curiosity satisfied, he surveyed the battlefield again. After a minute or two, he gave the others his conclusions. "It looks to me like Gabhart and the others had some advance warning," he said. "They could have seen the satellite track across the sky like we did, or mebbe they spotted the troops at a distance, or came across their wheel marks and knew what they meant. Wherever they were, whatever they were doing, they had enough time to get back here and recover some of their gear before the enemy showed up. We know at least two of them got into their battlesuits.''

"They must've put up a hell of a fight," Krysty said, "but it doesn't look like they did any damage to the opposition."

J.B. shook his head. "Even if they'd gotten all their gear up and running," he said, "they still didn't stand a chance. They were cornered, and then hit by a combined air and ground attack."

"How long ago did it happen, Jak?" Ryan said.

The albino brushed aside the surface of one of the blast pits until he came to damp sand. "Three days," he said. "Mebbe less, not more."

"And from the boot tracks we know the unit that hit them was around twenty-five strong, three wags, and at least one gyro," Ryan said. "It could have been a roving scout force, but it's hard to believe that their finding our friends was an accident. There's just too much country to hide in around here. Seems to me the attackers had to have scanned them from satellite, or they left sensors here that got tripped when Gabhart and the others came back to pick up their battle gear."

The companions had already encountered some of this remote-sensing technology. They were surrounded by a terrain littered with loose rocks of various sizes, any one of which might have been a camouflaged motion or sound detector.

"Correct me if I'm wrong, my dear Ryan," Doc rumbled, leaning on his swordstick, "but if your assumption is valid, then the die is already cast. In all likelihood, the enemy has tracked us here in exactly the same manner.''

'''Fraid so.''

"Which means that even as we speak, they are probably on their way to intercept us.''

Ryan didn't try to refute Doc's conclusion.

He couldn't.

After they had all recrossed the creek bed, J.B. took another look at the tire tracks. ''The opposition didn't make camp after the assault,'' he said. ''They just hit and git. From the tracks, it looks like they towed the missile gantry truck out of the hole we dug and drove it away with them.''

"We better get a move on,'' Ryan said. "If we head out the canyon mouth, we can see which way they came from.''

Jak nodded. ''I'm point.''

As the companions started to follow the albino, Ryan put a hand on Dean's shoulder. ''Wait a second, son,'' he said softly, drawing him aside. ''We need to talk.''

The boy looked up expectantly.

"Dean, listen close. Doc was right. Our situation is very bad, and it looks like it's only going to get worse. If the enemy is on their way, it may be a matter of minutes before they wipe us out. Your best chance to stay alive is to leave now with Krysty and Jak. To head back to the gateway with them and make a jump. To get as far away from here as you can.''

The boy was incredulous. ''Dad, you want me to leave?''

"What I want has nothing to do with it, Dean,''

Ryan said gently. "This is about you. About what you want. It's your life that's on the line."

"If I run with Krysty and Jak, they'll still find us, won't they? With that satellite and all the other white-coat gear they brought with them, we'll never ever be safe, will we? Not even if we run to the other side of the world?"

"I can't answer that for certain, but I won't lie to you, son. The chances are good they will find you sooner or later."

"And they will chill us when they find us?"

"Yes."

"Dad, are you telling me to go?"

"No. That's your choice."

The expression in the boy's eyes hardened; for Ryan it was like looking into a mirror. "Then I'm staying to fight."

"Are you sure that's what you want?"

"I'm sure, Dad. Come on, the others are getting a big lead—we'd better catch up."

As Ryan watched Dean run ahead, conflicting emotions surged through him. Even as his chest swelled with pride, he was crushed by the thought that his son had signed his own death warrant. Inwardly, he raged at the dire circumstances they found themselves trapped in, and at his own powerlessness to change things so far.

Rage was good.

Rage had helped him survive a thousand pitched battles. And every battle had tempered his body, his instinct and his spirit. If Ryan knew anything for certain, he knew this: if there was a way to win this struggle, he would find it.

He took up the rearguard position in the file as Jak led them along the rows of wheel tracks that paralleled the northern arm of the canyon wall. As Ryan walked along, he kept his eye out for defensive positions they could retreat to quickly—places to make a stand, the more enclosed the better, with entrances they could control. He wasn't the only one doing this; his companions knew the routine by heart.

When they reached the mouth of canyon, they could see the direction of the tire ruts leading in and leading out.

J.B. pulled his hat brim down to shield his glasses from the sun. "All the tracks head toward Slake City," he said. "The base for the invasion force must be that way."

"Not much between here and there," Krysty said. "No safe water, that's for sure."

"Trouble!" Jak cried. "Gyro coming!" He pointed at the horizon.

A single black gyroplane swept in low over the desert, flying out of the sun. That was just the tip of the iceberg. Far behind it on the plain, Ryan saw the spiraling pillars of dust that meant heavy vehicles were rolling toward them at high speed.

"The snake cave!" he shouted. "Triple red, let's go!"

The companions broke and ran for the side of the canyon. As they sprinted for cover, the whine of gyroplane's turbines grew louder. They were within twenty yards of the rock wall when a whistling shriek split the air. Oily desert shrubs blossomed in a line of fire to their left. Then a second beam of emerald light squealed over their heads and ripped into the sandstone cliff in front of them, making cascades of white sparks erupt from the red rock.

The warning shots didn't slow the companions, and none of them stopped to return fire. They knew that bullets were useless, and that their only hope was making the cave. They were almost to the wall when a blast of prop wind whipped dust into their faces. Behind them, engines howling, the gyroplane hovered, its rotor wash forcing them up against the wall in a swirling cloud of dirt.

Jak reached the entrance first and helped to pull the others into the angled slit in the cliff. Inside was cool darkness. Coughing and gasping for breath, the companions leaned against the crumbling sandstone.

The air attack broke off at once, but they could hear the gyroplane still hovering outside. Gradually, the rasp of their breathing slowed and their eyes adjusted to the cave entrance's dim light. From deeper in the cave came rustling sounds.

The rustling became a rattling.

"Shit!" J.B. snarled as he fumbled for a match. Light flared from the end of his small rag-wrapped torch. All around them the floor moved, uncoiling into dozens of thick-bodied, slithering shapes.

Mildred and Krysty instinctively drew their handguns.

"No bullets in here!" Ryan warned. "Ricochets. Stay back."

His panga knife scraped leather as it cleared his leg sheath. Grunting with the effort, Ryan cut a frantic, bloody path through the mutated rattlesnakes. This cave had kept the companions and Gabhart's crew in vittles—big, juicy, snake steaks—for better than a week. There was no choice now but to waste the rest of the nest—the rattler venom was agonizingly lethal. In the flickering torchlight he isolated, cornered and slaughtered the stragglers, using the flat of the blade to stun, followed by a quick backslash to decapitate.

With J.B. in the lead holding the torch, they crossed the sandy floor, stepping over headless, still thrashing bodies, moving toward the back of the cave. As they advanced, the ceiling and walls necked down, forming an archway that J.B. had to duck to pass under. Beyond the arch, the space widened into another domed chamber.

As Ryan approached the arch, his head brushed the ceiling. Pieces of loose rock and dirt came showering down.

"Watch out!" Mildred said, covering her head with her arms. "The roof's rotten."

Ryan ducked low to clear the arch. J.B. and the others were already examining the cave's back wall. On the floor a jumble of S-shaped snake tracks led up to it, then vanished. "There's a rad-blasted snake hole here!" the Armorer said, dropping to his knees. "Could be a way out!"

Jak fell to his knees beside J.B. and they both dug madly with their hands to deepen and to enlarge the hole.

From the mouth of the cave came the sound of heavy vehicles pulling up outside.

"Cover the entrance!" Ryan said.

Their weapons up and ready, the others took defensive positions on either side of the arch.

Ryan looked over his shoulder to see Jak squirming under the overhang of rock. J.B. passed him the torch through the hole, which plunged the cave into darkness.

From the cave's entrance an electronically amplified voice boomed, "You are trapped. Come out now and it will go much easier on you. If you make us come in after you, we will hurt you...badly."

Sounds of a scuffle and cursing came from the hole behind them. Moments later the torch popped back out and Jak scrambled out after it. "Dead end," he said, spitting out a mouthful of sand.

A beam of whistling green light speared through the middle of the cave, striking the back wall above Jak's head. He rolled out of the hole, out from under showers of fat sparks as the sandstone hissed and melted.

The companions drew back behind the curve of the archway, shielding their eyes from the green glare.

"You are outnumbered," said the electronic voice, much louder now to compensate for the piercing squeal of the laser beam. "There is nowhere to run. Surrender now or we will make this very unpleasant for you."

It already was unpleasant.

The laser beam was making the middle of the back wall glow like a huge ember. Sweat had already started to pour off the companions, and it was getting harder and harder to breathe.

Dean looked up at his father, eyes bright in the torchlight.

Ryan made a decision.

"Okay, okay!" he shouted. "We give up! Turn off the fireworks. We're coming out." Ryan signaled for everyone to keep their heads down.

The green light immediately winked off, but the red glow behind them continued. The rock wall was almost molten hot.

Boot heels crunched heavily on sand. The enemy had entered the cave. "Throw down your weapons," the electronic voice said.

Ryan looked at J.B. and pointed at the ceiling. "You know what to do, J.B.," he whispered.

As the one-eyed man started to step out from behind cover, J.B. stopped him with a hand on his shoulder. "Nah, let me do this one," he whispered back. He handed Ryan his M-4000 shotgun. "It'll make us even for all the times you've saved my sorry butt."

"Better screw on your hat," Ryan said, softly racking the pump gun's slide.

The Armorer grimly adjusted his fedora, then said to the others, "Everybody get ready to yell...."

His hands up, J.B. stepped into the line of fire, ducking under the archway. "Now, take it easy," he said to the tall, backlit figures just inside the cave entrance. "You know we can't hurt you. You don't have to prove anything more to us. We're giving up. See?"

He dropped to his knees in the sand and held his arms lifted high over his head.

Black figures approached with their laser rifles pointed at his head. One of them came within ten feet of him before it stopped. "Where are the others?" it said.

"Yahhh!" J.B. replied, bellowing at the top of his lungs.

"Yahhh!" Ryan hollered as he swung out from

behind the rock. The others yelled, too, as hard as they could, to keep from being deafened as the Smith & Wesson pump gun roared in the enclosed space. Orange flame from the muzzle-blast licked the ceiling. Ryan racked and fired, racked and fired as fast as he could.

On the third blast, there was a mighty groan from above, then in a cloud of dust, the ceiling of the entry chamber came crashing down.

Chapter Seven

Behind Dr. Huth, in the back of the lumbering bus, the three sluts were passing the time with a noisy dice game in which the winner got the right to bitch slap the losers across the face. Oblivious to their squeals, and to the pounding vibration of the rutted road, their satiated customers lay in a snoring heap on the mattresses.

Outside the bus, the landscape was uniformly bleak. To Huth's left, across the beige, featureless plain, were distant mountain slopes. Poisoned by radiation, they looked like monstrous heaps of brown dirt. To his right was the gray-green glacier of nukeglass, along whose southernmost edge they had been driving for more than half an hour. Though the Slake City phenomenon keenly interested him, the combination of surface glare and road vibration made it impossible for him to study its details.

Huth found it droll that the most significant act of this reality's whitecoats had been to supply the means for a civilization-ending, global holocaust. Four hundred years of creative, thoughtful inquiry into the diverse mechanisms of nature had produced thirty minutes of spectacular hell. From Huth's alternate-universe perspective, the nukecaust was nothing short of a blessing. The removal of ninety-five percent of the human beings from the planet had forestalled the real end-game scenario, which, as he had seen, came with the whimper of starving billions, not an earth-shaking bang.

When the driver started blowing the bus's horn, Huth lost his train of thought.

"Now arriving at Slake City," Mike the Drunkard announced as he tapped the brakes.

The lanky former whitecoat jumped quickly to his feet. He clung to one of the stainless-steel support poles in the aisle and squinted through the dirt-rimmed windshield. The repeated bleating of the horn roused the other passengers from their stupor. Eager to gaze upon the Promised Land, they lurched forward and pressed in close behind Huth, exhaling an eye-watering fog of alcohol fumes.

What they saw made them cheer and hoot and stamp their feet.

A short distance from the edge of the nukeglass, the Slake City encampment was just as Mike the Drunkard had described it. This was no typical Death-lands shantytown. No hodgepodge of rusted-out car bodies and scavenged fiberglass and scrap metal. It consisted of a cluster of shiny, black, segmented domes, the biggest of which was seventy feet in diameter. All of the structures were interconnected by black tubular walkways.

Huth's heart soared. The prefab mil-spec shelters were definitely the product of FIVE's technology. Made of the same synthetic, artificially intelligent material as the battlesuits, they could deflect conventional and laser attacks. Next to the clustered domes were a half-dozen, all-black, all-terrain assault vehicles, state-of-the-art killing machines designed for

high-speed pursuit and merciless interdiction. Closer
to the thermoglass massif, beside the start of a crude
road that cut over it, stood a group of huge black
semitrailers and tractors. These, too, had all-terrain
capability. On the far side of the domes, a half-dozen
attack gyroplanes sat on a landing field, lined up and
ready to scramble. From the number of otherworld
domes, vehicles and aircraft, Huth had no doubt that
his people had come across in force this time, and
that they had come prepared to stay.

Big Mike didn't stop the bus at the main compound, but drove on to a pounded rectangle of dirt
roughly one hundred feet square. Inside it, huddled
on the ground, were sixty to seventy people. The
seated Deathlanders didn't rise to their feet when
Mike parked the bus beside them, nor did they make
any sign of greeting or curiosity. Few of them, in fact,
even bothered to look up.

"Why are they just sitting there like that?" a man
standing behind Huth said. "Are they rad-blasted
dimmies?"

FIVE's top whitecoat could have answered the
drunk's question, but he didn't. He knew that no matter how many troops had crossed over to this reality,
there were certain jobs they wouldn't tackle themselves—dangerous tasks that were better left to an
expendable indigenous population. Because the Byram ville fools hadn't noticed or guessed the signifi-
cance of the silver bracelets and anklets worn by the
driver, the whores and all the people seated on the
ground, they were in for a very unpleasant surprise.
It pleased their former latrine engineer and kick toy
to keep it that way.

The woman standing beside Huth lifted one of her gigantic naked breasts and idly scratched the skin underneath it. "Hey, Big Mike," she slurred, swaying on her feet. "Where's them fancy new shitters you told us about? Gotta pee me a river."

"What the fuck is *that?*" cried one of the men, pointing out an open side window.

From a bulkhead doorway in the biggest of the domed huts a squad of black-armored creatures poured forth. They carried massive tribarreled longblasters. They jogged with grim purpose toward the bus.

"Giant fucking mutie roaches!" a young man exclaimed.

"Monsters! Rad-blasted monsters!" someone else shouted from behind.

"They're gonna eat us!" the woman cried. "Do something!"

There was nothing to be done.

Fear quickly sobered Huth's fellow passengers, but not before the black warriors had fanned out and surrounded the vehicle. There wasn't time for any of them to scoot out the door or crawl out the side windows. When they realized there was no escape from the horrors that waited outside, their fear turned to panic. Bleating like sheep, the passengers hurled themselves under the seats. Huth was the only one left standing.

Mike the Drunkard climbed from the driver's seat. He didn't waste energy trying to pry the passengers loose himself. Instead, he shouted down the aisle to his trio of sluts, "Get 'em out of here!"

The sluts advanced, wielding long, thick, black-tape-wrapped batons. From the looks on their faces, it was the high point of their day. It was their turn to do the prodding.

The pink-haired slut didn't swing her club at the legs of the first passenger she came across; she merely tapped him on the buttocks with it. There was a sharp crackling sound, and a fat blue spark jumped from the tip of the baton to the seat of his pants.

"Ee-yow!" he cried, jerking away from the baton tip so violently that he crashed the top of his head into the wall. As he scrambled onto the seat, he waved his hands in the air. "No, no...no more!"

"Get out!" the slut ordered him.

The man stole a sideward glance out the window, cringed at the black creature looking back at him and seized hold of the seat back's bar with both hands. He hung on to it, white-knuckled, and refused to budge.

When the pink-haired slut tried to touch the back of his hand with the electric prod, he deftly moved it out of the way, sliding it along the tubing but still maintaining his death grip. Obviously, this wasn't the first time a victim had tried the maneuver. The woman immediately countered by pressing the tip of the baton to the bar.

Blue sparks flew and the air crackled.

From the effect, Huth judged the voltage discharge was considerable. In an instant it brought the man bolt upright from his seat. He crouched there, shuddering, his teeth clenched, the tendons in his neck standing out like cables, unable to open his smoking hands and pull away from the pain. Only when the pink-haired slut drew back the baton and released him from the paralysis could he begin to scream. She waved her magic wand at him once more, and he took off down the aisle, running past Huth and down the steps.

The other two sluts gleefully attacked the remaining malingerers. Not even the strongest of them could withstand the shock treatment for more than a few seconds. One by one, they deserted their dark hidey-holes, then allowed themselves to be stampeded down the aisle and out the door.

Still clinging to his stanchion, Huth watched these events unfold with no small measure of delight. He was confident that one by one, the wrongs of his recent history were about to be righted, that he was about to resume his former, lofty place in the order of things.

From the bottom of the stairway, the pink-haired slut aimed her prod at Huth's scrawny behind. "And what about the bag of bones?" she asked.

"Nah, don't waste the battery," Big Mike answered. He grabbed the scientist by the scruff of the neck. Before Huth could protest, he was sent tumbling down the steps. The shovel landed in the dirt beside him.

"Better take that with you," Mike said. "You're gonna need it."

As Huth pushed up from the ground, spitting dust, the battlesuited troopers closed in on all sides, trapping the passengers against the side of the bus.

The woman didn't wait for a fancy two-hole outhouse to relieve herself; she didn't wait at all. As she cowered, monumentally topless, a wide, wet stain spread across the seat of her BDU pants. She wasn't alone in her sudden loss of bladder control. Two of the young men likewise soiled themselves before they dropped to their bellies and buried their faces in the dirt.

Huth was the only one who showed no fear. He straightened, brushed himself off and, leaving the shovel behind, stepped over to one of the helmeted soldiers. There was no insignia on the trooper's battlesuit, at least none visible to the naked eye. Not that Huth expected to see the word FIVE inscribed on the breastplate. He had already concluded that this wasn't a FIVE operation. As director of the Totality Concept, he knew that FIVE didn't have a backup trans-reality unit in place. Only the individual global conglomerates had the economic and technical clout to duplicate his great achievement. The research had to have been done in secret as it was a major treaty violation, subject to extreme punishment. Given the fact that his Earth was in its last days, the threat of punishment was no deterrent. You could only die once.

As Huth approached, the soldier reacted, and he found himself staring down the claw-foot flash-hider of a tribarrel laser. The muzzle was aimed at the bridge of his nose. Not only was the weapon capable of boring a hole clear through his head in a fraction of a second, but also it could simultaneously cook everything between his ears. The thought of his precious, genius-level brain reduced to a pea-sized cinder made him go momentarily weak-kneed.

"Stand back!" The order blasted out of the battlesuit's external speaker along with a squawk of feedback.

These were his people, Huth assured himself. He was a man of status, of renown, even. He spoke quickly, showing his empty, helpless hands. "I know how terrible I must look to you," he said. "And I know how difficult it's going to be for you to believe me, but I am Dr. Huth, director of the Totality Concept trans-reality program."

The soldier didn't respond.

Huth continued, and as he did, his voice rose in pitch. "I was sucked across to this world during the explosion," he said. "I have endured terrible hardships to get here and find you. See, see this?" He held up the embroidered FIVE on his lab coat's breast pocket.

The trooper's gauntleted hand moved to the plate beside the pulse rifle's trigger guard. Something snicked.

"No, don't do that," Huth groaned, realizing that the soldier had released the rifle's safety. "I know about FIVE. Omnico, Invecta, Mitsuki, Questar and Hutton-Byrum-Kobe. I know you're human under the battlesuits. How would I know all that if I wasn't telling you the truth? If I didn't come from the same reality as you?"

"Maybe you're psychic," said the digitalized voice. "Get in line with the others for your bracelets, or I'm going to fry your wormy little brain."

"Rad-blast it!" Mike the Drunkard shouted, hurrying down from the bus's steps. "Don't chill the dimmie bastard! If you chill him, I won't make my quota for today."

"You're bringing in the dregs," the soldier countered. "This skinny scab shouldn't count toward your quota, anyway."

"I know he looks kind of thin and wheezy," Mike

said, "but he's got a lot of work left in him. I've seen the man shovel shit, so I know what I'm talking about."

"If your shoveler doesn't move back three steps real quick, he's going to *be* shit."

Huth took the trooper at his or her word and retreated the required distance. Overcome by anguish, he threw back his head, clenched his fists and cried, "Somebody here has got to know me! I'm Dr. Huth! I developed this technology! I'm the reason you're all here!"

This admission drew murderous stares from the captive Deathlanders seated on the ground nearby. A few of them resonantly hawked and spit in his direction.

Huth fell to his knees and began to sob into his hands.

"Get over there with the others," the soldier said, poking him in the back with the rifle. "Do it now, or you're dead."

Then another amplified voice said, "Don't shoot. I know him."

Huth wiped his eyes as the battlesuited figure approached him. "Oh, thank you. Thank you!" he gushed. "You can't imagine the hardship and humiliation I've endured."

The figure said, "Cuff him."

"But…but…" Huth stammered as troopers quickly snapped laser manacles on his feet and wrists. "If you know who I am, why are you treating me like this?"

"Because I don't want you running off again."

Even distorted by the audio processor, the voice sounded vaguely familiar to him. "But I didn't run off," he protested, rising from his knees. "I was transported here by accident when the missile blew up the Totality Concept complex."

"There's no way to verify that, is there? Maybe you were part of the sabotage plan. Maybe you masterminded it. All I know for sure is that you're here and that my slave catcher snatched you up."

The voice suddenly clicked in Huth's memory. "CEO Trask?" he said, squinting hard at the opaque visor. "Is that you?"

The visor cleared.

What Huth saw inside the helmet struck him speechless for a second. He had known Dredda Otis Trask since she was a little girl. Her late father, Regis Otis Trask, had been one of his early champions. The elder Trask had promoted his career as a young whitecoat, had followed his rise to fame and influence and had been instrumental in his being appointed to the directorship of the Totality Concept, FIVE's most advanced and ambitious research program.

Regis Otis Trask and the other CEOs of FIVE were like figures from ancient history. Like the Caesars or the Borgias. These modern kings maintained their power through enormous, self-perpetuating bureaucracies, through favors granted or withdrawn, through webs of conspiracies. As with the Caesars and Borgias, their climb to the top was always bloody and violent. And once they were enthroned, the CEOs used their private armies to keep their positions. Their success was the result of cunning, not intelligence. Of brutality, not reason. No reasoning individual would have wrung out the resources of the world like the last drops of juice from an orange.

Remarkable genius though he was, Huth had come into the picture too late to do anything but delay the inevitable. There was no way to change the course of history that had already been set by the conglomerates, who had balanced markets, consumption and the taking of profits without regard to tomorrow. Over the course of their century-long reign, the conglomerates' viewpoint had shifted from "there's plenty to go around," to "let's squabble and backstab over the trickle that's left."

In terms of outright viciousness, the Trask daughter had been even more prone to excess than her father. She was always able to grab Regis's attention, which she treasured, by going one step further than anyone else was willing to go. Of course, there were never any negative consequences to her acts if they didn't produce, or if they turned out to be catastrophic. Her position as the only child of Regis Otis Trask had made her invulnerable before his death. When she was made CEO in his place, she remained untouchable. Dredda was the CEO who had pushed through FIVE's disastrous Beefy-Cheesie, Tater-Cheesie program, and she had personally coined the phrase "Let them eat rock."

She had repeatedly demonstrated that she had no scruples, foresight or concern for aftermaths. Huth had privately ranked her as one of the least intelligent of the CEOs he had ever dealt with. This combination also made her one of the most dangerous.

The female standing before him wasn't the same Dredda he'd seen two months ago. The weight and density of the bones of her face had increased, as had her gross size. He no longer looked down on her; they stood almost eye to eye. Though he knew he was taking a risk in asking for the details, his scientific curiosity got the better of him.

"You've certainly changed since I last saw you," he said.

"So have you," Dredda said, giving his shambling, bloodstained costume and missing teeth the once-over.

"I have been badly abused by the people here," Huth said. "In order to survive, I have been forced to do things too awful to describe. Being lost in Deathlands has been the most terrible experience of my life. But you? What happened to you?"

"A little genetic engineering," she said. "I'm bigger, stronger and faster. Smarter, too."

"Really?"

"I've gotten smart enough to know I don't need you anymore."

A great lump rose in Huth's throat. He was flabbergasted. "Surely, my expertise…"

"Is out of date," she finished for him. "My white-coats stole your technology, miniaturized it and made it portable. See those two big semitrailers over there? The trans-reality machinery is contained in them."

Huth looked at the trailers in disbelief. The original system he had developed had taken up an entire floor of a skyscraper. Recovering, he said, "Miniaturization was the next logical step, of course, that and reduced power consumption. Those improvements were already on the drawing board when I had my accident."

Dredda's digitalized laugh grated against his eardrums.

"My whitecoats figured out how to do all that six months ago," she said. "They also figured out how to make the trans-reality jumps consecutive."

"'Consecutive'? I'm sorry, I don't understand what you mean by that."

"Your system had a fixed starting point in the Totality Concept tower, which made consecutive jumps impossible. If you wanted to go to a different reality from Deathlands, you had to return to our Earth, recalibrate the corridor to arrive at a new destination, then cross over. Every new destination required a step back to Earth. Now the entire generating system moves with us every time we jump. Which means we can go from this reality to another, and another, and another, without every returning to the starting point. The only limit to the number of consecutive jumps is access to power at the terminus."

Huth stared at the glacier of nukeglass. Then it finally hit him. Power. That's why Dredda had come here. He could only blame physical hardship and a lack of calories for his failure to see it sooner—his mind wasn't working at its normal speed. "Reprocessing bacteria!" he exclaimed. "Of course, you're using reprocessing bacteria!"

"That's what those units are for." She indicated a pair of six-wheeled trailers standing beside the thermoglass.

At the ends of the huge boxes were hoppers, where the raw radioactive ore was dumped. They had chutes on their sides, so the rock dust byproducts of bacteria's digestion could be removed.

Dredda didn't have to explain the technology to him. It was twenty-five years old, developed when his world had been forced to cannibalize the energy contained in its one-hundred-thousand-warhead nuclear arsenal. Inside the black trailers, segregated colonies of bacteria performed a sequence of specific metabolizations on the inorganic material. The result, a concentrated, liquidized fuel, was then pumped through thick hoses into waiting, smaller tanker trucks.

"There's an enormous supply of raw material out there," Dredda went on. "This world has hundreds of other nuked-out hot spots to exploit. The only limiting factor is having a labor force of sufficient size to extract it."

Huth noted the lack of any shielding from the ore and the drippings of reprocessed nuclear fuel on the ground. The troopers were protected in battlesuits, but the seated Deathlanders weren't.

"What about rad hazard?" he asked.

"What about it?"

"Your workers are exposed."

"That's nothing compared to what they're going to soak up in the next few days. But you're going to see that firsthand."

"I know the technology," he insisted desperately. "You know I know the technology. I can help you maximize your efforts."

"How? You're nothing but a puffed-up bureaucrat."

"That's not what your father thought."

"You don't know what my father thought. He always said you were easy to manipulate because you were so vain. That's why he kept you on a leash all those years. Your techno skills are useless to me here. What I need is slaves.''

Huth couldn't help himself. The words leaped from his throat: ''Do you know how many degrees I have?''

''I'm sure they'll help you dig more ore,'' Dredda told him. ''Now, it's time to start walking. I don't need to warn you about those manacles. Step off the road and you won't be stepping anywhere ever again.''

With that, she roughly pushed him toward the other captives, who rose from the ground en masse at a signal from their guards. The mob of Deathlanders immediately surrounded him.

''So you're the one to thank for bringing these mutie bastards here?'' somebody growled.

The ''thanks'' that was dispensed was a blow over the right kidney that dropped Huth to his knees. As he gasped for air, the others began kicking and punching him, fighting one another to get in a good lick. Falling to his side, Huth rolled up in a ball and covered his head with his arms.

The beating was quickly broken up by troopers, who used the butts of their laser rifles.

''Start moving,'' Dredda ordered the lot of them. ''You've got eight miles to cover before dark. Any stragglers will lose a hand. As you can imagine, it's very hard to make your ore quota with one hand. No quota, no water. Fall down en route and the ore wags will drive over you. There's only one way to stay alive, and that's to keep walking.''

The ore wags started up and began pushing the crowd toward the beginning of the road. A double row of pulse-rifle-armed troopers kept them packed together nice and tight. As the others moved ahead, Huth hung back intentionally. He brought up the rear of the long file of humanity, not wanting to turn his back on his fellow slaves.

At the summit of the road's first low rise, a blare of familiar words and music made him turn and look over his shoulder. On the roof of the psychedelic bus stood Mike the Drunkard and his three lewd friends. The big man waved goodbye with his prosthetic hand, and the sluts blew extravagant kisses.

Chapter Eight

An instant before the cave's ceiling dropped, J.B. twisted on his knees and lunged, throwing a shoulder into Ryan's midsection, driving them both through the archway and into the alcove beyond. Ryan hit the sand on his back as the roof collapsed with a bass roar. The resulting rush of wind extinguished the torch, plunging the companions into a darkness filled with choking clouds of grit. The yelling stopped at once, replaced by groaning and coughing. As their eyes adjusted to the reduced light, the superheated rear wall glowed hellishly through the swirls of settling dust.

"Somebody find the torch," Mildred croaked.

Fumbling around on the sandy floor, Jak located it and passed it over to J.B., who once again sparked it ablaze. Over their heads, the ceiling of the second chamber had held. The front gallery, on the other hand, had caved in completely; where the archway had once stood was a solid floor-to-ceiling wall of tightly fitting boulders.

For the moment, they were safe.

In the flickering torchlight, Ryan searched the shadows for the face of his son. His forehead and chin powdered with red dirt, Dean blinked backed at him and abruptly sneezed. The others seemed to be okay, too.

"We got one," Jak said, moving to the barricade of rock. Grunting, he tipped some blocks away from the foot of the wall, where a helmeted head and battlesuited arms and shoulders poked out. The trooper lay face up, two-thirds buried under the fallen ceiling.

"Guess there's something even a battlesuit can't deflect," the Armorer said.

"Do you think it's chilled?" Krysty asked.

Jak snap kicked the head. The arms didn't move. "Mebbe," the albino said with a shrug. "Mebbe not..."

"Look, it dropped its tribarrel blaster," Dean said. He pointed at the butt of the bullpup-style rifle, which protruded from between two of the wall's boulders. Dean tried to pull it free, but couldn't budge it.

Ryan gave it a try, but had no luck, either. "The front sight or the pull-down front grip must be caught on something," he said. "Let's take the helmet off and see if the bastard's alive."

The companions had watched Gabhart and the others get out of their armored suits, so they knew where the helmet release mechanism was and how to operate it. J.B. pressed the small inset button on the outside of the battlesuit's collar and Ryan rotated the helmet. With a click and a hiss, it turned and came away in his hands.

Dix held the torch close so they could get a good look.

The trooper's face was pale and the features slack. The hair was cut so close to the head it might as well have been shaved. Blood oozed from the nose and mouth.

"Is it a man or a woman?" Krysty asked.

"Can't tell for sure," Mildred said. "Not without seeing the rest of the body."

Doc peered down and said, "No more extensive observation is needed, dear colleague. I'll warrant the skin on those cheeks has never seen a razor's edge."

The trooper's eyes opened. The mouth moved, and there was a wheezing rattle of breath. Realizing his or her predicament, the trooper panicked and began pushing and pounding at the rock, thrashing in vain to break free.

If a battlesuit couldn't repel tons of rock, Ryan thought, it couldn't be crushed by it, either. If the wild arm movements were any guide, the trooper was solidly pinned but not seriously injured,

Ryan knelt just out of reach. "You aren't going anywhere for a while," he said. "Might as well calm down."

Their eyes met and the trooper exclaimed, "Shadow Man!"

The unamplified voice was definitely female.

"She knows you?" Krysty said.

"No, she doesn't know me," Ryan answered. "She just recognizes me from the vid billboards of her Earth. My face was plastered on them twenty feet tall. It was part of a campaign to sell the migration to Deathlands and quiet the mobs."

The trooper's gauntleted hand reached up to her throat, her fingers applied pressure to the front of her neck, then she spoke, "We've got seven alive in here. Burn 'em out!"

"Fireblast!" Ryan snarled. He ripped her fingers away from the throat mike's actuator, then tore it out of the battlesuit.

He didn't even see her hand move in response, that's how fast she turned the tables on him. Quicker than a cat or a snake strike, the trooper gained control of his wrist, and she used it to pull him closer to her.

She was amazingly powerful. And not just for a woman, either. Her grip held him like the jaws of a machine. Ryan felt himself being dragged, all two hundreds pounds of him, on his knees over the sand. Before she could get her fingers closed around his throat, he picked up a chunk of rock in his free hand and smashed the flat side down onto her unprotected face. He had to hit her twice more before her grip weakened. He jerked himself away from her, cradling his numbed hand.

J.B. passed the torch to Mildred and, standing at a safe distance, leaned over the trooper. "She's still breathing," he said. "You just stunned her. Bloodied her nose pretty good but her eyes are opening. I'll be nuked, she's coming around already!"

"A most curious example of femininity," Doc remarked. "What say you, Mildred? Is this the future of the fairer sex?"

"She is a strange one," Mildred agreed. "Look at that brow ridge, and the density of the bone in her jawline. I'm sure it isn't acromegaly. There would be much more gross distortion than this at her age. Some other hormonal imbalance has to be involved. Whatever the root cause is, from how easily she got hold of Ryan and controlled him with one hand, she's a very unusual human being, both in her physical strength and her reaction time."

"She's nothing like Captain Nara Jurascik,"

Krysty said. "Ryan, were there others like this one on the other side?"

"If there were, I didn't see them, and I wasn't told about them. I think this is something new."

The creature came to, spitting blood and spitting mad. Her string of unintelligible curses was drowned out by the earsplitting squeal of a laser beam. Almost immediately the companions' side of the cobbled wall of rock started to give off heat; after a few more seconds, it was glowing red in the center at waist height.

"By the Three Kennedys!" Doc cried, throwing up an arm to shield his face as he backed away.

The air inside the chamber became scorching hot and difficult to breathe.

It was obvious to Ryan that their enemy had turned loose something a lot more powerful than the tribarrel longblasters they'd seen before. He had to yell to be heard over the laser's shriek. "When the beam breaks through, we're going to cook! Get under the wall! To the next chamber! Go!"

J.B. and Jak fell to their knees and, digging like terriers, widened the hole under the rear wall. Dean squirmed under first, followed by Mildred and Krysty.

Ryan was the last to leave the middle chamber. In the light of the torch, he could see that by pushing with her arms and madly squirming her torso back and forth the trooper was actually starting to pull herself out from under the wall. He could also see why she was so frantic to get free. The glowing spot had grown much bigger, and its reflected heat had become withering. As he watched, its center changed from red to yellow to luminous white. And then the white began to drip, spilling down the edges and angles of the boulders. The drip became a torrent. Rivulets of melting rock cascaded toward the floor and the trapped trooper.

Her gauntleted hands couldn't protect her from the rain of liquid rock. Beads of it rolled around and between her upraised fingers. She threw back her head and screamed, but it was lost in the screech of the laser and the explosive hiss as the cells of her face, eyes, skull and brain surrendered their water to four-thousand-degree droplets of quartzite.

An instant before the beam burned through the rock fall, Ryan squirmed down the hole, passing the torch and his scoped Steyr up to J.B. on the other side. As he climbed out, he found himself in a chamber so low he could only crouch. Then the laser struck the far side of the wall. The heat slammed his back through two feet of solid rock.

Crawling over the rattlesnakes that Jak had killed, Ryan hurriedly joined the others at the opposite end of the cramped enclosure.

"What are we going to do now?" Dean shouted over the squeal of the light beam. "There's no place to run. We're stuck."

Ryan knew that strategically their situation hadn't changed for the worse. He knew it couldn't get any worse. He took comfort in the fact that they had managed to take out at least one of the enemy. But it wasn't the kind of comfort his son was hoping for. Dean wanted a miraculous way out.

And there was none.

The facing wall glowed incandescent red. The air boiled. It was like being trapped in a bake oven.

"All we can do is survive as long as possible,"

Ryan shouted back. "Look for the chance to break free and fight back...and chill as many of the bastards as we can."

Then the whistling roar stopped.

Moments later, when their ears stopped ringing, the companions could hear scrambling sounds from the next chamber as troopers burst through the site of the cave-in.

Another digitalized voice boomed at them, this time from the other side of the hole. "You have ten seconds to crawl out of there," it said. "If you don't come out, we will roast you alive."

Ryan exited first, blinded for a moment by the headlamps of four battlesuits.

"Look who it is!" said one of the troopers as he ripped the Steyr out of Ryan's hands. "A celebrity POW!"

The other soldiers didn't seem impressed. Two of them began extracting the corpse of the female trooper from the melted rubble of the wall.

"You really shouldn't have done that, Shadow Man," the trooper confided. "It's going to piss off the she-hes, large. I'm supposed to report our battle casualties at once, but I'm not going to warn my CO about this one. She-hes tend to kill the messenger, if you know what I mean."

Then the trooper shouted down the hole, addressing the rest of the companions. "Everybody else out of there. Now!"

When Ryan and the others stepped from the cave, they saw what had been leveled against them. The laser cannon on one of three gigantic vehicles was pointed at the entrance.

At the direction of one of the dozen or so battle-suits, presumably the commanding officer, troopers scanned each of them with a detection device. Their hidden metallic weapons—belly guns, throwing stars, stilettos, straight razors—were located and confiscated. The device didn't manage to pick up Dean's bone blade, however. While they sat on the ground with their hands on top of their heads, the troopers removed the bodies of their comrades from the cave.

J.B. glanced at Ryan and winked.

They had chilled three in all.

Not bad for a first skirmish.

The troopers carried out the female last. She was quite a sight. The flesh of her face was horribly bloated, puffed up red and shiny around the blackened craters and pits that had been burned clear through her head. Her brains dripped out the pinholes in the back of her skull, swaying like strands of pink melted cheese.

The commanding officer let out an animal cry and rushed over to the body as it was carefully lowered to the sand.

Ryan could see the officer's face as the helmet visor cleared. It was another woman, of the same strange sort. The trooper had called his superior officer a "she-he." Which didn't figure to be an official term or a pet name the battlesuit grunts dared use in front of their superiors. It had a decidedly hostile and disparaging ring to it.

From the officer's screams and gestures, she was taking this particular death mighty hard. Much harder than Ryan would have expected. Not only was the scene she was making unprofessional from a military standpoint, but on the world where she came from, he knew a single human life wasn't worth spit. In full view of her command, the officer wailed and sobbed as if the two had been sisters, or mother and daughter. Rising from her knees, she sought a suitable outlet for her rage and grief.

She seized Jak by a hank of his white hair, jerked him to his feet, then locked her other fist around his throat. Jak's dead white face went pink, then shaded quickly to dark purple, his red eyes bulging from their sockets. The officer clamped her fingers on the top of his head and lifted him from the ground.

Jak kicked his legs and swung his arms, but his heels and fists bounced harmlessly off the battlesuit's armored plates.

The companions were already on their feet, but unarmed and facing a battery of laser rifles, they couldn't assist in the fight. They watched helplessly as the officer started to slowly unscrew Jak's head from his neck, like the lid of a glass jar.

"It wasn't him!" Ryan cried. "He didn't chill her."

The officer paused in her neck twisting. "Who was it, then?" she demanded.

"It was me. Shadow Man. I'm the one who croaked your girlfriend." He paused to flash the officer a broad grin. "I got to tell you, it was nuking big fun. Step over here, Jughead, and I'll do it to you, too."

The officer tossed Jak aside like a rag doll and charged. Six of her own troopers intervened and blocked her path. Straining with all their might, they

managed to keep her from reaching Ryan, who res-
olutely stood his ground, a smile on his face.

"The CEO will want them in one piece, Captain,"
a trooper reminded her. It sounded like the same guy
who had spoken to Ryan in the cave. "There'll be
big trouble for us all if we bring them back dead, and
she finds out that you took your own vengeance. If
you hand them over alive for her to deal with, there
could be a big reward."

Gradually, this idea seemed to sink in, and the officer stopped struggling in their grasp.

"The CEO will make them pay for what they did,"
the trooper went on earnestly. "All of them. And
they'll suffer, too. You know how they'll suffer. It'll
take them days to die."

"You're right," the officer said, throwing off the
restraining arms. She took a step back. "Why let
these scum die so easily? Where is the justice in
that?"

"No justice at all, Captain," the trooper agreed.

"Bind them securely and throw them in the back
of my wag."

The troopers pulled the companions' arms behind
their backs and tied their thumbs together with thin
plastic straps. Then they put larger straps on their
legs, linking their captives together at the ankles, so
if one ran, they all had to run; if one fell, they all fell.
The troops shoved Ryan and the others through the
rear cargo door of one of the big wags and made them
sit on the floor, alongside the lashed-down body bags
and the pile of their captured weapons.

As the rear door closed, the soldiers took their
places in the jump seats along the cargo bay walls.

There were no windows inside the vehicle. The only light source was the red glow of the instrument panel, which was well forward.

After strapping himself in, the trooper nearest to Ryan cleared his visor and said in a barely audible tone, "You really put your dick in it this time, Shadow Man."

His eyebrows were very dense and very blond. His skin was pale, and there was a tattooed teardrop at the outside corner of his right eye. Looking more closely, Ryan saw that the tear was actually made up of three tiny blue letters. PCS. Population Control Service. Ryan had seen the handiwork of the PCS in the other reality: vast, sealed, underground galleries choked with heaps of human skeletons. Too many bones to count.

"Captain Kira was the first officer to die on this mission," the trooper continued in a whisper. "The other two grunts don't count. They were good soldiers, but they were just regular men. Regular men like us are expendable. We can be replaced by Deathlanders, if need be. You never know, Shadow Man, maybe you'll be wearing my battlesuit someday."

Ryan wondered, and not for the first time, why the trooper was confiding in him. There had to be some personal risk involved. "Your officers are all women?" he said.

"No. Not women like your two friends, there. Not good for screwing or making babies. Like I told you, they're she-hes."

Ryan grimaced, not understanding.

"Genetically modified human beings," the trooper went on. "They aren't female, and they aren't male, either. They're a third gender created by the white-coats specifically for this mission.''

Mildred leaned forward. "Made from scratch, you mean? Cloned in a test tube?''

"No, these beauties started out just like you, honey.''

The trooper stiffened as the front doors of the wag rose and the driver and captain climbed in. His visor immediately fogged over and he said no more. Like his seven comrades, he sat like a statue in his shock-mounted jump seat.

"It would appear our new friend has a bone to pick with his superiors," Doc said.

"Same old military song and dance, even in jolly Super Techno World," J.B. commented.

Ryan had his doubts about that, but he kept them to himself for the time being. From what the trooper had told them, the separation of officers and enlisted men in the invasion army was absolute and based on genetically engineered differences. The male troopers were ordered into combat by creatures unlike them or anyone else they had ever known. Creatures who, it seemed, could both outfight and outthink them. All the talkative trooper knew about his future was that when he was chilled, someone else would inherit his battlesuit. Because of this, Ryan couldn't view the trooper's remarks as the typical grousing and back-biting of the lower ranks. Since when did well-trained, battle-hardened soldiers relate better to prisoners of war than to their own officers?

Once the wag got under way, the reason for the shock-mounted jump seats and cross-chest safety harnesses became painfully apparent. As the vehicle picked up speed, its yawing, pitching motion increased. Ryan and the others couldn't hang on to anything with their arms pinned behind their backs. As a result, they took a pounding on the cargo deck, bumping into one another, as well as the plastisteel floor.

No way could Ryan estimate their speed over ground. But from the vibration and G-force he felt, he knew he was traveling faster than he ever had before.

After what seemed like about fifteen minutes, the wag slowed to a stop. Their bodies numbed by repeated impacts, the companions found it difficult to stand when they were prodded from the deck by the troopers. The rear door opened and they staggered in a teetering file out into daylight.

J.B. scowled at the panoramic expanse of metamorphic nukewaste before them. "Slake City," he spit.

"Behold, the cloaca of the universe," Doc added.

Ryan took in the rest of their surroundings. The old man was right about the nukeglass massif. It was a cosmic butthole. But by Deathlands standards, the otherworlders' encampment clustered beside it was nothing short of magical. Everything was new and shiny. Nothing was cobbled together with rags and sticks and baling wire. There were towering black tractors and semitrailers, as well as other assorted all-terrain wags, and a fleet of attack gyroplanes. The living and storage quarters consisted of maybe twenty black domed structures, connected by sleek tubular walkways. Ryan's rough count of the battlesuited troopers was around one hundred. He also noted the tall stacks of fifty-five-gallon steel drums, every one of which had Baron Jolt's name stenciled on the side.

One of the troopers cut the straps on their ankles and thumbs while two others moved the body bags from the wag's cargo bay to the ground outside. The four remaining troopers held the freed companions at blasterpoint.

"Pick up the corpses," the captain ordered Ryan. "You killed them, you carry them."

One of the troopers poked him hard in the side with his pulse rifle's flash-hider. "Get a move on," he said. "And keep going straight ahead until the captain tells you to stop."

J.B. and Ryan hoisted one of the black plastic bags by the sewn-in handles at either end, and started walking in the direction the trooper had indicated. The other companions did the same.

They were force-marched with their burdens past a churned-up area of dirt. In one corner of the rectangle, four troopers sprayed carniphage foam from their back tanks onto an already heaping mound of the stuff. Brown goo spread out in a shallow pool beneath the creamy bubbles.

As chewed up as the ground was, it was impossible to miss the litter of severed hands and feet, or the fact that they all had suckers on the palms, fingers and soles. One trooper kicked these grisly relics into a pile for foaming, while another made a neat stack of dull silver bracelets.

"Stickies," Jak said as they passed by. "Lots stickies."

Ryan grunted in agreement.

Stickies were a race of degenerate, crazed chillers

with incredible strength. They used the suckers and the adhesive secretions in their hands and feet, and their rows of needle teeth to rip their victims apart. Some people believed they were accidental nuke-spawned mutations; others claimed they had been bred on purpose for hunting sport or sideshows. Regardless of their origin, stickies had first appeared in scattered wild bands decades after skydark. It was hard for Ryan to imagine how so many of them had been caught at once, unless the troopers had interrupted one of their breeding orgies.

When they were within fifty feet of the largest of the black domes, the companions were ordered to stop. "Put down the bodies there," the captain said. "Sit beside them. Do not move." The officer then walked across the compound and entered the dome through a bulkhead door.

As Ryan and the others sat there, waiting for they knew not what, a huge truck appeared over the rise in the thermoglass and rumbled down the road toward them. Its cargo box was heaped to overflowing with tons of gray-green glass. Before the loaded wag reached the encampment, another identical truck departed, its cargo box empty. On the road in front of the second wag were perhaps a dozen spindly humanoid figures, forced to walk ahead of the massive bumper.

Some of the stickies had survived the foam yard.

"I sure don't like the looks of that," Krysty said as they watched the stickies march up the slight grade. "There's nothing in that direction but a bastard slow death."

Meanwhile, the loaded truck pulled up beside a

tractorless semitrailer and dumped its cargo of glass into a big hopper at one end.

"It's some kind of industrial operation," Mildred said. "Though what they could want with chunks of Slake City, I can't imagine. The invaders must be hard up if they're trying to use stickies as slaves."

"Hard up or just plain dim," J.B. said. "Everybody knows you can't train stickies to do anything. Their instinct gets in the way. All they want to do is eat, fuck and chill."

The bulkhead door in the big dome swung inward, and ten black-armored troopers rushed out on a dead run.

"Uh-oh," Dean said.

Ryan leaned close and said, "Our hands and legs are free. Stay focused, son."

Standing between the ten running battlesuits and the body bags were several troopers who were guarding the seated captives. The guards' counterparts bore down on them so quickly they didn't have time to get out of the way. Instead of going around the immobile grunts, the newcomers shoved. And when they shoved, the troopers' battlesuits offered them no protection. The guards' boot soles left the ground and they flew aside, crashing to earth with arms and legs spread wide. The troopers who had narrowly missed being bowled over backed warily away.

The ten newcomers paid no attention to the men they had knocked senseless. They surrounded the body bag with the she-he in it. Dropping to their knees in the dirt, they removed their gauntlets and their helmets. From their speed and strength Ryan already suspected that they were she-hes; seeing their heads confirmed it. They had the same rugged bone structure, the same nearly shaved skulls as the dead thing in the bag.

The bag's zipper was drawn down to reveal the devastated face.

Tenderly, they slipped off the dead one's gauntlets. Then each put a cheek to the already cold fingers.

Ryan could see the tears streaming down their faces, but the only sound was the low grinding noise coming from the semitrailer's hopper. The other, presumably male troopers were giving the she-hes plenty of room to express their grief.

After a few minutes, the officers rose to their feet and turned to confront the captives. At a silent signal, troopers seized Ryan by the arms and dragged him away from the others. He was thrown facedown in the dirt before ten pairs of gleaming black boots.

"I remember you, Ryan Cawdor," said the figure looming over him. "Do you remember me? Dredda Otis Trask?"

Ryan squinted up at a face he vaguely recalled. "You were one of the CEOs of FIVE," he said. "I saw you on a vid screen. You and the others asked me questions about Deathlands."

"Disaster seems to follow wherever you go, Shadow Man. The loss of our dear sister Kira is impossible to measure. She was a resource that can never be replaced. My other sisters want to beat you to death, here and now. But I am in charge. And I have to look past the simple and the pleasurable answers. My responsibility is to our future." She gestured to the troopers. "Bring him inside. Manacle the others."

Ryan was jerked to his feet and hauled across the compound toward the big dome. He didn't struggle as the troopers pushed him through the bulkhead door, which opened onto an anteroom intersected by numerous tubular corridors. The light source was a strip of material that ran like a spinal cord along the top of the hallways. He was marched a short distance, then left alone in a room with the former CEO.

The chamber was dark gray in color. The only decoration was the light strip across the ceiling. The Spartan furnishings consisted of a cot, a rack for a battlesuit, a tier of electronic machinery and a tall silver tank with a locking wheel on the lid.

Dredda set her helmet and gauntlets on the cot.

Seeing the former CEO up close from behind, Ryan was amazed at the breadth of the base of her neck. It formed a wide triangle of muscle that tapered only slightly as it climbed the back of her skull.

"You were never offered the opportunity to join us before," Dredda said as she turned. "I see now that was a big mistake. You could be a very valuable asset. You have abilities and experiences that our own males lack. You could teach us much about your world. And in return we could make you one of its rulers."

Ryan said nothing.

"Doesn't that prospect interest you?"

"I never thought of myself as the ruler of anything but Ryan Cawdor. Always seemed a big enough challenge for me."

"Perhaps I should have explained the alternative first. If you don't cooperate, you and your companions will be marched to Slake City's ground zero, and there perform hard labor until you die.''

''What do I have to do to avoid that?''

''Use your knowledge of the people and terrain to help us organize our attack plans. We would prefer to subdue the local populations and consolidate our gains as quickly possible. Once that is done, we will need to replace the existing barony system with something more efficient. When Deathlands is under our control, we will move to the other continents of this world and conquer them in the same manner.''

''Seems like a mighty tall order for a hundred or so troops.''

''You can help us there, as well,'' Dredda said. She walked over to the tall canister and put her hand on it. ''Inside this canister are my extracted eggs and the eggs of all my sisters. They await fertilization by a suitable male donor. By implanting the fertilized eggs into host mothers, we will reproduce our kind. In a single generation, we can produce thousands of female offspring who, after a chemically accelerated maturation process, will undergo the same genetic transformation we did.''

''You want me to fertilize all your eggs?''

''It's not that daunting a task, I assure you. We can store sperm for decades, just as we can store our eggs.''

''And the host mothers, where would you get them?''

''From the general population of Deathlands. The two females in your group would make prime surrogates. If they submitted to the procedure, it would save them from Ground Zero. Which one are you sleeping with, by the way? My guess is the red-haired one. Or are you servicing them both, Shadow Man?"

He didn't dignify the question with a response. "What about the males who are with me?" he said.

Dredda shrugged. "Their only use to us is in the mines."

"If I do what you ask," Ryan said, "it'll only make more mutie freaks like you. Frankly, I'd rather chill you all, or die trying."

"Maybe a few days in the mines will change your mind," Dredda said. "Unlike the bumbling idiots who held you on my world, I do not make mistakes. I leave no escape holes. You will cooperate with us, or you and your friends will die."

While Dredda put on helmet and gauntlets, Ryan considered making his move. The opportunity for a one-on-one fight was there, all right, and he had the advantage of being able to launch a surprise attack from behind, but he knew the troopers outside the room would join the action as soon as they heard the sound of a scuffle. After his experience with the she-he Kira, he was pretty sure he couldn't drop Dredda with a single punch or kick. And there were no weapons in the room to help him out. In the end, he decided the situation wasn't right and he didn't have the right tools for the job. Swallowing his fury, he let the former CEO shove him back out the door.

"Manacle this one, too," Dredda told the troopers waiting in the corridor. "Send them all to Ground Zero in the next convoy."

Seconds later, Ryan found himself sitting on the dirt with his companions, his wrists and ankles circled with bands of plastisteel. He shook the wrist cuffs. "What the blazes are these things?"

"They're what chopped off the hands and feet of the uncooperative stickies," Mildred told him. "There's a laser built in. It's activated by remote control."

"Whitecoat guillotines," Doc said. "If you go beyond a preset distance limit, you lose your extremities. The surgery is bloodless, but not painless you can be sure."

"What did the head she-he want from you?" Krysty asked Ryan.

"She wanted me to join them. To act as a guide and strategy maker. And she wanted me to be the father of all their babies."

The redhead's eyes flashed. "She wanted you to fuck them all?"

Ryan almost laughed, despite himself. "No, it was nothing that personal, lover. Dredda Otis Trask wanted to collect my sperm to fertilize their extracted eggs. Seems to believe I have some kind of special genetic qualities they need in their she-he offspring. Makes me think the ex-CEO has swallowed her own line of Shadow Man advertising bullshit. She wanted you and Mildred to carry some of the babies."

"Forced motherhood?" Mildred asked.

"It's either that or die," Ryan said.

"Die," Krysty said without hesitation.

Mildred nodded. "Die is good."

"They're gonna send us to the same place they sent those bastard stickies, aren't they?" J.B. said, pushing his glasses up the bridge of his nose with a callused thumb.

"Yeah, old friend," Ryan replied, "that's where they're going to send us."

Chapter Nine

The companions had been sitting in the sun for more than an hour, listening to the moaning, crackling sounds of the nukeglass, when the ground began to shake under them. The first tremor was short and sweet, no more than a second or two, and it was followed by a long pause. Then came a fifteen-second skull-rattling quake that sent the guards to their knees, raised clouds of beige dust and turned the domes and the wags into black blurs. As the quake growled on and on, the earth beneath them became plastic, if not liquid. Ryan and the others were lifted, twisted and dropped by the waves passing through it.

Somewhere deep in the bowels of the earth a great switch flicked off, and the shaking was over as suddenly as it had begun. The guards stood, brushed off their weapons and life in the Slake City encampment resumed as if nothing unusual had happened.

"Whew!" Dean said. "That was some ride."

The moaning sounds had turned into a low roar, punctuated by sporadic, dull crashes as distant, damaged sections of the vast glacier collapsed under their own weight.

"It's a lucky thing we weren't out there on the glass when it hit," Krysty said.

"As if we didn't have enough to worry about," Mildred added.

Ryan didn't say anything, but at that moment he was thinking that if a person had to take the last train West, getting swallowed up by an earthquake was a whole lot better than taking a week or two to die of rad poisoning.

Shortly after the quake, a gaudily painted, gas-powered bus pulled into the camp. It stopped beside the churned-up dirt rectangle and began disgorging its passengers to the primal beat of a boom box. Dazed, the new arrivals staggered and fell down the steps, only to find themselves ringed by battlesuited troopers and pulse rifles. They watched in shock and disbelief as manacles were clapped on their wrists and ankles.

As the new slaves were bound, the bus driver, a giant of a man in a squashed canvas fedora, counted them off on the fingers of his false hand, this while three particularly scabrous-looking sluts danced and cavorted obscenely on the roof of the bus.

Downwind, the smell of grain alcohol coming off the wag was overpowering. From that and the state of the passengers, it was obvious what had happened.

"Big bastard got the poor bastards stoned and tricked them into coming here," J.B. observed.

"Those prancing scum have sold their fellow human beings to the invaders as if they were domestic animals," Doc said. "For that heinous act they should be flayed alive."

"Look closer, Doc," Mildred admonished him. "The driver and the sluts are slaves, too. They're wearing the silver bracelets, just like us. They're just trying to survive."

"Helplessness is a state of mind, madam," the ancient academic countered testily. "That is a lesson I learned a long, long time ago, under conditions of hardship and privation too painful to relate. Mildred, even in the most dire circumstances, we human beings have the power to make our own choices, to either live by our own rules or to embrace the rules of others. Look again at the slave catchers and tell me they are not enjoying themselves tremendously.''

"He's got you there," J.B. said.

Mildred hated losing an argument with the old man, and rarely ever conceded defeat, but from her expression she knew he was right this time. Bracelets or not, the slave catchers needed chilling.

The companions watched the bus driver use a hand-powered pump to refill his fuel tanks from the tier of steel drums marked Baron Jolt. Once this was done, the big man climbed back in the wag, and he and his sluts drove back the way they'd come, disappearing in a spiral of dust.

"Off to collect another busload of fools," Krysty stated.

"Before they do," Doc said, "may God strike them dead. Or better still, afford me the opportunity."

A loud rumbling noise made them all look toward the massif. A pair of ore trucks appeared over the rise, rolled down the road and pulled off onto the plain near the domes. The companions watched the wags dump their cargos into the semitrailer's hopper. They had a much closer view of the operation this time and could see that the loads consisted of chunks of nukeglass and various other, seemingly unsorted debris. When both wags had been emptied, the troopers ordered the whole group of slaves to their feet.

"Walk ahead of the trucks," one of the troopers

told them. "The road is clearly marked. If you step off the road, you will lose your hands and feet. If you fall behind, the trucks will crush you. It's eight miles to where you're going."

It was a stock speech, delivered without inflection. It could even have been a recording.

In response to the slowly advancing ore wags, the assembled slaves, companions included, began to move forward, and as they did so, they were funneled onto the road by bracketing phalanxes of troopers.

"Stay together," Ryan warned the others.

The mob that surrounded the companions was mostly made up of men, aged from their late teens to early sixties. There were a few women, too, and some of them carried small children. They all walked with stooped shoulders and lowered heads. Some cried brokenly into their hands; others stared blankly at their feet. Clearly, they knew enough about Slake City's singular, unnatural wonder to realize they were on a one-way trip.

"What's it like where they're taking us?" Dean asked his father.

"Don't know, son," Ryan said. "Never heard of anybody going out that far on the nukeglass and returning to tell about it."

"We're coming back."

"That's right. We're coming back. Keep that thought front and center in your head."

After the first gradual rise, the road began a slow descent as it wound towards the sunken epicenter of the twenty-mile-wide blast crater. The trailing ore trucks kept the slaves moving at a steady, five-mile-an-hour pace.

Even this late in the day, the heat and glare off the glass was tremendous. The landscape before them was completely devoid of life. There was no soil for plants to grow in. No standing water. There were no birds flying overhead. There was just glass.

Glass, glass and more glass.

The roadbed underfoot was a uniformly light shade of gray green because it had been etched for better traction. On either side of the roadway, the glass's coloration was irregular, and in some places it edged almost to black. In those spots, large shadowy objects lay entombed many feet down. Buried things, in some cases huge things, caused erratic humps and dips to appear in the surface. There were also great, yawning holes filled with fractured, room-sized sheets of glass. The road had to be diverted around these massive cave-ins. There were truly mad shapes on the surface, too, like breaking waves frozen in time, like floes of dirty icebergs, separated by banks of ground glass, blown by the wind into glittering heaps.

"We'd better cover our noses and mouths," Mildred said as she knotted a bandanna around her head. "We don't want to inhale or swallow any of that glass dust. Try to keep it out of your eyes."

The companions did as she suggested.

When the slaves moving alongside them saw what they were doing, they followed suit, tearing off strips of their clothing to protect themselves.

Even over the engine and wheel noise of the ore wags, Ryan could hear the crybaby sounds of splitting glass. Beneath his boots, the road surface was crazed with an interlacing of fine cracks caused by earth tremors and the weight of passing loaded trucks.

They trudged around a series of spires, maybe fifty feet tall, set along the perimeter of a wide rectangle. As the sun angle changed, Ryan could see dull orange monoliths inside the spires—encased by nukeglass were the rusting steel girders of a ruined skyscraper. Farther on, they came across a field of smaller spikes, perhaps one-tenth as high, created by the crystalline growth of some melted components. The elevated areas were few in comparison to the low spots, which ranged from small, star-shattered cave-ins a few feet wide to great sprawling bowls of glass blocks hundreds of yards across.

Evidence of recent human activity, the narrow holes hacked into the thermoglass by Slake City's scroungers, disappeared after they had walked less than a mile. The farther they went, the hotter it got. The crater's concavity seemed to focus and intensify the sun's rays. As they walked, the horizon line on all sides shrank away. Snowcapped mountain peaks were gradually blocked from view by the rim of the crater, until there was only sky and glass.

Three miles in by Ryan's reckoning, the first of the slaves collapsed. A man in his fifties with big overhang of pot belly and a wild shock of white hair suddenly clutched at his chest and dropped onto the roadway. He fell into a fit, his body twitching, his eyes rolled up in his head.

Everyone but Mildred stepped over or around him and kept on moving. She knelt and started to try to help the man, but J.B. grabbed her shoulder and pulled her away.

"There's nothing you can do for that one," he said. "We can't carry him. You can see he's not going to make it. We've got to keep going." He forcibly dragged the woman along with him.

They had only gone a dozen yards, when from behind, they heard the wheels of the first wag crunch over the body.

"Fuckers," Mildred said. "Dirty fuckers."

She didn't look back.

Inside of another mile, two more people fell beneath the huge wheels. After the third fatality, the trucks stopped and the slaves were allowed to rest and were given a cup of warm water each. There was pushing and shoving in the water line. The companions stayed together and made sure they all got their rations.

"What's that?" Dean said, pointing at another entombed object on the side of the road. "Looks like gold."

The afternoon sun flashed off something buried under humped-up layers of glass. It was, in fact, gold. It was the gilded head and shoulders of an enormous statue with arms extended, its hairline melted down into its chin.

"That is all that is left of the Angel Moroni," Doc said, removing his neckerchief to mop his brow. "A great statue that used to adorn the east tower of the Mormon Tabernacle. The place of worship was completed in 1893, three years before I was time-trawled by whitecoats, before the life I should have lived, the death I should have died were stolen from me. I remember showing newspaper pictures of it to my beloved wife and my cherished children...." He suddenly choked and his voice trailed off.

With tears in his eyes and the sweat peeling down

the sides of his face, he swept his arm wide, making the kerchief flutter as it took in the bleak panorama. "What consummate wickedness conceived this nightmare? What spavined pelvis birthed this abomination of God's beauty?" As Doc spoke, his voice changed. It grew deeper and more resonant, as if he were projecting his words to some larger audience only he could see.

Ryan looked from face to face. Doc wasn't the only one showing the effects of the forced march under skyrocketing temperatures. All of them were breathing hard under their bandannas, their foreheads flushed and slick. But there was something else, too. It was there, in their eyes, like a passing shadow. Not just simple exhaustion, but a growing sense of doom.

"I put it to you, my dear esteemed colleagues," Doc said in summation, "that here, at last, we come face-to-face with the hard and bitter fruit of our civilization's ignorance and arrogance."

No one could argue that.

No one tried.

When the downhill trek resumed, as they approached ground zero, the focal point of the nuke's blast, they were confronted with even wilder and more fanciful hellscapes. They circled immense frozen whirlpools of dirty glass. They looked down into the seemingly bottomless pits of crevasses, voids the nukes had drilled thousands of feet deep into the bedrock, which were then glazed over or backfilled with cascades of molten thermoglass.

As Ryan walked he tried to keep his mind focused and alert by paying attention to these bizarre details. It was difficult because he was light-headed, having sweated out a lot more water than he'd taken in. Then he heard moaning sounds, more distinct and directional than before.

"There," Jak said, raising his pale arm to point ahead on the right, just off the road.

Ryan was treated to a strange sight. Five stickies lay marooned on a flat-topped spire of glass. Even from a distance, they didn't look human—a combination of their hairless skulls, their flat, black doll's eyes, their tiny nostrils centered in moist flab and their rows of yellow nail-point teeth. Ryan assumed the killer muties had panicked and tried to run, probably because the earthquake had frightened them. The attempt had cost them their sucker hands and feet. Then the plain of glass around them had collapsed, again probably due to the earthquake, leaving them stranded on the raised hourglass of a pinnacle. Because they had no hands or feet, they couldn't stand, let alone jump the required forty feet to safety. Forty feet over a deep chasm lined with huge chunks of broken glass.

Ryan had never heard stickies make noises like that. So desperate. So fearful. They certainly weren't the familiar, soft kissing sounds of a chiller pack on the hunt. While the slaves silently marched past them, the stickies moaned and waved their handless arms for help.

"As if we would, if we could," J.B. said.

The matter was settled by the rumbling gait of the ore wags. The vibration caused the pillar to crack at its narrowest point, tipping the screaming stickies off into space. When they hit the razor-sharp edges of the blocks below and began to slide, they were sliced and diced, backs, fronts, thighs, faces, cut through the bone. Their screams suddenly stilled, they tumbled to the bottom of the chasm, leaving long, bloody smears on the glass.

Without shedding a single tear, the file of humanity struggled on.

After another quarter mile of descent, the lowest point in the crater came into view. Their final destination. Ground Zero. It was a pancake-flat depression, roughly circular, five hundred feet across and stippled with shallow dimples like the rind of a mouldy orange.

In the light of the late-afternoon sun, the glass looked more gray than green. To illuminate the area at night, it was ringed by a battery of klieg lights on tripods. In the center of the ring were three great holes in the glass; the holes swarmed with laborers going in and out. Parked beside the mine entrances were ore wags. They were being loaded by hand from crude carts on skids. From the edge of the ring of lights, battlesuited troopers stood guard with laser rifles. There was a large holding tank, presumably for water, which had its own guard. There were no sleeping or cooking facilities, but there were long, open-flame heaters to keep the workers from freezing to death after the sun went down. In some of the shallow depressions, bodies were curled up—whether sleeping or dead, it was impossible to tell.

The group of fresh slaves was met at the end of the road by troopers who forced them into a long single file. As they passed a checkpoint, under the muzzles of triblasters, they were given another cup of water to drink and a large plastic badge was pinned to their chests.

After the last badge was handed out, one of the troopers addressed the crowd in an overamplified voice. "When the badge glows green, you are in an area of glass worth mining, and the glow will be bright enough to work by. If you bring out ore that doesn't register bright enough green, you will get no water. If you don't fill your sledge to the top with ore, no water. If there are problems with quality or quantity, everyone assigned to that sledge pays the same price. No water."

Ryan looked down at his badge. It was already faintly glowing. There was no need to ask what that signified.

They were in a death zone.

"Bubblehead over there talked about giving us water," J.B. said, "but he didn't mention anything about food. I think that means we're on our own in that area."

"Might as well hang up a sign—Abandon Hope All Ye Who Enter Here," Mildred said.

"We cannot abandon that!" Doc stated emphatically. "Standing at the gates of hell, it is our only shield."

The troopers started using their rifle butts to herd the milling slaves in the direction of the mine entrances. At a second checkpoint, the companions were each handed short-handled pickaxes and mesh bags for carrying ore. When all of the new slaves had been given tools, the guards retreated to the outside of the ring. There were no further instructions, and the slaves weren't forced underground at blasterpoint. Their captors knew that thirst would do that quickly enough.

Ryan and the others filtered over to one of the mine entrances. Beside the round hole was a cut-down oil drum with the words Baron Jolt stenciled on the side. Stuffed inside the drum was a man with matted gray hair. Obviously the victim of laser manacles, he had no hands or feet.

While the companions watched, a slave came out of the mine, walked up to the half drum, unzipped his fly, hauled out his wherewithal and proceeded to empty his bladder. The gray-haired man groaned in protest, raising his wrist stumps to keep the warm spray out of his eyes and mouth.

"Do you know who that is?" J.B. asked. "That's Baron Doyal himself. From baron to urinal, man, talk about a tough world!"

Ryan was already circling to the other side of the entrance, where a group of slaves squatted in front of a ten-foot-long propane burner that served as a night-time heat source. They were using two-foot lengths of stiff wire to toast small, elongated objects over the open flames.

The objects had four stumpy little legs and long tails.

Rats.

One of the slaves who was watching the others cook, a big, dirty, bearded man with spiral brands on his forehead and cheeks, slipped in from behind and deftly snatched another's rat on a stick. There was a brief scuffle for the hot food, which its original owner quickly lost. He seemed in very bad shape and was far too weak to reclaim his meal. The stronger slave gleefully chomped down the well-browned rat, bones, crispy tail and all.

The robbed slave turned away from the barbecue and staggered back toward the mine entrance, presumably with the intent of chasing down another dinner.

Ryan did a double take as the man stumbled past. Though his face and hands covered with weeping rad sores, though he was missing hair in big patches and most of his teeth, there was no mistaking him.

"Colonel Gabhart?" Ryan said.

Chapter Ten

Dredda leaned her head forward and peered over the edge of the abyss. Striated nukeglass lined both sides of the yawning chasm. After a sheer drop of five hundred feet, the almost vertical walls began to curve together, like the folds of a glistening gray wound, one bulging over the other, forming a black crease of impenetrable shadow.

Below the crease, the bottom fell out.

Because of the way the walls overlapped, the maximum depth of the second level of the crevasse couldn't be accurately measured by overflight sonar; certainly it was in the thousands of feet, more than enough to keep scavenging animals from reaching Kira's corpse.

Their battlesuit helmets off, their stubble-shaved heads lowered, the ten surviving Level Four females clasped gauntlets in a mourning line along the verge of the Slake City precipice. Their dead comrade lay in a body bag at Dredda's feet.

As Dredda looked into the plummeting abyss, she flashed back to her father's state funeral, a miles-long procession with millions of mourners lined up to pay their last respects to the ornate armored coffin that was guarded by a full military escort—tanks, APC wags, combat troops and hovering gyro squadron. She realized that what she had felt as her father's body rolled past the CEOs' reviewing stand was nothing, absolutely nothing compared to the emotion she was feeling now. At the time, she actually believed that she had suffered a terrible, life-shattering loss. At the time, she actually believed that she had loved her father more than she could ever love anyone. Now she knew that she had deluded herself in both cases.

It was a matter of perspective. There was no way to appreciate real loss until you experienced it. You couldn't understand real love until you felt it.

The way Dredda viewed that whole experience now, she had been merely an actress, reading from a script written and produced by Regis Otis Trask. According to that script, Dredda was as incapable of emotion as her father. With his lifelong neglect, his unreachability, he had trained her well for the part; a parent's unconditional love was never part of their relationship. A cold, grasping octopus of a creature, Regis Otis Trask had planned, consciously or unconsciously, for her to turn out the same, a perfect reflection.

And she had not disappointed him.

The octopus Dredda, despite the flow of tears at her father's elaborate funeral, had been secretly glad that he was dead because it meant she would finally come into her own. The tears had been a sham, an act for the vid cams recording the reactions on the reviewing stand. She had milked the drama of the moment to consolidate her control over the mid-and upper-level technocrats. That was her father's technique to a tee.

She pushed those dark memories out of her mind and visualized the face of Kira, recapturing the power of her beauty. Beauty lost. Kira, like Dredda, like the others, had not yet fully blossomed. And now she never would. Potential lost. Her companionship, and the joy it brought, was likewise gone, forever. Love lost. Real tears streamed down Dredda's cheeks. Real grief twisted her heart. Her pain was physical and it was enormous.

Curious what a little dose of virus could do.

It had given her sisters, where before she'd had none.

It had given meaning to her life, where before she'd had none.

Not only did the Level Four females have an implanted genetic heritage in common, but they also had a shared experience of transformation and a common, connected future that was still unfolding. They were, in fact, much closer than sisters.

This wasn't some sort of insectlike hive consciousness, but rather a clan consciousness, an intense kinship that they all felt. Every one of them believed that they, the ten, were at the core of something as yet incomplete, something mysterious and new. Something more perfect. Something magical with its own unique destiny and right to exist. The crescendo of their world had sent them hurtling across realities, as if everything, all four billion years of its existence, had led up to that single pregnant moment.

Despite the changes they had undergone, the sisters, Dredda included, still saw themselves as women, only much improved. They knew that the male troopers called them ''she-hes'' behind their backs. Even though it was scientifically untrue, since there was nothing male about them, they allowed the practice to continue because the reference to their strangeness and physical prowess had discipline value. It kept the enlisted ranks in line without the need for demonstrations of force.

In both universes, it had been fashionable at one time or another to speculate that there would be no wars if women ruled the world. There was no way to test the hypothesis, of course, since women never had that kind of absolute global power in either reality. Dredda and her sisters subscribed to a slightly different idea. They believed that there would be war, but only one. This, because women, if granted the means, would conquer utterly; they would do the job right for the sake of their offspring. Women, because of their biological function, their much more intimate connection with the future, were prepared to take this longer view. And stick to it. History taught that in victory, men always had sympathy for the male foe they had vanquished, that they always took pity because they could see themselves in his position, as if war were a jolly game to be played over and over with alternating winners. Men were the reason that nothing ever got solved. The Level Four females didn't view war as a game. Or jolly. They believed that if they waged it once, and properly, they would never have to face it again.

The "they" part was something Dredda hadn't anticipated. When she'd taken the Level Four plunge, she'd realized that she would have no control over how she changed or what she became. She'd done what she'd done for a reason, a sound reason, because she felt she had no choice. It was another case of being backed into a corner, then leaping before looking. After only a month in Deathlands, her previous existence seemed like a dream that belonged to someone else. A parade of empty acts and pointless accomplishments that fulfilled someone else's plans. Dredda was becoming herself in a way she never imagined.

The idea that on Shadow World she could be ruler of everything—a living god—was no longer the stimulus that drove her on. The Alexander the Great, or Regis Otis Trask syndrome—"I win! I survive!"— had been replaced by "We win! We survive!" The appetite for power and the aptitude for beating animate and inanimate into submission was still alive and well, but it was now a cooperative venture.

The death of Kira had forced the sisters to examine their own mortality, something their heightened physical abilities had made seem remote, at best. Kira's tragedy had shown them that in some circumstances, being stronger and faster wasn't enough to save their lives. It also showed them that they needed to produce offspring as soon as possible, to replace those lost in battle. If they were the ultimate survivors of their world, Ryan Cawdor was the ultimate survivor of his. Which was the reason why Dredda wanted his genetic material. With it and the viral transformation process, the sisters could birth a legion of indomitable warrior daughters, which their portable Totality Concept technology could then spread across the unmapped realities, like seeds on fertile ground.

"What we have lost today cannot be replaced," Dredda said to the others. "A piece has been ripped from our hearts. Kira was brave and strong. And she loved us as we loved her. Her love and her bravery made us proud. Whatever we do after today, whatever we conquer, wherever we travel, she will always live in our memory.''

With that, Dredda bent and gently tipped the body bag over the edge. It made a slithering sound on the glass, growing fainter and fainter. The black bag slipped over the bulge five hundred feet below and disappeared into the shadowy crease. The sisters held gauntlets in silence. Moments passed, stretching longer and longer. There was no sound of impact.

As they turned from the chasm toward their waiting wags, Dredda noticed something strange on the side of Mero's neck. It looked like an abrasion from the collar of her battlesuit. ''What's that there on your neck?'' she said.

''It just appeared overnight,'' Mero replied. ''It itches a little, but not too much. I think it might be from the battlesuit.''

''That's odd,'' Dredda said. ''I've got some minor irritation, too. But it's on my shoulder. Could be from friction.''

They had been living in the battlesuits for weeks now, and only getting out of them in order to sleep. Under the circumstances, abrasions weren't unexpected, even with the lubricant sprays they used to coat the inside of the armor.

Dredda knew that she and the others were spending way too much time in their battlesuits, but to be outside the artificially intelligent armor was almost unbearable. Without her suit, without the deluge of information it provided, without the access to its nanosecond-response lethality, she felt incomplete if not crippled, and disconnected from her sisters. They felt the same.

"Jann," she called, waving over the medical officer. When the blonde she-he stepped up, Dredda said, "Mero and I have got superficial skin rashes. Could be from our battlesuits."

Jann looked at the side of Mero's neck, noting the small patch of redness near the suit collar. "When we get back to the base," she said, "I'll give you both a topical ointment. An antiinflammatory and local anesthetic. And I'll take skin cell scrapings for analysis. I don't think it's anything important, but it never hurts to make sure."

Chapter Eleven

When Colonel Gabhart spun at the sound of his name, he lost his balance. Ryan caught him as he fell, and since he seemed too wobbly to stand, helped him to a seat on the ground.

"Shadow Man?" the colonel said, squinting up through eyelids so puffy they were nearly swollen shut. "So the murdering bastards got you, too. What about the others?"

"Sit still," Ryan told him. He beckoned to the companions and they came running.

When they saw how ravaged the colonel was, they couldn't hide their shock. They were speechless.

"I guess I'm pretty messed up, huh?" Gabhart said, trying to laugh and choking.

"Take it easy now," Ryan cautioned him.

Mildred pointed at Gabhart's badge, which glowed bright green, even in daylight. "He's really giving off the rads," she said. "Try to touch him as little as possible."

"How long have you been here, Colonel?" Ryan asked.

"Twelve days." He nodded in the direction of the trooper standing guard at the water tank. "The fuckers won't give out extra water. When you start to get the nuke sickness, you get so damned thirsty."

"What about Captain Jurascik?" Krysty said. "Is she here, too?"

Gabhart shook his head. "She died the day before yesterday. It was horrible."

"Was it from the radiation?" Mildred asked.

"No," Gabhart said, "it was from the stickies. The geniuses from my world who are running this operation captured a big group of stickies to help work the mines."

"They're trying to put stickies to work?" J.B. said. "That's crazy! You can't train stickies to do anything."

"They didn't figure that out until it was too late," Gabhart said, "after they'd already let them loose in the mines. They actually thought they'd scared the sucker-fisted bastards into cooperating. Must be close to a hundred roaming free underground. They can't get rid of them now. It's a maze of crevices, side tunnels and air shafts down there."

"Stickies can squeeze through some mighty small spaces," J.B. agreed. "Got weird mutie cartilage. It lets them squash down their skeletons. Even their skulls compress a little."

"But the laser cuffs…?" Ryan said.

"They only activate after you run a certain distance from the center of the road," Gabhart said. "The stickies aren't running away from anything. They like it in the mines."

"The lasers can't be selectively activated?" Ryan said.

"There's no way to target individual slaves, if that's what you mean. The only way to get rid of the stickies now that they're loose is to trigger all of the cuffs on all the slaves, which would make the entire work force useless. The stickies are hiding deep in the mines. That's where they jumped me and Jurascik. There was nothing I could do to help her. Nara was weak from the rad sickness, much worse off than me—most of her hair had fallen out, and she was coughing up blood. Stickies attacked and separated us, and then they dragged her off.''

"Killed her," J.B. said.

"Fucking ate her," Gabhart stated, bitterly. "There's nothing to eat around here, except whatever you catch yourself under the glass. That's why the stickies like it down there. The food comes to them. As you get weaker, you make easy meat. Easier than rats, because the mutie bastards have to chase them. Believe me, the stickies are the only ones getting fat around here.''

With a great effort, the colonel forced himself to his feet. "Got to get back down there," he said. "Got to make my ore quota or no more water today. Thirsty. I'm so damned thirsty."

"We'll go with you," Ryan said. "What do we have to do?"

"Pick an empty sledge from over by the mine entrance," Gabhart said, "and push it down the hole."

The ore carts consisted of battered metal boxes, five feet by three feet, that sat on pairs of crude, ski-like, metal runners. Each box had a number scribed into the side. Ryan and the companions chose one of the sledges. Shoving it ahead of them, they followed the colonel down into the mine.

"He's not long for this world," Mildred whispered to Ryan. "He's in the terminal stages of radiation exposure. The linings of his intestines and lungs will start to slough off soon. The internal bleeding will be massive. Then he'll collapse and he'll never get up.''

That was pretty much what Ryan had figured.

''Be sure and keep your bandannas on,'' Mildred told the others. ''We've got to try to keep from inhaling the radioactive dust.''

The entrance angled down steeply between gray glass walls for about twenty-five feet, then the floor leveled out. The companions used a rope tied to the rear of the box to brake the empty cart on the way down the slope. As they descended, another cart, this one fully loaded, was being hauled up by four slaves using a rope tied to its front end. There was just enough room for the two sledges to pass side by side.

A short distance farther on, the main shaft branched in two, and the fork was guarded by a pair of troopers. The area where they stood was brightly illuminated by klieg lights on tripods.

''Too many bodies on that sledge,'' the trooper on the left said as they pushed their cart toward him. He used the muzzle and butt of his pulse rifle to shove Doc, Mildred and Jak to one side. ''You three, go back up top and get another one. The rest of you go that way,'' he told Ryan and the others. ''Move it.''

There was nothing Ryan could do about the split up.

''Do not fret,'' Doc assured him. ''We'll be fine.'' Jak nodded.

''See you later,'' Mildred said as they turned back for the entrance.

A short way down the right-hand tunnel, which angled down slightly but steadily, Ryan and J.B. helped

Gabhart get into the sledge box. It was either that or abandon him. No way could he keep up.

As they pushed on, Ryan stared into the eyes of the people coming the other direction, pushing or dragging heavily loaded carts. They were exhausted and terrified, their faces and hands bleeding, their radiation-sensitive badges glowing like spotlights on their chests. The greenish pall cast by the badges made them look like zombies.

It wasn't long before they started seeing people dead and dying in the dark corners of the shaft. Some of the dying ones appeared to be delusional; others were having out-and-out fits, foaming at the mouth while they rhythmically bashed their heads against the wall.

Nobody paid them any mind.

There was nothing anybody could do for them.

The side tunnel continued its gradual descent, one foot of vertical drop for every hundred feet of horizontal distance. The available natural light grew dimmer the farther they went, filtered as it was through a growing thickness of glass overhead.

Gabhart raised his chin from his chest and said, "This tunnel dead-ends around the bend ahead. We've got to leave the sledge there. Past that point, the turns are too tight for it to pass. Somebody will have to stay behind and guard the cart, or the other slaves will steal our ore. As you've noticed, there's no honor among the damned."

At the end of the tunnel a group of half-filled sledges sat parked. Each cart had at least one miner standing in it or in front of it, with a short-handled rock ax ready to defend the cargo.

Ryan stopped their sledge against the tunnel side wall and helped Gabhart out. The colonel pointed to the numerous man-size tunnel openings in the walls. "We've got to go in one of those crevices, follow it until we find the seam of the hot stuff, then hack it out with our axes, bag it and drag it back here."

"You aren't going anywhere, Colonel," Ryan told him. "You're too damn weak. Just sit here with J.B. and Dean, and rest. Krysty and me will go in, check it out and bring back the first load."

"Watch out for the stickies," Gabhart said. His voice cracked and whistled in his throat; he was badly drained from the effort he'd expended. "They like to hide in the low-rad spots where the badges don't give off much light, and then they get hold of you from behind. Once they get hold of you, you don't get away."

Gabhart sucked in a ragged breath, then continued. "Be careful of cave-ins while you're hacking ore. When the glass comes down, it comes down huge, and it cuts like a band saw. Another thing, keep those rags over your noses and mouths. We've got Mindburst mushrooms growing down here. They're one of the few things that seems to be able stand the radiation. It's just them and the rats. The rats live off the mushroom caps, but they'll take a piece out of your nose if you fall asleep in the wrong place.

"You'll find the mushrooms sprouting up along the horizontal cracks and seams in the glass. Any place there's a ledge. If you breathe in their spores, you'll start to hallucinate within minutes. If you breathe too much, you'll collapse and fall into a fit. If you accidentally get stoned on Mindburst down here, you're as good as dead. You'll get lost. And one way or another, you'll get killed. There must be a thousand ways to die in this hellhole, and none of them are quick and painless.''

''A trooper talked to us on the way in,'' Ryan said. ''He told us about this third-gender business. What do you know about it?''

''The women, the officers, had some genetic engineering done before they came over from our Earth,'' Gabhart said. ''The men are scared of them, and with good reason.''

Gabhart's lips, which were crusted over with a mass of scabs, cracked and started bleeding a thin line down his chin. Though his eyes were almost shut, and his voice was losing its power, he kept talking. ''When I first arrived at Ground Zero, the troopers spoke to me because I used to be one of them. They talked out of earshot of their officers, of course. As far as the she-hes are concerned, the male troopers are expendable, like us slaves. They take better care of the troopers, of course, because they're more difficult to replace, you know, because of the training and so on. It's the same old story. Everything is a product. Everything has a price.''

''Do you think the troopers would turn on their officers if given the chance?'' Ryan asked.

''No way of telling that, Shadow Man. These are conglomerate mercenaries, not FIVE regular army. Their allegiance is to themselves, first and foremost. I'd say they'll stay loyal to the officers as long as they think they might end up paying for a rebellion with their own blood. If the odds change, and it looks like there's no penalty, it could be a different story.''

J.B. and Ryan had a dozen other, critical questions that needed answering, but before either could speak, Gabhart's head drooped his chest and his mouth went slack.

"Fireblast!" Ryan said.

"He's not dead, just unconscious," Krysty told him. "I can see him still breathing."

"From what Mildred told me," Ryan said, "he may never wake up. He's on his last legs. If he comes out of it while we're gone, J.B., get as much info as you can from him."

"Gotcha."

Ryan and Krysty picked axes from the pile at the bottom of the cart. The tools had wickedly curved points at one end; the other end was flat, more like a hammer. The reason was obvious. That way, two axes could be used to split apart pieces of nuke ore too big to lift: one acting as a wedge, the other as a sledge. They also each took one of the roughly woven bags.

"Be careful, Dad," Dean said.

"Always, son. You, too."

He and Krysty stepped into the nearest side shaft. The opening was as wide as Ryan's arm span, and a couple of feet taller than the top of his head. It looked as if it had been hacked out with a laser. There were no tool marks on the walls, just smooth glass; it almost looked polished. And the floor, walls and ceiling all met at near right angles. Inside the shaft, the level of available light dropped even more.

"Look at our badges," Krysty said.

They were definitely glowing brighter. But they weren't bright enough to light up more than twenty feet of tunnel ahead.

They had only walked thirty or so yards when the darkness in front of them began to dance with green lights. From deeper in the fissure, three slaves appeared, single file, dragging the loaded ore bags behind them. Their badges were like tiny beacons on their chests. The blurry circles of light they cast bounced and quivered as they walked.

Ryan and Krysty put their backs against the wall, their axes ready to fend off a sudden attack. No words were exchanged. Not even a nod to acknowledge one another's existence.

After the slaves had passed, Ryan and Krysty stood there, staring at the glass wall opposite. Their badge lights penetrated the solid mass, allowing them to see deep inside. There were shadowy, mysterious shapes, distorted by folds and masses of bubbles, obscured by irregular, unidentifiable pieces of large and small debris.

"Gaia knows what all's in there," Krysty said.

"Yeah," Ryan said, "it's a treasure chest of busted-up shit."

Around a tight turn that would have blocked an ore cart, they came across the first of much smaller intersecting tunnels, obviously hacked by hand. As they approached it, a man's head and shoulders popped out of the narrow hole in the wall. Before they could reach him, he had scrambled out with his ore bag. Growling like an animal, he threatened them with his ax, the pointed tip of which was worn into a tiny mushroom, like an expended bullet.

"Easy," Ryan said, raising his own ax as he stepped between Krysty and the guy. "We don't want your ore."

The slave scuttled past them with his bag, his back to the wall, feinting with short swings of his weapon. His arms and hands were a mass of barely healed cuts. There were deeper gashes across his forehead and cheeks. His trousers and shirt were slashed from glass edges; his spindly thighs were visible between the long tatters.

Ryan knew the looks of wild animals caught in traps or mortally wounded, awaiting death. He knew the looks of human beings as they faced that same terrible unknown. But what was in the slave's eyes was something even more desperate, even more despairing. The man's expression said that he knew his life wasn't worth living, but he couldn't let go of it yet.

As Ryan and Krysty moved deeper, the available light became nil, but their badges grew brighter, casting forty instead of twenty feet ahead of them.

"Wait," Ryan said, stopping.

"I thought I heard something, too."

It wasn't the intermittent crying of the glass, which was something they had gotten used to, like the sound of the wind. This was the moan of a human being. And it was punctuated by the whack of an ax. Over and over again. Then came a crash of falling glass.

"Let's take it slow," Ryan said.

As they advanced, at the edge of their green circles of light, they could see a single dim figure. Moving forward, they caught the frantic rise and fall of the ax it was wielded two-handed. A slave was hacking away at the face of the right-hand wall. Puffs of glass dust exploded at every impact. Chunks of glass lay at his feet.

The slave turned to blink at their badge lights. His nose and mouth were uncovered, and snot swayed in long strands from his chin. His pupils were mere pinpoints. "You've got to help me get her out!" the man cried. "We've got to save her!"

With that, he returned to the wall, slamming his ax into it.

"Save who?" Ryan said as he and Krysty came closer.

"Hold on, honey," the man cried as he reared back for another blow. "Hold on!" He was bleeding from deep cuts on his forearms and hands.

"Who is it?" Krysty asked him. "What is it?"

"My baby, she's caught in there," the man said. "Can't you hear her calling me? Can't you see her? Are you deaf? Are you blind?"

When the man lowered his ax, Ryan looked into the crude crater he had fashioned. Much deeper in the matrix was a dark, elongated shape. Something was entombed.

"That's definitely not a baby, mister," Ryan said. "It looks more like a big rock."

Not understanding, perhaps not even hearing, the man rambled on, "Her name is Charla. She's only four...she calls me Poppy Deary."

Ryan shook his head.

"Idiots!" the man cried, and resumed smashing the wall with his ax. Foam bubbled from the corners of his mouth, and as he swung his tool, it flew in sticky streamers along his neck.

A big hunk of glass tumbled to the floor. From deep in the wall came a crying sound, shrill, quavery. It grew louder and louder.

Rearing back for another blow, the man said, "I'm coming, honey. I'll save you!"

"Out of here!" Ryan told Krysty. "Now!"

They turned to run back the way they had come. They got no more than a few strides before the ceiling and walls crashed down behind them. There was a rush of wind, and Ryan took the stinging blast of glass fragments on his back, protecting Krysty with his body.

When the dust cleared, they found the man partially buried in jumbled pieces of glass. His head was connected to his body by the slimmest of threads, a single strip of muscle and skin. His still jetting blood glistened black on the edges of the glass.

The cave-in had exposed the entombed object that had cost him his life.

It wasn't a rock after all, but a dirty void, a nothingness. A gap left by a section of predark wooden log or telephone pole that the nukeheat had charred to ash.

Jutting out of the cavity was one end of a piece of predark Unistrut metal framing. About a yard of the U-shaped metal channel was showing; the rest, a slightly shorter length, was still embedded in the wall of glass. Ryan leaned closer and looked at the exposed end. Molten nukeglass had filled the inside of the two-inch-wide half tube of steel. The cave-in had fractured away most of the glass outside the free part of the Unistrut, leaving behind a three-inch, green fringe of crude, razor-edged spikes that stuck up from the channel opening like nightmare hacksaw teeth.

"Poor bastard didn't know what he was doing,"

Krysty said. "Had to be from the spores Gabhart warned us about."

"Yeah," Ryan agreed. "There must be some of those mushrooms around here close. Keep an eye out. We don't want to stumble onto them by accident."

They found the Mindbursts a bit farther on. In the green light of their rad badges, little button shapes clustered along the seam of the floor and wall. They were dainty looking, with small, rounded caps. Ryan noticed a peculiar sweet but sharp smell they seemed to give off. Holding his bandanna tight around his nose and mouth, he bent closer and saw some of the caps had been gnawed down to stumps. Scattered about were dozens of tiny, half-moon-shaped black turds.

"Like Gabhart said, the rats must eat them," he said as he straightened.

"And their crap fertilizes the next crop," Krysty said.

They moved past the corpse caught in the glass fall, and continued down the tunnel until they found an intersecting shaft that was stand-up height. The space inside it was much narrower. There was hardly enough room to swing their axes. But their badges glared like searchlights, so they knew they were in the right place.

Working together carefully, they excavated the base of the walls, using their axes to crack big blocks of it free. The ore wasn't all that dense; their bags were severely stretched by sixty or seventy pounds of the stuff. With Krysty in the lead, they headed back for the sledge.

When they reached the site of the cave-in, she exclaimed, "He's gone!"

"What?" Ryan said.

"The stoner, he's gone!"

Ryan pushed past her. One look told him she was right. Someone or something had shifted the chunks of glass and pulled the body free. All that was left were strips of shredded clothing.

He turned to Krysty. In the glow of his badge he saw her prehensile hair drawing up into tight coils.

Then he heard soft kissing sounds from the darkness.

Chapter Twelve

It was nasty-hot underground.

Gradually, the heat of the day had built up inside the tunnel, until by late afternoon it was an airless furnace. In the greenish twilight of rad badges and glass-filtered sun, crouching human forms made animal growling sounds as they circled.

J.B. watched yet another fight unfold beside the row of sledges at the shaft's end. The rock axes made mean hand-to-hand weapons. He wondered what one of them would do to the helmet of a battlesuit. Probably nothing, he decided, or the otherworlders wouldn't have passed them out so freely. Probably couldn't even get near a helmet with one; the ax head would clang harmlessly sideways before contact, just like a 9 mm slug.

The odds were stacked against the lone guy trying to protect his cart. He had three raggedy-ass thieves coming at him, taking turns ducking in and out trying to get him to commit himself and expose a weak point for the others to attack. These were the same three scumbags who had been working over the end-of-tunnel sledge line up for half an hour. They took note every time somebody dumped a bag of ore in a cart. Then they would wait until the guard was alone and close in and take some of it. Sometimes all it took was a show of force to get what they wanted; other times, like this one, it took more.

If J.B. hadn't been charged with protecting the boy and Gabhart, he would've walked over and stuck his ax in, and put an end to the harassment forever. As it was, he could only be a spectator in other people's trouble. The boy didn't like doing nothing about it, he could tell.

The guy guarding the cart finally made a move, took a big swing at one of the thieves. And missed. The other two were on him before he could get the ax back up to block. They didn't hit him with the pointy ends. That would've been too merciful. Instead, they shattered his left elbow and right collarbone with the flat sides of their ax heads. His arms hanging limp, the poor bastard staggered against the wall and slipped down to his butt.

The thieves didn't bother finishing him off. He was already done for. Unable to lift another piece of ore, he'd earned his last cup of water.

None of the slaves standing around the other sledges did or said anything. They watched the thieves push their sledge over to the wounded man's cart and take every piece of ore he had. Even though the slaves knew the three bastards would surely victimize them next, they were relieved that it had happened to someone else this time.

Everybody down here was crazy, J.B. realized. And with good reason. The bastard place was death row with festival seating.

The thieves started shoving their loaded cart back toward the mine entrance. In so doing, they had to pass J.B. and Dean. The Armorer took a good, long look at them. All three wore overcoats so greasy it was impossible to tell what their original color had been. Their side pockets bulged with dead rats, the tails sticking up stiff as sticks. From their expressions, they thought they had surviving Ground Zero all figured out. They didn't collect ore for water or hunt the dark tunnels for food. They stole it, which meant they lived longer because they didn't spend as much time in the high rad zones.

One of them, a guy with long, matted hair pulled into a ponytail and a wispy chin beard, looked into their cart. An appraising look. Just to see how the ore collection was going, for future reference. All he saw in there was Gabhart, unconscious.

"What are you looking at?" he demanded of the man in the fedora and wire-rimmed spectacles.

"Dogshit, walking," J.B. replied.

At once, Dean had his ax up and ready to strike. J.B. rested his, nice and relaxed, on the rim of the cart. He smiled at the thief. He already had his moves worked out, although he figured that after he dropped this one, the other two would light out in a hurry.

The Armorer's stance clearly unnerved the ponytailed guy. The usual reaction to threat was tension and retreat, not gleeful anticipation. The other thieves seemed uninterested in backing up a confrontation over personal honor; there was nothing in it for them—the cart was empty. Though he had been insulted, Ponytail didn't push the matter any further physically. "Hey, I'm just making the best of a bad situation," he snarled back. "Just like you'd do if you had any balls."

"We got nothing for you scabs," J.B. said. "Fuck off."

"We'll be back," Ponytail promised over his shoulder.

"Looking forward to caving in your head."

"J.B.," Dean said, "the colonel is waking up."

Gabhart stirred in the bed of the cart. He moved his arms and opened his eyes. "Damn, I dreamed I was already dead," he whispered. "It was a happy dream."

"Come on," J.B. said, "let's get you out of there."

He and Dean helped the colonel to a seat on the floor of the tunnel, propping his back against the wall.

"We need to know more about these manacles," J.B. said to him. "How do they work? What sets them off?"

Gabhart stared at him blankly for a moment, and J.B. thought he was going to pass out again, but then he spoke. "They're linked to the satellite's ground-position locator, which divides the planet surface into grids. A comp somewhere in the Slake City compound controls which grid sectors trigger the cuffs. When you cross into one of those sectors, the lasers automatically fire. The slaves at Ground Zero have one activation setting. Slave catchers have another. Ours is on either side of the road and outside the mines' perimeters."

"Can we get them off without setting them off?"

"No. If you try, they'll fire. They have to be deactivated at the control source."

"How do we do that?"

"Smash the comp. If there's no link with satellite, there's no way to trigger the cuffs."

"Sounds easy enough."

"There's another possibility, of course. There could be a fail-safe measure in place."

"What would that be?"

"When the satellite signal is broken, all the cuffs activate."

J.B. caught the boy staring at the dull silver bands around his wrists. He put his hand on Dean's shoulder and gave it a gentle squeeze. "Nothing for you to worry about now," he said. "We're a long way from making that move. But if it turns out that's our only chance to get free, we've got to take it. We've got to find a way to get back there and pull the plug."

"My mouth is so dry, my tongue's split," Gabhart said. Then he suddenly doubled over, wrapping his arms around his stomach. "My guts hurt," he moaned. "Feels like they're on fire."

"Hang on, Colonel," J.B. said, kneeling beside him. "Try to hang on. We need to know about the battlesuits. Do they have a weak point?"

Gabhart sagged over onto his side.

"Colonel? Colonel?"

Gabhart couldn't hear J.B. He had passed out again.

PUFFING, DOC TRIED to stay close to Jak's heels as he scrambled through the maze of side tunnels and man-size crevices. In the light of Doc's rad badge, the albino's long hair reflected back a shocking green, and he moved with an economy of motion and a split-second decisiveness that the old man couldn't hope to match. It was more a glide than a trot. Effortless. Silky smooth.

They had already dumped off one load of ore. About 150 pounds of it. By Doc's estimate, it was going to take thirty more trips to fill up the cart. At fifteen to twenty minutes per trip, it would be eight to ten hours before they'd have more water.

Not something to dwell upon.

Doc was relieved when Jak slowed his breakneck pace down the tunnel. They began looking into the intersecting crevices and holes for a likely place to collect more superhot ore.

As Doc glanced down one of the narrow side seams, a set of eyes flashed back in his badge's light. It was so startlingly close that he jumped back a step. There was a rustling noise, then the eyes were gone.

"What in Hades was that?" he cried.

"Stickie," Jak said. "Crawling through the cracks. From inside walls up into ceiling. He's over there now. Hear him?"

Doc had to admit that he couldn't hear anything except the sighing of the nukeglass, but he took the youth's word for it. He felt damnably naked without his LeMat. The pickax he'd been issued was no substitute for nine .44-caliber lead balls.

The corridor they were following zigzagged back and forth before it opened onto the high-domed expanse of a partially collapsed bubble. A huge interior space, it was too broad for their badge lights to reach the other side. They could see the ceiling, though. To Doc it looked like a vast, curved mirror, blurred by swirls and ripples.

Jak found the place unattractive, for strategic reasons. "Too big, too dark," he said. "Can't stay here."

Then they heard a cry from the far side of the bubble.

"Help me. Help me."

A man's voice, certainly, Doc thought. But where exactly was it coming from? "I can't see where he is," he said to Jak.

"Me, neither. Mebbe a trap. Could be stickies."

"Most stickies cannot form words."

"Could have a prisoner, use him as bait. Making him talk."

"Shall we not inquire further?" Doc said. He didn't wait for Jak's reply. He cupped his hand in front of his mouth and shouted through it into the darkness, "What is your situation?"

"I'm caught in a cave-in," the voice said. "My legs are pinned and there's a block edge against the inside of my groin. It's too heavy to move. If I try, it will sever my femoral artery. Please help me...."

"Whoever he is, he has some knowledge of anatomy," Doc said. "An educated man, perhaps. A rarity in these wild parts and unhappy times. Shall we take a closer look?"

Jak scowled and shook his head. "No."

"We can be circumspect, my dear Mr. Lauren. Just a reconnoiter. If we do not like what we see, we are off."

They worked their way around the edge of the bubble, picking a path of least resistance over the slick planes and treacherous edges of the ceiling's glassfall.

"Cover badge," Jak said, as he put his hand over his own.

When Doc did the same, the bubble was plunged into pitch darkness, except for a muted glow of green on the ground about one hundred feet in front of them.

They watched it intently for several minutes.

"Nothing's moving," Doc said at last.

Jak uncovered his badge and nodded.

"Are you still there?" Doc called across the rubble.

"Yes, I'm here."

Doc and Jak closed in on the man's position. As they did, there was an explosion of scurrying tiny feet. Low dark forms scooted away in all directions. Like shadows, flitting at the corners of Doc's eyes, the fleeing rats were almost too fast to follow.

They found the man almost completely buried in glass block. His head, his arms and one leg stuck out of a collapse that had come from the wall and ceiling above. A block of at least a hundred pounds straddled his hips and held him down. Doc and Jak shone their badge lights onto his face. The man had no front teeth. There were old bruises on his eyes and cheeks.

"Are you cut anywhere?" Doc asked him. "Once we start lifting off the glass, it could release pressure on a wound and you could bleed to death."

"I don't know. I can't tell. I've been pinned here for a long time. My arms and legs are asleep."

Jak and Doc set aside their axes and working carefully, lifted the glass from his body. His torso and limbs were covered with a myriad of shallow cuts and gashes, but none of them serious.

Freed, the man stood shakily.

"Thank you, thank you," he said. "I didn't think anyone would help me. Before you came, others passed by and did nothing. They stood over me and then walked on. They left me to be eaten by stickies or rats. This place is wicked and evil. And it's full of wicked, evil people.''

"Do you know something of human anatomy?'' Doc said. "You used a medical term a moment ago.''

The glass-fall survivor's eyes lit up and he started to say something, then changed his mind. When he spoke, his words were guarded. "Medicine? Oh, no. Not really. I just pick things up here and there. My name is Huth, by the way.''

After Doc had completed the introductions, he asked, "Where are you from?''

"Out east,'' Huth said. "I've been wandering on my own for quite a while, now. Never thought I'd end up in a place like this.''

From its shape and cut, the jacket Huth wore looked like the remains of a lab coat. The uniform of a scientist. Doc had very bad associations with coats like that. He glanced at the lapel. Something had been embroidered there, just over the pocket, but the threads had all been picked out.

"How did you come by that jacket?'' he said.

"Oh, this? The same place I got the pants and shoes. The garbage dump over in Byram ville. Some poor guy died in these pants. I don't know the story about the coat. I just picked it out of the rubbish pile before it burned up.''

The story satisfied Doc.

"Is it just you two working on a sledge?'' Huth said. "If it is, maybe I could join you. We could combine forces.''

"We already have a third person,'' Doc told him. "Why are you working alone?''

"I had some trouble back at the camp. Made some rather unpleasant enemies, I'm afraid." He indicated the bruises on his face.

"And you did what to deserve that?"

"It was my fault," Huth said. "There was a misunderstanding and it got blown out of all proportion. I said something to the guards that I shouldn't have said. A lie to gain their trust. I was just trying to find a way to get out of here, but it didn't work. In fact, it backfired completely when my fellow laborers took what I'd said for the truth. What about my joining you? The guards allow as many as five people to a cart."

"Let me talk about it with my friend here."

Doc and Jak withdrew slightly, and conferred in whispers.

"We could use a fourth on the sledge," Doc said. "He could help us fill it faster."

"Not like him," Jak said. "Has bad smell."

"Everybody down here has a bad smell, lad. It is the stink of fear. I say we take him back to Mildred, and then have a vote. The majority will decide. How about that?"

"Still don't like his smell."

"KEEP BACK!" Mildred warned, brandishing her pickax. To show she meant business, she swung the tool in a short, quick arc against the rim of the cart, making the steel clang and sparks jump.

The situation wasn't good.

In her brief time in the mines, Mildred recognized two distinct kinds of robbers. The sneaky kind, who usually worked alone. They walked past a cart and tried to filch a chunk or two of glass on the run. And the barefaced kind, who always worked in groups. They attacked without provocation in order to drive you away from your load, which allowed their accomplices to move in and help themselves.

The bearded, filthy man who taunted Mildred by spinning out of range and skipping away wasn't the sneaky kind. He was part of a four-thief pack. His pals watched with amusement from beside their sledge along the far wall. Their cart was nearly full. A feat that had been accomplished without their leaving the cart-loading area. Like a mosquito, the bearded guy kept darting back to test her reflexes. A huge mosquito, clad in foul-smelling rags and strips of black plastic bag. The guy was over six foot four, and his face had been mutilated by spiral brands on his forehead and cheeks, Deathlands tattoos. A tuft of black hair sprouted from the tip of his nose.

Mildred knew she would have shot him if she had been armed. Shot him dead, just for smiling at her like that. Her temper was barely under control, her nerves fraying. She found the idea that she was going to have to use lethal force to defend 150 pounds of nuke rubble that was slowly killing her both absurd and infuriating.

She had already witnessed some pretty hairy fights over much smaller quantities of ore. The struggles had all been between men, because they made up ninety-five percent of the slave population. In the mines, the strong victimized the weak. To the four thieves, Mildred, a woman, was the easiest of easy targets. A pushover, in fact. It was only a matter of time before they made their play on her. Mildred bent and with her left hand scooped up some of the fine glass dust that collected in the corners.

She hadn't given away the fact that she had fighting skills. All she had shown them was a few measured swipes of her ax. Demonstrating that she was willing and able to inflict bodily harm.

When they all started to move toward her at once, spreading out to close in on all sides, Mildred let her body relax. The axes they wielded had short handles, just like hers, which meant they'd have to get in close to land a blow. She had the cover of the cart, and a wall to protect her back. Those were the only strategic points in her favor, aside from the fact that the thieves were only after ore and she was trying to save her life.

The tattooed giant came at her first, waving his ax, again taunting her by offering his animalistic face as a target and then skipping out of reach. Mildred ignored him. She had to let the enemy come to her in order to save her strength. If they could wear her down physically, they would concave her skull. She held her ax in her right hand, point down, ready to block or strike.

A fat, sweaty bald guy, who outweighed her by close to one hundred pounds, closed in with a sideways shuffling gait. Like the tattooed man, his clothing consisted of a heap of tatters, fabric and plastic. The maneuver was intended to move her away from the cart, either by intimidation or brute force, so the others could plunder it. The fat man edged closer, trying to get her to take a swing at him. He was willing, it seemed, to take one for the team. With the thick coat of blubber that protected most of his body, Mildred realized that doing him sufficient damage was going to be difficult. The fat man was smiling at her, too. As if she didn't have a chance. As if this was fun.

The other slaves, the nonthieves, watched the proceedings in sick fascination.

She could expect no help from them.

Mildred had drawn an imaginary line on the tunnel floor. It was the distance she knew she could cross in a single step with power; it defined her killing range. When the fat guy sidestepped over the line, Mildred flung her left hand up at his face. A cloud of twinkling dust scattered into his eyes and up his nose as he gasped in surprise. The powdered glass cut him like ten thousand tiny razor blades.

"Unnhhh!" he cried, covering his eyes as he staggered back.

Mildred power stepped, bringing her ax up side arm, and two-handed it into the center of the fat man's throat. The point made a wet, slapping sound as it sank in to the start of the handle. She turned with the man as he gagged, ripping the curved ax out of his neck.

Blood jetted from the gaping hole where his Adam's apple had been.

He clutched at his ruined throat, his mouth opened wide, but no scream came forth.

Mildred used her momentum, planting her feet and twisting her torso. Uncoiling from her hips and legs, she backhanded the flat end of the hammer in a tight arc that ended at the base of his unprotected skull.

Bone crunched sharply and the fat man jolted forward. His knees buckled under him.

From the way his face hit the floor, Mildred figured he was dead before contact.

His friends figured the same thing.

"You bitch!" Bristle-nose cried. "You chilled Bucky. We're gonna pound you to a pulp!"

"You're going to need a longer handle than that if you're going do it from over there," she said.

"Get the bitch!"

Mildred moved into her original position, the wall to her back, the cart protecting her left flank. She guessed that a three-man charge was coming next. An attack from all sides, which she couldn't turn away. But what the thieves had just seen her do to their friend Bucky made them cautious. They didn't want to get too close. They took short swings at her, their blows coming up way short. Mildred didn't overreact, didn't commit herself. She didn't retreat, either. To do that would have given them an opening.

The stocky robber with running sores on his cheeks tried to edge in along the right-hand wall, close enough to land a blow.

Though Mildred saw it coming, she was barely able to duck the right-handed, sidearm blow. The man's ax point crashed into the wall. Mildred countered by bringing the flat of her ax down onto his wrist. Something snapped. The robber let out a shriek and released his ax handle. The weapon clattered to the floor as he jumped back, clutching his forearm.

"She broke my wrist!" he moaned.

Mildred was on him before he could take another step and before the others could recover from their shock. She swung the square end of her ax head against the side of his skull, a single two-handed blow to the temple that sent him sprawling. He hit the floor flat on his belly, arms and legs splayed, and didn't move.

Mildred could see he wasn't breathing.

The thieves could see it, too.

"Maybe this wasn't such a good idea," the third robber muttered out of the corner of his mouth. His long, greasy hair was plastered to the sides of his narrow head.

"Shut up, dimmie," Bristle-nose growled. "When we chill her and take her ore, it means double water rations for us. Come on. She must be getting tired. Let's take her out before she recovers."

Mildred was feeling the effects of her exertions. The ax definitely seemed heavier than a few moments ago, but she was so pumped with adrenaline it didn't matter.

Two thieves were down for the count, and the others were still coming at her. She realized she was going to have to kill them both. And the only way she could do that was to exploit her relative maneuverability, make them get in each other's way.

Bristle-nose moved along the far side of the cart; Greasy-hair came next to the wall. They closed in, with axes raised to strike.

Mildred let them come. They were trying to time their blows in unison, figuring she couldn't deflect both, so one would have to land. When they struck, she darted away from the wall, under the arcs of their swings. She hip checked Greasy-hair as she passed him. Already committed and off balance, he slammed into the wall, then bounced into Bristle-nose.

For a split second, his back was turned toward her, his arms locked up in his companion's.

Mildred brought the hammer down behind his left ear, which protruded from between the oily plaits of dark hair. Again, she struck with the flat end—she couldn't risk getting the point stuck in his skull.

A light blow to the mastoid would have just knocked him out.

It wasn't a light blow.

Blood and bone sprayed across both Bristle-nose and the wall.

As Mildred retreated, the huge robber surprised her by throwing his partner's limp body on top of her. Her feet tangled and she went down hard on her behind.

Before she could get up, the bearded guy had her throat in his huge, powerful hand. He squeezed her neck, closing her airway and shutting off the flow of blood to her brain. He held the point of his ax raised high over her head. He was grinning at her again, showing off his corroded yellow-and-brown stump teeth.

"This is for Bucky...." he said.

WHEN DOC AND JAK heard the hubbub, they were within a few strides of the sledge-loading area.

"That's Mildred," Doc said.

Jak dropped his bag and broke into a dead run. His speed was truly amazing. By the time Doc exited the side tunnel, the albino was already halfway across the main tunnel. The older man's heart skipped a beat. A big, filthy man was leaning over Mildred, holding her pinned by the throat while he prepared to strike a killing blow. As fast as Jak was, he couldn't close the gap in time to stop the tragedy.

The teen realized that, too, and didn't even try. Instead, he threw his ax, timing the toss with a forward lunge, putting his full body weight and momentum behind it. The ax sailed end over end in a whistling blur. It spiked into the top of the big guy's head with a solid thunk.

The ax hit so hard that it drove the tattooed man off his feet and sent his face smashing into the wall. The ax tumbled from his fingers. Mildred rolled away and catlike regained her feet as the man's legs buckled under him. His cheek and nose slid down the glass, leaving a wide smear of blood.

"Close one," Jak said, looking at the broken heads of the four corpses that lay around their sledge.

"Too close," Mildred said, wiping the sweat from her forehead with the back of her hand. "Thanks for the help."

Jak grunted.

Unable to free the ax point from Bristle-nose's skull with a straight pull, he used the sole of his boot to try to lever it loose. It wouldn't come out. The ax was buried past the handle.

"Shit," he said, letting go of the ax and allowing the head to drop to the floor. He left his ax where it was and picked up the one the dead guy had dropped.

The chilling Jak and Mildred had performed made a big impression on their fellow slaves. They were so impressed that during the fight none of them had moved to steal the robbers' ore, which sat in an unattended sledge. Now that the battle was over, none dared make a move for it.

"Those were some very bad men," Huth said. "They were the ones who knocked my teeth out." He pointed at the nearly full cart and said, "Aren't you going take their ore?"

"Divvy up," Jak said to the milling slaves.

The laborers looked at him, then at one another in astonishment.

"Go on, do what he says," Mildred told them. "The thieves stole it from you in the first place. Everybody take a chunk until it's gone."

For Ground Zero it was a very unusual proposition.

Instead of dog-eat-dog, every man for himself, it was more like all for one, one for all. The very prospect of decent, humane treatment made some of the slaves start crying—those who could still remember what their lives had been like before Slake City.

"Who's the tall, skinny geezer?" Mildred said as the redistribution of wealth began.

"His name is Huth," Doc said. "He wants to join our efforts to fill the sledge."

Mildred shrugged. "The more the merrier."

Chapter Thirteen

"What are you doing!" Krysty cried in disbelief. "We've got stickies all around us!"

Ryan stopped hacking at the wall with his hand ax.

"Is it the spores?" she said. "Ryan, are you seeing things?"

"Watch for the stickies," he told her. "If they rush us before I'm done, I need you to keep them off me."

With that, he resumed his wild attack on the nukeglass, making dust and splinters fly. He used the pointed end of his ax to chip out a wide, crusty hole around the buried part of the piece of Unistrut. He hadn't lost his mind. He had a plan. In a close-quarters fight against dozens of stickies, he knew that the axes would be next to useless—they had too short a range. Clonking the muties on their bald, flabby heads meant letting them get close. Getting close to a stickie's suckers meant big trouble.

He needed something longer, something that would allow him to take advantage of his height, weight and strength.

With a last whack he cracked loose the U-channel. All five feet of it tumbled to the floor. At the end he'd just freed was a big, oblong clump of glass. Kneeling, he rested the clump on the floor and used the point of his ax head to clip off the excess material. He cleaned the nukeglass from that end of the Unistrut, scraping it right down to the metal. This gave him an all-steel handle, two feet long.

The business end of the new tool was three feet of green glass splayed teeth, some huge, some small—all razor sharp.

Smaller was better.

The weapon's edge had to be able to deliver a blow without losing its teeth. Ryan knew that the closer the teeth points were to the channel opening, the less likely they would be to snap off.

The kissing sounds from the darkness were a lot louder now.

There was no time for fine work.

Using the flat end of the ax head, he spawled off the longest points of glass in quick, powerful strokes that left them shorter, but just as wickedly sharp.

"They're coming!" Krysty cried over her shoulder. "I can see their eyes! Ryan, there are too many of them!"

He snatched some scraps of the dead man's clothes from the floor and hurriedly wrapped the cloth around the makeshift handle to protect his hands from any spurs of glass he might have missed.

"Get back!" Ryan shouted.

Krysty's eyes widened at what he held.

A yard of sawtooth horror.

She ducked under his left arm and got behind him.

When Ryan saw all those sets of eyes bouncing down the shaft toward him, he said, "Fireblast!"

Stickies moved at tremendous speeds in short bursts; they also defied the laws of gravity. With the suckers on their hands and feet, they ran upside down along the ceiling and sideways along the walls.

Ryan closed his mind to the impossibility of the task. Deal with them one at a time, he told himself. One stroke at a time.

The narrow walls of the tunnel would only permit a looping, overhead, figure-eight slash. That he had freed a terrible weapon was evident when the first stickie launched itself at him.

With a screaming hiss, he brought the blade down at the join of hairless head and scrawny neck. At impact, there was a crunch, then the head leaped free and caromed off the side wall. Blood fountained from the neck stump as the body jittered wildly at his feet.

It wasn't a clean slice.

Chunks of wet flesh and shards of bone torn out by the sawteeth were flung against the ceiling as Ryan rolled his wrists, swinging the edge over in a tight arc. The backslash caught the next stickie as it leaped from the wall on his left. The rows of nested spikes ripped into the creature's exposed midsection, gutting it in an eye blink from groin to breastbone. The force of the blow sent the body spinning back into those who ran behind, knocking two of them flat.

The others clawed over them to get to Ryan.

It was all eyes and bared teeth for as far as he could see.

Ryan looped the jagged sword back and forth, driving with his legs and hips, grunting with the effort of each blow. They were coming too fast, from too many angles, so there wasn't time to aim for their necks. He just hit them wherever he could, across faces, across chests.

Contact was all he was after.

The nukeglass sword did the rest.

Its splayed teeth opened gaping trenches in flesh and bone. Wherever they touched, devastating wounds appeared. Bowels spilled in slimy coils from half-split torsos. Jaws were torn off whole along with tongues and teeth.

And still they came.

The ceiling, walls and the floor of the tunnel ran slick with stickie blood. Ryan's boots began to slip and slide in the viscous stuff. It had the same effect on the stickies—their suckers couldn't get firm holds on walls and ceiling.

The more blood that was spilled, the wilder they got. Though they could no longer run along the ceiling and walls, they threw themselves at him from the floor, leaping over the corpses of their brethren.

Ryan shut out the fatigue in his arms and shoulders, and kept the nukeglass sword windmilling, making his lower body do most of the work, driving all of his two hundred pounds into each strike.

Though he clobbered them, they wouldn't stop.

Their bodies piled up, clogging the crevice, forcing Ryan to retreat to clear his swing. The heap of dead stickies worked in his favor, by effectively narrowing the corridor. Only by clawing over the remains of their fellows could they come at him through the gap, one at a time. They fought one another to clear the opening, to meet death upon the edge of his gruesome sword.

"Ryan!" Krysty cried desperately.

He glanced over his shoulder and saw a hairless mutie perched on her back, its sucker fist caught in her hair, its needle teeth bared to bite the side of her lovely throat. Spinning, Ryan angled the glass blade across the stickie's neck. The body jolted, and the head tumbled off the ragged stump, which spewed gore to the ceiling.

The dead hand was still caught in her hair. The corpse's body weight pulled her backward.

Ryan couldn't bear the sight of it touching her. Growling a curse, he rolled his forearms, whipping the sword over, slashing its hacksaw teeth against the wrist joint. Arm and hand separated with a snick. The spasmodically clutching fingers released.

When he whirled back, he faced a pair of onrushing stickies who had cleared the gap in the corpses. They were already too close for him to swing the ax. He sidestepped their frantic, arm-waving charge and used the tip of the business end of the Unistrut like a lance, jamming it through the needle teeth and into the mouth of the creature on the right. In the same motion, he ripped the sword down and out, splitting tongue, jawbone and throat down to the collarbone. The other stickie's outstretched fingers brushed his face, but either it was going too fast, or his face was too bloody for the suckers to attach.

As it moved past him, sliding on the floor, Krysty stepped up and nailed it with a full-power whack of her pickax. The combination of her speed and its momentum made for deep penetration. The stickie's forehead dimpled in around the point of the ax, and Krysty jerked it off its feet and onto its back. She stomped the ax handle, freeing the point by popping up a divot of the stickie's skull.

Because the flow of stickies had slowed to a trickle, Ryan was able to take his time. He measured his sword strokes, timing them so necks and sawblade made contact at the maximum power point of his swing. Detached heads careened off the walls, bouncing into the dark.

Then the rush stopped altogether.

From atop the high pile of bodies, dolls' eyes in bald heads and flabby faces stared at him. As if suddenly it had dawned on them that he was royally kicking their asses.

As the stickies turned to run, he followed them through the gap, his boots slipping on the slick flesh and spilled guts. The stickies' traction was even worse than his. They were used to relying on their suckers, and the suckers did them no good on the wet floor. They squealed as their feet and hands slid on the edges of the broken glass and were cut to pieces.

Ryan gained on them easily. Running right up their backs, he chopped their legs out from under them. He dropped three more like that before he stopped, panting. On his way back to Krysty, he finished off the badly wounded stickies with single blows to the neck.

It was only after he had crawled through the gap that he realized he was covered with blood. It dripped down his arms and face and from the tips of his hair.

"How many did you chill?" Krysty asked.

"Don't know for sure," he said. He looked down the tunnel, heaped with pale bodies and body parts, with tangled, twitching wrecks. Ryan sagged against the wall, breathing hard. "Never saw so many of the bastards in such a small space."

After a moment or two, he straightened and said, "Dump the ore out of your bag."

"Why?"

"Just do it."

Ryan set aside the Unistrut sword and tipped his bag full of ore onto the floor. Then he picked up one of the bald, severed heads by its eye sockets and stuffed it in the bag.

"Ryan?" Krysty said. "Are you all right?"

"Put them in the bag," Ryan told her. "Get as many in as you can and put them in the bag."

Because the stickie heads were lighter than the ore, and because the bags stretched somewhat, they could pack a lot inside and still carry it. Ryan's sack topped out at ten.

"Okay, now what?" Krysty said.

"Take them back to the cart."

"I don't understand."

"You will."

Ryan was already moving, dragging the bag behind him, his glass sword in his other hand.

When he exited the crevice and started toward J.B. and Dean, the boy jumped up and shouted, "Dad, are you all right?"

"Fine," Ryan said. "Don't worry. It's not my blood. It's theirs."

With that he poured the heads into the sledge.

The other slaves standing cart guard heard the series of hollow thuds and ventured close enough for a look. Their jaws dropped.

"I'll be nuked!" the Armorer exclaimed.

Then Krysty stepped up and did the same thing, tipping her overstuffed bag into the cart.

Thunk-a-thunk-a-thunk.

Blood-smeared faces, gaping needle-toothed jaws, blank eyes looked up from the bottom of the box.

"Ryan, what's going on?" J.B. asked. He stared at

the bloody and flesh-fouled nukeglass blade. "And what the hell is that?"

"We'll be back in a minute," Ryan said. "Come on, Krysty."

They made two more trips to the kill site. Ryan used the Unistrut sword to chop the heads off the stickies who had died of other wounds. They loaded their bags with grisly trophies. When they reappeared the second time, the slaves left their own sledges and gathered around to watch the dumping. The third time, they cheered as heads rolled.

And they kept on cheering. The noise they made in the tunnel was tremendous.

"I counted fifty-four, Dad," Dean said.

"That's a shitload of heads," J.B. commented. "What are you gonna do with them, Ryan?"

"Cash them in, of course."

Ryan looked over at Gabhart, who lay curled on his side on the floor, unconscious and barely breathing. "Help me get the colonel in the cart, then let's push it into the fresh air."

The other slaves deserted their posts to follow.

Ryan, J.B., Krysty and Dean shoved the sledge back to the main tunnel's fork, past the pair of troopers, who didn't notice anything was wrong until they saw the mob following. Then it was too late to intervene.

As they pulled the sledge out of the mine and onto the flat, the mob spilled out, as well, and spread out over the dimpled ground, passing the word that something exciting was about to happen.

Ryan and the others pushed their cart past the others waiting to be unloaded, right up to the head of the line. No one complained. They glanced at the cargo, grinned and waved them on.

The trooper standing beside the ore truck looked into their cart. There was no way to gauge his surprise through the opaque visor, but he paused for a long moment before he said, "We don't give water in exchange for heads. Only ore."

"Fuck that!" said one of the slaves whose sledge was waiting to be unloaded. He reached into the companions' cart, grabbed a bald head for himself and quickly placed a double armload of ore on the ground beside the cart.

The idea caught on quickly.

Everyone with a sledge waiting to be unloaded did the same thing. In a matter of minutes, their cart was empty of heads and a pile of ore stood beside the cart.

"How about some water now?" Ryan said to the trooper.

Another cheer went up as he waved them over to the water tank. "Give water to sledge number seven," he said.

The slaves who had traded seemed delighted with the deal they had made. Hooting and hollering, they began booting the stickie heads around Ground Zero like soccer balls. Even the rad-sick ones, too weak to stand, managed smiles at the ghoulish antics. The major horrors of the slaves' everyday existence had been reduced to kick-toys.

Ryan ignored the raised pulse rifle of the trooper guarding the water tank, opened the tap, stuck his head under it and rinsed the blood off his hair and face. There was so much blood that it stained the wide puddle beneath the spout a rosy pink. After he had cleaned himself off, Ryan filled a cup and took it over to Gabhart, who had been moved to one of the shallow depressions in the glass. He and Krysty got the colonel to swallow a few tiny sips.

"Damned guards can't do a rad-blasted thing!" J.B. said, slapping his thigh in delight. "Whoa! Dean, look at that kick! That one's outta here!"

The troopers were unprepared to deal with death-sentenced slaves having fun on their own killing ground. They didn't know what to do, so they did nothing.

"Ryan, lover," Krysty said, "you just opened the floodgates of hope. Life in Hell is never going to be the same."

Chapter Fourteen

Dredda entered the doctor's quarters without knocking. "You have something for me?" she said to Jann, who sat at a small desk.

"Yes," Jann said, pushing up from her chair. "I took some scrapings from Mero's neck. And I found a similar patch of discoloration on myself, which I also sampled. Before giving you my analysis, I'd like to examine you, as well, if I could."

"Of course," Dredda said. She immediately unbuckled the torso plates of her battlesuit. They came away in two halves, front and back. They were overlapping and airtight. Underneath the armor, she wore a sleeveless gray T-shirt. She pulled the T-shirt off over her head, the hard muscles of her back outlined and jumping under her pale skin.

Jann used a magnifying loop to look at the area of redness on her right shoulder, which had spread from a small patch on her shoulder cap to cover half of her shoulder blade. The entire area was tender to the touch, and the edges of the patch, where they contacted normal-looking skin, had a slight yellowish crust on them.

After a moment or two, Jann said, "I'll want a scraping from you, too. If you don't mind."

"Fine. Do it."

With the point of a fine-edged scalpel, the doctor

teased some of the irritated tissue onto a slip of plastic. She took the sample over to the microscope on her desk and examined it more closely. When she drew back from the binocular eyepiece, Jann said, "It looks like we're all infected with the same creature."

"Infected?"

"Come over here and see for yourself."

Dredda bent over the microscope. What she saw were clusters of single-cell organisms, like stars on a midnight-black field. They all looked pretty much the same to her. They were oblong and globular in shape. They had waving, whiplike strands at either end. These strands seemed to propel them around—all of the creatures were jumping about erratically. If she looked hard, she could see right through their outer skin or cell wall. Tiny gobs of indefinable stuff moved around inside of them.

"What is it?" she said as she straightened.

"An organism of some sort," Jann said. "A bacteria or a fungus. We don't have an exact counterpart for it on our world. From the samples I've taken and cultured, it appears to be a relatively slow breeder for a prokaryote. The population doubling time is in hours, not minutes."

Dredda pointed at the microscope. "That's what's causing the rash?"

"Yes, I'm almost sure of it."

"Almost?"

"It's the simplest solution I can come up with. But at this stage I can't rule out the possibility that the rash is caused by something internal, and the organism on the skin is simply attracted to the irritation for feeding purposes. We may have brought these organisms with us from our Earth.''

"You just said they weren't like anything found there.''

"Because of its rapid breeding cycle, this kind of organism is prone to mutational changes. The differences that are apparent may have something to do with the Level Four procedure.''

"How so?''

"Genes could have jumped from the engineered virus to these organisms by accident.''

"Couldn't the mutation have been produced by the nukecaust in this reality?''

"That's a possibility, too.''

"Is this dangerous?'' Dredda asked.

"At this point, it doesn't seem so. Though it's spreading rapidly, it appears to be a superficial topical infection. I'm going to treat everyone who is infected with an antifungal ointment and see what happens. That's all I can do without more specific information. I'll need to check the male troopers to see if it's showing up on them, as well. And it wouldn't hurt to look at the Deathlanders, too.''

"How quickly can you test all the possibilities?'' Dredda asked. "Are the battlesuits involved? Could they be infested with these things? Can our armor be sterilized? Jann, this matter is a top priority. Our security may be at stake. I want it settled as quickly as possible.''

"That could present a major problem, I'm afraid. There's only one of me. I could use some help in this.''

"You can call on as many of the sisters as you need."

"I need trained help." Jann paused, then said, "I understand you sent Dr. Huth to the mines?"

"So?"

"You could bring him back. Let him work with me."

"I'm not sure what use he might be."

"I'm just a medical doctor," Jann said. "A diagnostician. A surgeon. Dr. Huth is a genius at research. He can help me nail down the organism's life cycle in short order. And once that's done, it's possible that the only solution to the problem will be biochemical. That's way outside my field of expertise. I'm concerned that if the organism continues to spread on our bodies, it could become life threatening. We can't afford to wait and find out. By then it might be too late to do anything about it for any of us. If Huth is no use, we can always send him back to Ground Zero."

"You can have Huth," Dredda said, "but I do not want to be forced to order the sisters out of their battlesuits for any length of time. That is completely unacceptable. Do you understand?"

"Of course."

After Jann had applied ointment to her shoulder and back, Dredda pulled on her T-shirt. "What is the status of the egg-fertilization program?" she asked. "I want to get our embryos started as soon as possible."

"We are ready to begin anytime," Jann said. "Once we have the male factor, we should be able to start implantation of host mothers within a week to ten days. I take it Shadow Man hasn't changed his mind about being a sperm donor?''

''I haven't given him a chance to yet.''

''It's important that he isn't left out at Ground Zero too long,'' Jann said. ''There could be irreparable damage to his reproductive cells, which would make them worthless to us.''

''I have no intention of *ever* bringing Shadow Man back here,'' Dredda told her. ''He's nothing but trouble. He's going to die at Ground Zero.''

''But the sperm for our in vitro procedures—''

''Shadow Man doesn't have to cooperate for us to get what we want from him.''

Chapter Fifteen

Nightfall at Ground Zero found all of the companions seated around a corner of the propane burner, taking turns cooking their dinners over the leaping rows of flames. The sizzling flesh and smoking droplets of fat filled the air with a gamy perfume.

Krysty was right, Ryan thought as he looked around. Hell had definitely changed for the better.

The thieves who had made their living by preying on the weak or sick were nowhere near the burner. They kept to the shadows along the edge of the ring of klieg lights, leaving the honest slaves to complete their meager meals in peace. Even the most hardened robbers were going to go hungry this night. Those who had attempted to steal food from their usual targets had been soundly beaten by their fellow prisoners, and turned away. An unspoken mutual-defense policy was in effect. The slaves would no longer permit individuals to be isolated and victimized.

As Dean cooked his rat shish kebab, three skinned, headless bodies threaded nose to butt on a long piece of wire, he said, "You know, these things may be kind of greasy tasting, but the crispy parts are real good. I especially like the crunchy little feet."

"Not a lot of food on these critters," J.B. commented, "but it sure sticks to your ribs."

"One rat goes a long way," Ryan agreed.

Doc belched discreetly into his fist, then said, "I find it helps to try to imagine it as roast squab."

"That takes one hell of an imagination," Mildred said. She stared dismally at the charred carcass on the end of her wire spit, a single bite missing from the backstrap. Mildred was having trouble choking down her meal; in fact, she couldn't even raise it to her lips.

"Same sort of dark, oleaginous meat," Doc stated.

"The metallic aftertaste is what gags me," Mildred said. "Like I've swallowed a bullet."

"A robust burgundy would certainly help to wash it all down," Doc admitted.

"If we had a robust burgundy, we could forget the fucking rat," the Armorer offered.

Jak didn't need to pretend the meal was anything but what it was. The mutie albino had lived wild and free his entire life, gladly accepting whatever Deathlands had to give. For him, protein was protein, whether it flew, walked, swam, slithered or crawled. He held a roast rat by the tail and chewed the head and shoulders noisily, using his back molars to pulverize both flesh and fine, fragile bones.

"What happened to your new friend?" Mildred asked Doc. "The guy who helped us load up our sledge. I figured he was going to eat with us, but I haven't seen him since we came out of the mine."

"That gentleman seems to have vanished, I am afraid," Doc replied. "And just when I was about to introduce him to Ryan and Krysty. I am sure he'll turn up later."

"If you're not going to eat any more of that rat," Ryan said to Mildred, "let me give it to Gabhart. See if he can keep it down."

"I'll come along with you," she said. "It's time to check on him again, anyway."

Downwind of the blue-and-yellow flames of the heater, Gabhart lay curled in a tight ball. He shivered violently, though he was sandwiched between insulating layers of rags they had stripped from the dead thieves.

Mildred gently touched his forehead. "Fever's a whole lot worse."

"Is he conscious?" Ryan asked.

"Colonel?" Mildred said, giving him a little shake. "Colonel, come on, wake up."

There was no response.

"Is this the total collapse you were telling me about?" Ryan said.

"No, he hasn't sloughed off his lung or intestinal tissue, yet. I'm afraid this is just the prelim."

"Bad way to go," said J.B., who had joined them.

"He could still come to?" Ryan asked.

"Anything's possible," Mildred admitted. "Miracles do happen, occasionally. It's a whole lot more likely that he'll slip into the terminal stage of the sickness without ever regaining consciousness. That would be the kindest thing for him."

Ryan turned to the Armorer. "Tell me again what he said about the manacles. Tell me everything."

J.B. repeated the story he had already related, almost word for word.

When he was done, Ryan said, "So, it sounds like the cuffs won't cut off our hands and feet as long as we stay on the road."

"That's how I read it, too," J.B. agreed.

"And the road runs all the way back to the camp,

where they keep the comp that controls the cuffs.'' Ryan scratched the dense black stubble on his cheek. "If that's the case, then all that's keeping us here are the guys in the battlesuits.''

"Pretty big 'all,' if you ask me," Mildred said. "It's the same 'all' that's going to laser us into chunks even if we make the camp and break up the computer.''

"We've got to take this one small step at a time," Ryan told her.

Then he turned to J.B. and said, "Gabhart said nothing about a way to defeat the battlesuits?''

"Never got to ask him the question. He conked out on me, first.''

"It's possible that there's no way to defeat the battlesuits," Mildred said. "At least not with what little we've got here at hand. I mean, all we have for weapons are pickaxes. If a centerfire slug can't get close to one of those suits, how the hell is an ax going to do any damage?''

After a long silence, Ryan said, "We need to sleep on it. Mebbe something will come to us by morning.''

"Mebbe the colonel will wake up and give us what we need before he croaks," J.B. said.

The companions crawled into the shallow, circular dimples in the glass's surface, downwind of the heater, and out of the direct glare of the encircling klieg lights.

Krysty and Ryan curled up together in the same dimple and quickly fell asleep.

AN HOUR BEFORE DAWN, Ryan awakened to Krysty's warm, soft lips brushing his.

"Mmm," she said. Her fingers tangled in his hair, and she pulled his mouth onto hers.

"You did real good yesterday," she said as she drew back. "You deserve a proper reward."

From the way her hand lingered on the back of his neck, Ryan knew she wanted to give him more than just another kiss.

"This hellhole is the wrong place for love," he said.

"There's no such thing. Let me show you."

Ryan winced slightly as her fingers found and fondled him through his clothes. His grimace didn't deter her one bit. And despite his misgivings, her stroking produced the desired effect almost immediately.

"See what I mean?" she said, smiling up at him.

Ryan didn't say anything.

Krysty snuggled closer. "We may never get another chance, lover," she whispered, her lips once again brushing against his. "You wouldn't want to die knowing we'd missed it, would you?" The tip of her tongue tickled lightly over his lips and pushed gently between his teeth.

They kissed deeply.

Ryan was the one who pulled back. The taste of Krysty's mouth and the feel of her tongue lashing against his seemed to steal the air from his lungs; the intimate contact left him hungry for more.

He pushed up to his knees and looked around. In the hard light of the kliegs, no one else was stirring. The other companions were out of sight in their own dimples.

"Do it quiet," he told her as he lay down beside her.

"Quiet as a mouse, lover," she said, unfastening his fly with practiced fingers.

Krysty did try to keep it under wraps; he had to give her that. Biting her lower lip and digging her nails into her palms, she managed to stifle herself while he thrust into her over and over again. But in the end, she couldn't hold back. She arched up from the glass and let out a piping cry.

Ryan covered her mouth with his hand and finished in a sprint, along with her. Afterward, they lay in each other's arms for a long while, finally falling into a light sleep.

It seemed as if they had only just drifted off when they were awakened by the *thwup-thwup-thwup* of approaching rotor blades. The noise got louder and louder and then the gyroplane's landing lights speared down on them from the black sky. As the aircraft descended onto a flat spot outside the ring of klieg lights, Ryan and Krysty had to turn their heads and shut their eyes to avoid the wind-whipped glass dust.

The gyroplane's arrival roused all the slaves. Raising their heads above the edges of their dimple beds, they watched the aircraft's doors open and three troopers step out.

"Is Dr. Huth here?" one of the new arrivals shouted. "Is Dr. Huth still alive? He's been summoned back to the main camp."

A tall, lanky man sitting on the other side of the compound jumped to his feet. "Here!" he cried. "Here I am!" With that, he hurried across the flatland, towards the troopers.

"What the blazes?" Doc said, scrambling to his feet. "The man's a doctor?"

People began to boo and curse and shake their fists at the frantically running man.

A slave standing near Doc said, "He's not a medic. He's a stinking whitecoat. He's the bastard who brought all these black-suited fuckers over here." The slave bent, grabbed a stickie head by the chin and mouth and lobbed it in Huth's direction. "Bastard!" he cried.

Several others launched similar missiles, which landed with dull smacks on the glass.

Ryan picked up an ax from the ground and in a blur of arm motion, sent it spinning over the compound. His lead was right on target; the arc of the throw was a bit high, though. The tool cleared Huth's head by about a foot and skittered across the glass. Seeing the merit in what Ryan had done, and the fact that the guards had exacted no penalty for the attempted murder, other slaves looked to their tools, as well. As the whitecoat zigzagged toward the gyroplane, he dodged a veritable rain of hurled pickaxes.

Covering his head with his arms, Huth moved behind the protection of the troopers' battlesuits. The armor deflected the barrage of tools; it provided an invisible shield that sent the projectiles veering off at steep angles. When the troopers raised their laser rifles to fire on the mob, the downpour of axes stopped.

"Ryan, I am at a loss here. I thought the man was just another slave. What is going on?" Doc said.

"I know Huth," the one-eyed man said. "I met him in the other reality. He was the director of the Totality Concept on the alternate Earth. He developed the trans-reality technology for FIVE and set up the first expeditionary force led by Colonel Gabhart. How

he ended up at Ground Zero on this Earth is anybody's guess.''

''Maybe he's just lucky?'' J.B. said.

Doc turned to Jak and said, ''It would appear my
initial induction concerning his education was correct
after all. The man has obviously earned advanced degrees.''

''Told you,'' the albino said. ''Bad smell.''

''If not that, a sorry state of affairs to be sure. We
should never have saved the miserable wretch. I can
only blame myself for that. You were right, my dear
Jack. We should've left him there to feed the rats,
then his existence might have served some greater
ecological good.''

Jak grunted in agreement.

It soon became apparent that the new batch of
troopers hadn't completed their mission at Ground
Zero. After securing Huth in the gyro, they joined the
mine guards and marched with them in formation,
pulse rifles at the ready, driving a wedge into the milling slaves. It wasn't clear until the last moment what
their intentions were. At a silent signal, they charged
into the mob, using their rifle butts to club back those
who didn't move out of the way fast enough. They
beat a path straight toward Ryan and the others.

At a shout from Ryan, the companions pulled together into a defensive hand-to-hand formation. J.B.,
Ryan, and Jak took the front, Mildred and Krysty
guarded the sides and Doc and Dean covered the rear.
All of them stood back to back.

''Use your axes to deflect their gun butts,'' Ryan
said as the troopers bore down on them.

The battlesuited soldiers split ranks around the

point of contact, surrounding the companions. When they attacked, they did so all at once.

Ryan dodged a rifle butt to the face, then used the curved point of his ax to hook the weapon's trigger guard. He gave a mighty jerk and pulled the rifle out of the startled trooper's hands. The trooper just stood there, watching as it sailed off over Ryan's head. Instinctively, the one-eyed man fired a roundhouse left punch into the side of his helmet.

Ryan was surprised that his hand made contact without being deflected by the armor's EM shield. It made good contact, too. The helmet didn't give at all under the punch, and the blow hurt his knuckles. If it stunned the trooper, he didn't show it. Before Ryan could block, a gauntleted hand was wrapped around the front of his throat.

Ryan tried to counter by swinging the ax into the man's side, aiming for his kidney, but the point hit something solid long before it hit the target. A very strange something. Power in, power out. With the same force he had applied to the blow, the handle was ripped from his grasp. The ax bounced away on the glass. And his arm went numb all the way to his armpit.

J.B. paused in his own self-defense long enough to side-kick the trooper's weight bearing leg, right behind the knee. Nothing happened. J.B.'s boot hit it square, but the armor kept the leg from buckling.

Then J.B. had all he could handle. A rifle butt caught him in the ribs, and he twisted away to avoid a second blow.

In this kind of free-for-all brawl, it was impossible to keep track of anything except what was right in front of you. The troopers had the same problems, too. Everybody was juking, swinging, ducking. Either hitting or being hit.

Ryan half turned to the left and stepped around the trooper's right hip. The instant he got his weight shifted, he had the guy. He bodyslammed the soldier to the ground, driving his shoulder into him. Ryan knew he'd made an impression on the guy because the hand around his throat let go. The trooper didn't move for a couple of seconds. In those seconds, Ryan tried to get his helmet off so he could do some more serious damage. He hit the release button, but before he could twist the helmet off, another trooper came to the rescue, clubbing him with the stock of his laser rifle.

Ryan snap-kicked the trooper in the middle of the chest, shoving him back a good yard and putting his gun butt out of range. The armor didn't dent or buckle around the kick, even though he had put a good deal of heel into it. Mebbe Mildred was right, he thought, and there was nothing they could do about the battle-suits.

"Dad! Dad, they've got Krysty!"

At Dean's cry, Ryan whirled. Battlesuited troopers had separated Krysty from the companions' fighting square. They had her surrounded and were battering her with their gauntleted fists.

Ryan threw himself at the nearest trooper, grabbing his arm from behind as he raised it to hit Krysty. He jerked the man off his feet and sent him spinning away.

J.B. tried to break through, as well, and for his

trouble got a rifle butt in the side of the head that dropped him like a rock.

Ryan lunged forward, through the gap he had created. Krysty was already slumping to the ground, unable to fight off the rain of blows from all sides. Before Ryan could reach her, he took a gun butt from behind that made him see stars and put him on his knees.

The follow-up blow to the base of his skull knocked him out, but only for a second.

As he heaved himself up from the glass, the troopers had Krysty by the arms and were dragging her away. Her head drooped like a broken doll's. Her eyes looked dazed, and there was blood on her mouth and cheek.

Ryan growled a curse and charged after them.

When they saw him coming, the troopers leveled their pulse rifles at him, muzzle first and waist high.

"Stop where you are or we'll fire, Shadow Man," one of the troopers warned him.

Ryan stopped. He had no choice. There were too many weapons in too many hands. He could see he couldn't get any closer without being sawed in half. "Let her go, you bastards!" he shouted.

"Don't worry," the trooper told him, "we're only going to borrow your red-haired friend for a little while. We'll bring her right back when we're done."

With the sights of their weapons sweeping the surrounding crowd, the troopers backed their way across the flatland to the cargo door of the gyroplane. As Krysty was hustled inside, the slaves started shouting angrily and they surged forward, rushing the landing site. More axes sailed through the air, and two of the klieg lights shattered and winked out. This forced the guards to fire a series of warning shots to cover the aircraft's departure. Though the shots weren't that close, most of the slaves hit the deck to avoid the energy pulses.

Ryan didn't go belly down on the glass and he didn't duck. He stood rigidly upright, watching grimly as the gyro with Krysty in it lifted off. The black aircraft rose into the sun, which was just breaking through banks of gray clouds on the horizon.

"We'll get her back, Dad," Dean said as the gyro wheeled away toward the Slake City camp. "We'll get her back."

Chapter Sixteen

Krysty came to inside the gyro, buckled into a contour seat by a cross-chest harness. The cramped interior's red lights swam as the aircraft made a sudden, gut-wrenching takeoff. For a moment the G-force had her stomach down around her boot tops.

When the pressure eased, she noticed the man sitting in the seat next to her. He had a high forehead and long skinny legs. Filthy and dressed in fetid rags, he smelled like a slaughterhouse on a hot day. He wore a big smile on his gap-toothed face.

"What are you grinning at?" Krysty demanded.

"The turn of my fortune at last," he said. "Moments ago I was doomed, like you and your friends, to die a terrible, lingering death. Now I am saved." He showed her his manacle-free wrists.

"Lucky you."

"No, it has nothing to do with luck," he said. "Dredda Otis Trask finally came to her senses." Still grinning, he tapped the side of his head. "What's in here is priceless, you see. I have a track record of success that belies my chronological years. My rise to professional prominence was meteoric. I assure you I have solved problems whose complexity and implications would crack your tiny mind. On my own world, statues were raised in my likeness. Halls of academe were named after me. I was emulated and bitterly envied by my peers."

"Are you crazy?"

"Hardly, though what I have endured would have certainly driven lesser spirits mad. In the other reality, I was the wellspring of invention. I helped to postpone the collapse of human civilization by more than a decade. And I discovered a pathway to other universes."

"You brought the battlesuits here?"

"That's correct. I met your lover, Ryan Cawdor, in my reality. When I saw him outside the mine this evening, I took cover. I was afraid that even in my current condition he would recognize me. Our last encounter was less than cordial."

"He would have torn your head off."

The whitecoat ignored her comment and went on. "It was most amusing to meet your version of Dr. Theophilus Tanner in the flesh. You see, he was an important figure in the history of my world's science. Not because of any discovery he made. He was a pivotal laboratory subject. As in your reality, my whitecoat predecessors trawled Dr. Tanner from the past, then expelled him to the future. However, instead of materializing in Deathlands, which of course never existed in my reality, he reappeared in my era, in the middle of a carniphage alert. He died on the spot.

"A detailed examination of frozen samples of his tissues taken before his expulsion was the key to my cracking the barrier between dimensions. It's a difficult concept to explain, even to someone with the proper academic credentials. To simplify is to oversimplify, in this case. Suffice it to say that the changes in his cellular structure brought on by the trawling event revealed certain specific physical mechanisms that had up until then not even been hinted at. My research into the nature of these mechanisms produced the miracle of reality transfer.''

Huth leaned closer to her and said, "I opened the door.''

As he spoke, her prehensile hair reacted, visibly shortening as it drew up into ringlets.

"Amazing,'' he said as he reached out to touch the red strands, which coiled away from his grimy, split-nail fingers like a nest of snakes.

"Careful, it bites,'' she said.

"A most remarkable mutation,'' he said. "Although I must admit, it's adaptive function is puzzling to me. Tell me, is the movement voluntary? Or is it automatic? Is your hair's retractability produced by a linkage with your other senses, or does it possess some sensory array of its own?''

"Fuck off.''

"I'll have to cut some of it off for testing when we get to the camp. It could well be the basis for an entire new branch of cybertechnology. Yet another prodigious feather in my cap.'' The whitecoat sank back into his seat, a dreamy expression on his face. "This world is full of such mystery and promise,'' he said.

"You sorely need killing,'' Krysty remarked as the gyroplane banked.

After it landed on the Slake City airstrip, the cargo door opened and a pair of troopers leaned in and unbuckled Krysty from her seat. As they pulled her out, the whitecoat said, "I'll be by soon for a sample of that hair."

Krysty didn't struggle in the troopers' grasp. There didn't seem to be much point. She was way outnumbered and with the cuffs on her hands and feet, even if she broke free, she wouldn't get far. Instead of wasting her energy, she conserved it, letting them half-carry her along. The troopers took her through the airlock door of the biggest of the domes and from there down a series of tubular, antiseptic corridors.

As they advanced, Krysty kept her eyes open, looking for the comp that controlled the manacles. As Colonel Gabhart said, it had to somewhere in the Slake City complex. But all the doors they passed were closed and none had visible markings on them. It occurred to her as she was hurried along that she might not even recognize the electronic brain when she saw it. The only comps she had ever seen were the ones the companions had come across in the redoubts—predark government caches of machinery and supplies. Those comps were a century behind what these invaders had. The science of Deathlands had come to a crashing halt in the year 2001.

The troopers took her through a doorway into a small dome that was blindingly lit. Unlike the corridors, the structure had not one, but a half-dozen light strips across the ceiling. From the furnishings, it looked like an operating suite or a dissection room.

Two she-hes stood in the hard light, beside a low black table with blood gutters running down the sides. One wore a battlesuit without a helmet; the other had on a tight-fitting, sleeveless gray T-shirt and loose gray pants. Krysty was struck by the size and definition of the second one's arms. Beneath the smooth, pale skin Krysty could see every jumping sinew. The bulk of the muscle wasn't feminine, but it wasn't masculine, either. There was something very different about it. It was more fluid. More supple. Not only powerful, but fast. Very, very fast.

Standing beside the operating table was a small black cubicle on wheels with a plastic hose coming out the top. There were LCD readouts on the side. Krysty didn't like the looks of it one bit. It reminded her of the tissue sampling apparatus she had seen Gabhart use on a cannie. The cannie had failed the tissue test, and been immediately foamed. Also next to the table were two-wheeled trolleys with instruments under clear plastic domes, and neat rows of injectable medicines in little bottles.

"Don't be alarmed," the she-he in the battlesuit told her.

Then she dismissed the pair of troopers. "You can go now," she said. "We don't need your help."

Krysty took in the handsome, androgynous face, the intense eyes, the confident expression. The queen bee of this nasty hive indicated a chair next to the wall. "Please have a seat over there and take off your coat," she said.

"Do I have a choice?"

"No, of course not. I'm Dredda, by the way. And this is Jann. She's a medical doctor. She'll be examining you."

As Krysty sat, the other she-he moved to the side and rear of the chair. Before Krysty could react, Jann locked an arm around her neck and plunged a hypodermic needle through her shirt and deep into her shoulder.

"Yeow!" she cried.

She couldn't get free of the arm. Jann pushed the plunger home, shooting burning pain into her muscle. Then she jerked out the needle, leaving a spreading patch of red around the tiny hole in the fabric.

"Sorry to be so rough," Dredda said, "but we don't have time to wrestle with you."

"What the hell did you shoot into me?" Krysty demanded, rubbing her wound.

"Don't get upset," Jann told her. "It's perfectly safe. It's just something to relax you."

It was already becoming apparent to Krysty that she had been drugged. Her head was growing heavy, and her tongue was starting to feel thick. Her fingertips and toes were starting to tingle. She tried to get up from the chair, but the she-he pushed her back down easily. Her legs had no strength.

"You can't fight the effects of the sedative," Dredda said. "You might as well stop trying."

Dredda and Jann picked her up under the arms and dragged her limp-legged over to the table.

Krysty was fully conscious, but paralyzed. She had feeling in her limbs, but she couldn't move them. She could think, but she couldn't talk. The she-hes laid her out on her back on the operating table, then Dredda started pulling off her boots. Jann slipped the jumpsuit from her torso, unzipping it and rolling the fabric down over the points of her hips. Then the two of them pulled off the jumpsuit and her panties.

Jann took a pair of stirrups from under one of the trolleys and attached them to the either end of the table. The doctor lifted her feet and hooked them inside, spreading her legs wide.

Unable to raise her head, unable to give voice to the string of curses that filled her head, unable to defend herself, Krysty felt tears of impotent fury slide down her cheeks.

You bastards, she thought, you filthy bastards.

"Pick up her head so she can see what's happening," Jann said to Dredda. "It's a quick and painless procedure," the she-he assured Krysty. "The sedation was necessary only because we assumed you would resist."

Dredda slipped a hand under her neck and gently raised her head from the table. What Krysty saw made her shudder. Below the flat, pale plane of her belly, above the tuft of red hair atop her pubis, her entire crotch was in full view and easy reach of the muscular creature who stood between her splayed knees. After pulling on a pair of transparent, skintight gloves, Jann attached a long, thin instrument to the hose emanating from the low cube beside the table.

Gaia, protect me! Krysty thought, shuddering as uninvited fingers deftly opened up her most private place and inserted the hollow, pointed tip of the instrument.

The box beside the table began to hum and from deep inside her the instrument started making sucking, slurping sounds.

"Your lover, Shadow Man," Dredda said, "refused to give us his seed for the in vitro fertilization of our eggs. But he couldn't refuse you. You gathered the necessary material for us. A little vacuuming up is all that's required. As Jann said, it will be painless and quick.''

Dredda set Krysty's head back down, leaving the redhead to stare unblinking at the domed ceiling. The extraction procedure took two or three minutes. They were very long minutes for Krysty. She lay there while the doctor probed her inner recesses with the suction tip, her face burning with anger and shame, more humiliated than she had ever been in her life. When it was finally over, Jann gave her another injection, which caused the paralysis to gradually subside. After a few more minutes, she was able to sit up and pull her clothes back on.

Whereas before Krysty had been speechless due to the drug, now she was speechless due to fury. She looked wildly around the room for a weapon, her green eyes flashing.

Dredda noticed the way she was staring at the instrument tray. "Maybe you should rethink that. First of all, you'll never reach it before I do. Second, I might accidentally injure you in the process."

Krysty glared at Dredda. "What are you?" she said. "What kind of thing are you?"

"You and I are not that different, actually. We have much of the same body chemistry. We have exactly the same emotions. The same yearnings. I just took advantage of an opportunity. I made a conscious choice to never be a victim."

"That's not something anyone can control," Krysty said. "Turnabout is the nature of the universe. All universes."

"I realize you think we have done you an injustice, if not an injury," Dredda said. "But we have the need to reproduce. It's biological, it's built-in, and just like you, we can't do it alone. We had to have his seed.''

"You're not really human anymore. The only way you can reproduce is in a jar.''

"We had to have our eggs extracted,'' Dredda said. "The genetic procedure we underwent would have damaged the eggs. In order to change ourselves, we had to give up motherhood, and the normal way of achieving it. That doesn't mean we can't love our offspring the same way you do, or that we don't want to see them grow and prosper.''

Krysty glowered at her.

After a pause Dredda said, "How would you like to help us in another way? It could be beneficial to you.''

"I know, you want me to carry the thing you're going to manufacture. No, thanks.''

"It would be half his.''

"It's the other half that turns my stomach. Like I said, no, thanks.''

"There could be rewards.''

Krysty shrugged.

"For one thing,'' Dredda continued, "you wouldn't have to go back to the mines. You could avoid that horrible death. And if you are cooperative, there may be another benefit that you haven't considered. You are a remarkable female specimen. Both Jann and I agree on that. You could join us. Become the first sister from Deathlands.''

"You'd adopt me?''

"Not exactly. You would take a dose of the same virus that we did. You would undergo the same physiological changes. You would come out the other side a force to be reckoned with. No man could ever stand up against you. You would wear the battlesuit and wield its full, awesome power. We sisters are more than female, and you could be, too.''

''More than a woman,'' Krysty said. ''And all I have to do to earn this honor is to bear…how many of your brats? Four? Eight? Twelve? Do you kill the male babies before or after they're born?''

''You don't understand what we are doing, where we are headed. Sacrifices have to be made. You can't possibly appreciate that until you walk in our shoes, until you become one of us.''

''Just being in the same room with you makes me want to puke,'' Krysty snarled. ''You don't deserve the joy of offspring. You deserve to be made extinct.''

''Have the guards take her to one of the holding cells,'' Dredda told Jann. ''Let her think about it for a while.''

The doctor grabbed Krysty by the arm. She twisted and fought, but she couldn't break Jann's viselike grip unless she called on Gaia. And at that moment, she wasn't prepared to do so. There was no point.

As Krysty was dragged to the door, Dredda picked up a slim, stoppered vial of pearly fluid and waggled it at her. ''Thanks again for the help. There is enough Shadow Man here to make us an army.''

Chapter Seventeen

Shortly after the gyro took off from Ground Zero, there was another confrontation between the slaves and their battlesuited keepers.

The cry went up from the doomed miners, "We want water! We want water!"

To emphasize their point, some of the slaves at the back of the crowd hurled their pickaxes at the trooper standing watch on the water tank. The flying axes clanged harmlessly off the fifteen-by-fifteen-foot metal cylinder and the stout steel framework that raised its bottom four feet above the glass.

"No ore, no water," the trooper announced.

This was the normal routine. No one got water in the morning until they returned with a load of ore.

Emboldened by the troopers' recent failure to act, some of the slaves tried to take matters into their own hands. They rushed the water tank.

"A real bad idea," Ryan said as he and the companions took cover in the dimples.

This time the troopers opened fire on the trouble-makers without hesitation. Obviously, it was a plan worked out well in advance. It wasn't a wholesale slaughter because the workers were needed to mine ore. The guards performed selective mutilations, targeting those who were already showing the effects of the radiation.

Lasers whistled, their green beams lacing through the charging mob from three sides.

Slaves dropped here and here, squealing in pain.

And the smell of burned meat drifted over the compound.

Those who hadn't been singled out, scattered, abandoning the wounded men flopping about on the glass. Some waved their blackened stump arms. Others, more grievously subdivided, could only lay there and moan. None of those who had been hit were dead. None would die soon. All of them faced horrible suffering.

"The least you could do is finish them off!" one of the slaves shouted through cupped hands.

And for his trouble, he got a green beam through the middle of his stomach. It cauterized his bowels and severed his spinal cord, and passed on to drop the man standing behind him, and the man standing behind him. It would have kept on dropping slaves, but the others jumped aside.

Skirmish over.

Status quo intact.

The slaves meekly picked up their axes and started funneling back into the mines. Their first cup of water was hours of toil away.

As the companions fell into line with the others, Ryan and J.B. gathered up Gabhart and brought him along. The colonel was still unconscious. After they had selected a pair of sledges to use, Ryan and J.B. carefully laid him in one of them.

"Mildred, what can we do?" Ryan asked. "Gabhart isn't coming around, and we need what's in his head or we're all going to die just like him. Slow and ugly."

"I don't know what to tell you, Ryan."

"You're a doctor, we need to wake him up. Give us some options."

While they talked, the other companions eased the two sledges down the entrance's slope by their ropes.

"Hard to do that," Mildred said.

"Why's that?"

"I took a solemn oath not to injure my patients," she said as they joined the others on the flat of the main tunnel. "Pain can be used to rouse people from this kind of state. But as a physician I'm sworn not to inflict it unnecessarily. As a physician, I know that the colonel's better off unconscious when his body gives out."

"There are more people to think about here than him," Ryan said. "People who aren't sick yet. Dozens of people. Some of whom are your friends."

"I know that. I know that."

"Triage, my dear Mildred," Doc said. "This calls for triage. A sound medical practice since the days of Hippocrates. Treat those with the best chance to survive. Leave the others to the grace of God."

"Waking him isn't going to kill him," Ryan said, "and if it does, by your reasoning, it would be for the best. Mildred, we can't wait. Krysty can't wait. We need the information now."

"Trouble is, it isn't just triage. I'm going to have to keep hurting him to keep him awake. It's more like torture. And I don't like it."

"Just tell us what to do and we'll do it!" J.B. said.

Mildred shook her head. "No, I know what to do. I know when to stop. I have to be the one to do it."

When they reached the fork in the tunnel, the pair of guards stationed there split up the companions. This time Mildred, Dean and Ryan took Gabhart into the left-hand passage, and Jak, J.B. and Doc took the right.

When Ryan's group reached the end of the tunnel, they parked their cart out of the way against the wall.

"Let's get him out on the ground," Mildred said, gravely.

She and Ryan lifted the limp man out of the box and stretched him out on the tunnel floor. The other slaves pushing sledges into the tunnel paid them no mind.

Mildred knelt beside him and took his pulse. "It's fast and thin," she said, putting his hand on his chest. "His breathing is very shallow. We'd better get on with this."

That said, she put the ball of her thumb against his left eyelid and pressed down hard on the hidden eyeball. Gabhart's legs jerked, and his arms thrashed. His head came up from the floor, his mouth open, gasping. The colonel didn't have the strength to keep his head up. Dean caught the back of it as it dropped, keeping it from hitting the floor.

Mildred leaned right into his face and said, "Colonel, you've got to stay awake. You've got to answer Ryan's questions."

Gabhart's eyes opened. There was something wrong with them. They seemed to focus in midair. It wasn't clear if he could still see. "Ryan?" he croaked through cracked, bleeding lips.

The one-eyed man took his hand and squeezed it hard. "I'm here, Colonel. We need to know more about the battlesuits. It's vital."

"Okay," Gabhart said, and his eyelids closed.

"Is it true that the EM shields only deflect things that are made of metal?" Ryan said.

"No. Things have to be subsonic, too. They'll deflect laser beams, coming at the speed of light."

"Colonel, we need a weak point. You've got to give us something to attack."

"Power supply," Gabhart said, grimacing. "The suits use the same kind of nuke fuel as the wags. Without fuel, there's no EM pulse, no combat arrays, no com link. Without fuel, a battlesuit is just so much light armor. It will stop conventional bullets, particularly where the plates overlap, but they will dent it, and if fire is poured on top of fire, the slugs will eventually penetrate. Unenergized, it will not deflect laser pulses, either. The fuel is highly concentrated and highly radioactive. It has to be shielded from the suit-wearer's body."

"How is the fuel stored?" Mildred said.

"Each suit has a fuel reservoir."

"Where is it?" Ryan said.

Gabhart's eyelids fluttered shut and his face went slack. Blood trickled out of the corner of his mouth and down his jawline to his ear.

Mildred gouged him again, pressing her thumb into his eye socket. Again the colonel came violently awake, moaning pitifully at the pain.

"You've got to try to stay with us," Mildred said. "Try to concentrate." Her face was starting to look drained in the eerie greenish light.

"Where is the fuel reservoir?" Ryan repeated.

"In the crotch of the suit," the colonel said. "Fuel and shielding are both heavy. For balance they need to be as low to the ground as possible and spread out."

"What's the reservoir made of?" Mildred asked.

"The reservoir is a flat, hourglass-shaped bladder sandwiched between sections of armor," Gabhart said. "The bladder itself is very flexible. It has to be to allow full range of leg and hip movement. Nuke power is transferred through the crystalline structure of the battlesuit. It is has its own inorganic circulatory system."

"How do we drain the reservoirs?" Ryan said. "Colonel?"

Gabhart was out cold again.

"His breathing is getting worse," Mildred said. "His lungs are starting to fill with blood."

"Do it," Ryan said.

Mildred had tears in her eyes as she awakened the colonel for the third time.

When the man stopped groaning, Ryan repeated his question.

Gabhart seemed to gather himself. His eyes focused on Ryan's face. "Once the suits are fueled," he said, clearly but with tremendous effort, "they can't be touched with energy or lead, or metallic hand weapons. There's a nipple for draining the used-up fuel and pumping in fresh. If you lift up the edge of the crotch plate the nipple is on, it will move about an eighth of an inch. The gap exposes one end of the bladder.

"Can they be punctured?" Mildred said.

"They are made of plastisteel but they can be cut with a sharp point, so long as it isn't metal."

"Dean, give me your blade," Ryan said.

The boy pulled his bone knife from his boot.

Ryan showed the colonel the serrated tip of the catfish spine. "Will this cut them?"

"Probably. The fuel is very dangerous, though."

"Explosive?"

"Not under normal conditions. But it's toxic. Don't get any of it on bare skin. If it gets on your clothes, strip them off at once. It is fairly viscous. Drips slow unless it is pumped hydraulically…which is how the reservoir is normally drained and filled."

"How much of this stuff is in each suit?" Mildred said.

Gabhart opened his mouth to answer. His eyes suddenly widened, almost bulging out of their sockets. Then blood gushed from his mouth and nostrils. He choked and sputtered, spraying gore as he strangled on the lining of his own lungs. His heels drummed on the tunnel floor, while his arms thrashed.

"Hold him down!" Mildred said.

They grabbed his arms and legs and pinned him to the glass.

"Let it go, Colonel," Mildred told the desperately struggling man. "Just let it go. It's done. It's over. You did good."

With a last, bubbling wheeze, Gabhart relaxed, his eyes fixed and staring at the ceiling.

"Brave man," Ryan said.

"Came a long way to die so hard," Mildred replied.

She gently touched the colonel's eyelids, closing them. "Did you get what you needed?"

"Thanks to Gabhart, I've got the start of a plan," Ryan said. "It's gonna take all seven of us to pull it off. We're going to need a couple of empty battle-suits."

"Is that all?" Mildred said.

"Let's get the colonel buried and start loading the sledge. We'll meet up with the others topside."

TWENTY MINUTES LATER, Ryan, Mildred and Dean pushed and dragged their full cart out of the mine. After they had traded ore for water, they hung around the compound until the other companions showed up.

Seeing that Gabhart wasn't with them, Doc said, "Did the colonel shed this mortal coil?"

"About thirty minutes ago," Mildred told him.

"Did he talk?" J.B. asked.

Ryan filled them in on what the colonel had said before he died. Then he quickly sketched out his plan.

"Problem I see," the Armorer said when he was done, "is the suit-to-suit communications. If one of the guards hears his pal in trouble, he'll either come running himself, tribarrel blazing, or he'll call in the others. Either way, we're cooked meat."

"It just means we've got to occupy them both at the same time," Ryan said. "Occupy them so they don't have a chance to think about calling for help."

"Get one to leave his post," Mildred said, "while we strip the other one."

"Jak, you're the fastest runner," Ryan said. "Think you can make one of them chase you?"

"Which?"

"Take the guy guarding the right fork," Ryan said. "The other one is more my size."

"Take him and lose him?"

"No. Lead him back to the fork."

Jak nodded, then headed toward the mine by himself.

The companions paused a moment to give the albino teenager a good head start, then pushed their empty sledges after him. When they reached the main tunnel's fork and the klieg lights, there was only one guard in evidence and he had his back turned toward them. He was staring down the right-hand fork, with the muzzle of his pulse rifle pointed at the floor.

J.B. jumped in the front cart's ore box, and Ryan, Dean, Mildred and Doc started pushing it as fast as they could. On the slick surface, it picked up speed in a hurry. They aimed the sledge at the trooper, who whirled at the last second and tried to step out of the way. Ryan countered, throwing his weight to the outside, which caused the sledge to veer sharply. Before the guard could get his pulse rifle up, the bow of the sledge crashed into him and carried him hard into the wall.

An instant after impact, J.B. jumped out and onto the trooper, pulling him headfirst into the cart's box. This tipped the guard's legs into the air. While the man fought to get free, wildly kicking his legs, J.B. sat on the back of his helmet, pinning him to the bottom and sides of the sledge. The Armorer used his boots to keep the trooper's hands off his throat mike's activator.

Mildred grabbed one flailing leg, and Doc the other. Ryan slipped between the two with Dean's dag-

ger in his fist. His fingers found the battlesuit's fuel
nipple fill, then the edge of the armor plate. He pried
up the plate and thrust the point of the bone blade
under it. The dagger point slipped in perfectly. Its
serrated edge slashed deep into the fuel bladder. Ryan
ripped it back out, splitting the bladder wide open.

"Look out!" he cried as a thick fluid, lemon-
yellow in the light of the kliegs, gushed out and splattered onto the floor.

"Kill the fucker!" shouted a passing slave. "Gut
him!"

Others stopped their carts. They, too, began to
shout encouragement.

This was something worth watching.

J.B. reached down and pushed the helmet's release
button, then he screwed the helmet off the battlesuit's
collar. Then he knee-dropped on the back of the guy's
head, driving his face into the bottom of the cart.
After two knee-drops, the trooper went dead limp.

"He's out," J.B. said.

"Get him onto the floor," Ryan said.

When they had the guard on his back, they started
unbuckling the battlesuit. They removed the torso
plates first, then arms and gauntlets, and finally the
crotch panel and leg attachments. Under his armor,
the trooper wore gray underwear with an Omnico
logo. The companions tore it off, then tore up his
underwear.

Mildred pointed out the angry rash across trooper's
lower back and down his right leg.

"Try not to touch it," she warned the others.
"Could be some kind of off-world scuzzies."

After they tied and gagged him with strips of his

own clothing, they dumped the trooper back in the cart and shoved it to the side.

The spectator slaves moved in around the sledge. They took turns leaning in and punching or spitting on the defenseless guard.

"That rash could be contagious," Mildred told Ryan as he reached for the armor. "Could be something living in that battlesuit."

"The least of my worries," he said, buckling on the torso plates.

Ryan had trouble getting on the gauntlets and boots because of his manacles. It was a very tight fit, especially over his ankles, but with help he managed it. He was careful with the crotch panel, which still dripped a feeble trickle of fuel.

"How does it feel?" J.B. asked him when he stood.

"It's a lot lighter than it looks." He rotated his arms. "Flexes good, too. I got a full range of movement."

Doc handed Ryan the helmet, and the Armorer helped him screw it on.

"Can you see out of it?" Mildred said.

"Kind of," Ryan said. She couldn't hear him. Without power, the voice amplification didn't work. Neither did the oxygen pump. There was no air in the suit. And the visor began to fog over from his breath. He unscrewed the helmet at once.

"The suit's ventilation system is shut down," he said. "Lend me your ax, J.B."

Ryan laid the helmet on the floor and with powerful blows of the ax, punched a series of ragged holes in its back, just above the join with the battlesuit collar.

"There," he said. "That should do it."

"A no-tech solution," J.B. stated with a grin. "Pure Deathlands."

Ryan picked up the trooper's laser rifle. Although it looked bulky, it was light and quick in his hands. The bullpup design came up fast to his shoulder, and its balance was nose forward and sweet. Gabhart and his crew had shown them how to read the charge-indicator LCD. The indicator read full. Enough power to saw through a hundred yards of igneous rock.

"Where did the cart with the trooper go?" Mildred said.

The sledge wasn't where they'd left it.

It was nowhere to be seen.

"The other slaves must've taken him into the mine when we had our backs turned," J.B. said. "By now he's dead meat."

There was nothing for the companions to do but wait around the fork for the mutie albino to show up.

"I wonder what Jak did to get the other trooper to chase after him?" Dean said.

"Whatever it was, it sure worked," Ryan said.

"Must've pissed him off, large," J.B. agreed.

"There's no denying the fact," Doc concluded, "our young Jak is a most enterprising fellow."

Chapter Eighteen

As Jak walked down the tunnel, he didn't have a clue what he was going to do. He didn't have a clue until he saw the orc sledge coming his way, up the right fork, on other side of the klieg lights.

It was full of big blocks of glass.

Nonmetallic glass.

Something twinkled in the blood-red seas of his eyes. A smile twisted his pale lips and he laughed out loud. Why hadn't he thought of that before? Why hadn't any of the others thought of it?

Though Jak was a man who usually communicated in terse, fractured English, it was no indication of his mental powers. The albino teenager had a keen native intelligence, a quick, decisive mind and an instinct for making the right move at the right time. Some people might dismiss this talent as a survival urge, something he shared with the lower beasts, even the insects, but it was much more complicated than mere reactive hardwiring. Jak had put together Gabhart's last words with the problem he faced and the tools at hand, and come up with a viable solution. It was real-time synthesis, under pressure of certain death.

He timed his loping stride so he arrived at the guard station a second before the sledge did.

"Whoa!" he said, holding out his hands, grabbing the front of the cart and stopping it.

"What do you want?" said one of the slaves doing the pushing. "Get out of the way, you white-haired runt!"

Jak walked around the trooper's side of the sledge. He looked into the box and said, "Ore's no good. Not rad hot enough."

"What's the holdup?" the trooper said, coming closer.

Jak reached into the cart and hefted out one of the big, rectangular blocks, bending his knees to take the weight, which was considerable. "This," he said, turning and opening his arms.

A hundred pounds of nukeglass fell with a satisfying crash onto the soldier's boots.

No EM pulse.

No deflection.

"Nuking hell!" the cart-pushing slave exclaimed. He gawked at the block, which covered the black boots up to the shins.

Jak couldn't see inside the trooper's helmet, but his body language—all scrunched over, barely holding onto his laser rifle—said what had just happened didn't feel good.

Before the soldier could move, Jak took another, smaller piece of glass and slammed all twenty-five pounds of it onto the top of his helmet. The pulse rifle clattered to the floor beside the block.

At this point, the cart-pushing slave and his partners silently backed away from their sledge and made themselves scarce, hightailing it toward the mine entrance.

The trooper bent and retrieved his rifle. Then he used it like a pry bar to lever the block off his boots.

By that time, Jak was running down the side tunnel, his shoulder-length white hair flying.

The trooper didn't hesitate. And he didn't call for help from his pal in the other fork of the tunnel. As soon as he got free of the block, he charged after the albino teenager.

Jak actually had to slow down so the trooper could keep him in sight as he ducked into one of the crevices at the end of the tunnel fork. He didn't want him to lose hope and give up. On the other hand, he didn't want to give him a clear shot with the pulse rifle.

The passage ahead ran straight for maybe thirty yards, before splitting off into narrower corridors. Jak knew where each went, having out of habit already memorized various routes through the underground maze. His red eyes, which had limitations in bright sunlight, worked well in the green gloom of the shafts. He saw the other slaves coming long before they saw him. He saw their surprise when they blinked and found him running, bagless and full tilt, down the passage straight at them.

They were even more startled by the whistling shriek of a laser rifle in the enclosed space. A beam fifty times brighter than their badges sliced through the cavern's pall. Diving to avoid the energy pulse, they dropped their ore bags and flattened themselves to the floor.

The shot was high and to the right, just past Jak's shoulder.

The draftsman's line of green light hit the wall in front of him.

And melted it.

Instantaneously.

Unlike plain old rock, there was no red glow of the heat-up stage, no incandescent center before it began to drip. At the laser's impact point, the glass immediately liquefied. And the damage spread out around the initial hole, like ice melting around a blowtorch flame. There was no steam, but there was smoke. Harsh, throat-rasping smoke. The liquid glass poured down the wall and melded with the floor as it quickly cooled.

Jak suddenly saw how the invaders had cut the tunnels leading to the high-rad areas. With their shoulder-fired energy weapons, they could carve out immense caverns in the glass in a matter of minutes.

As Jak raced for the turn in the corridor just ahead, another slave appeared around the bend, lugging his ore bag. The trooper fired again. And again he missed high, perhaps because he was shooting on the run. This time the pulse opened a two-foot-wide hole near the top of the wall. The slave who ducked under the shot was caught in a molten glass waterfall that poured down over his head and back. He managed to stand for a split second as it cascaded over him, then he slowly sank to the floor, unable to scream because his lungs had already been scoured out. As he slumped, his flesh burst into flame. By the time Jak reached the turn, all that remained of the man were the charred bones of his legs, which stuck out of the smoking blob of glass.

Jak ducked around the corner and sprinted. The sound of his own breathing was loud in the narrow corridor. But not loud enough to drown out the sound of heavy boot falls behind him.

The tunnel went through a series of zigzags before

a crevice on the left offered him the detour he was looking for. He slipped through the crack and followed it as it doubled back to join the main shaft. The trooper couldn't fire at him. He was a hundred feet behind and his target was not only out of sight, but pulling away.

Jak knew his real trouble was going to come when he got back to the sledge loading zone at the end of the side tunnel. There were no sharp turns in the shaft there to give him cover. And there was a long straightaway before he reached the fork. All he could do was pour on the speed, try to get as big a lead as possible.

Head bobbing, arms pumping, he burst through the end of the crevice, vaulting past groups of slaves who stopped loading their ore and craned their necks around to follow him.

Ahead was the hard glare of the klieg lights.

He dashed madly for it.

"Look out!" someone shouted from behind.

Jak veered away from the tunnel wall just as a thin green beam squealed past him. Trigger pinned, the trooper swung the laser rifle back, trying to slice him in two.

Jak threw himself down and rolled.

Chapter Nineteen

Dredda unbuckled her torso armor and pulled her sleeveless T-shirt over her head. "How is it?" she asked Mero.

"A lot worse," Mero said. "See for yourself."

Dredda looked in the hand mirror her sister changeling held up. The small patch of red had spread from her shoulder to the middle of her back and down her arm. It oozed clear, sticky fluid like a second-degree burn. Even more disturbing, the infection was starting to impact movement and nerve function on the right side of her body.

Mero put down the mirror and picked up a tube of topical lotion. She carefully applied it to the irritated area.

"That stuff doesn't seem to be doing any good, does it?" Dredda said.

"It isn't helping mine, either," Mero replied. "It just keeps spreading and spreading."

There was a knock at the bulkhead door.

"Yes?" Dredda said.

Huth opened the door and stuck his head in. He had shaved his face and his head. He was dressed in clean gray fatigues. His gaze immediately dropped to take in the small, hard-nippled breasts that Dredda didn't bother to conceal.

"What is it?" Dredda demanded of him impatiently. "What do you have for me?"

"I have some preliminary results," Huth said as he slipped into the room. "I repeat, they are preliminary, but I think we can draw some reliable conclusions from them."

When his focus again dropped to her chest, she angrily grabbed her T-shirt and pulled it on. Men, she thought. Hardwired stupidity was standard equipment.

"Let's have it," she said.

"The organism that is causing the problem is everywhere," Huth said.

"Everywhere?"

"Correction. It's everywhere I've been able to examine in the last five hours. I've found it inside and outside the domes. It's inside the wags and gyros. It's in all of the battlesuits. It's in the soil surrounding the compound."

"Do you have a treatment for it that works? The ointment Jann gave us does nothing."

Huth reached in his pocket and took out a white plastic tube. "This formulation will heal your irritations. It won't solve the problem, however."

"Explain."

"This organism will adapt to the formulation," he said. "That is guaranteed. In days, in perhaps hours, it will produce offspring that are immune."

"So, find another formula."

Huth shook his head. "Ultimately, that route leads to total disaster. If we attempt to keep one-upping this organism, in the end all we will succeed in doing is selectively breeding a generation that cannot be stopped by any means at our disposal."

"There is nothing we can do?"

"As I said, there are temporary measures."

"How widespread is the infection now?"

"Almost everyone has it. The transgenic females and the male troopers. The Deathlanders do not seem to be affected, however."

"Because the organism is native to this planet?"

Huth frowned. "Evidence on the organism's origin is uncertain. It is difficult to tell whether it is a native species or whether it has spread locally since your arrival."

"You mean we brought it with us? I thought it was unlike anything on our world."

"That's true, but it doesn't eliminate the possibility that it changed, either in transit or after it came here. There is also the possibility that your treatments made you susceptible to a species native to Deathlands."

"But the male troopers didn't have the procedure."

"If the engineered virus wasn't completely burned out of your systems, it's possible that you infected the troopers or the organism, or both. Genes could have been inadvertently transferred."

Dredda recalled her haste to get out of Level Four quarantine, warnings of whitecoats unheeded.

"At present this organism is only attacking the surface layer of skin," Huth went on. "But as the colonies grow on infected individuals, they will begin to penetrate deeper. If they get past the muscle and into the body cavity and internal organs, death is the only foreseeable outcome."

"We did not go through hell to be defeated by something as small and insignificant as this," she told him. "Can't we sterilize the environment?"

"We can clean the battlesuits and the interiors of the domes and wags, but we can't keep the organisms out because they are already too well established locally."

Dredda paused for a second, then said, "What about you? Have you got it, too?"

"That's a critical point," he said. "Currently, I am infection free. And I've been here much longer than you. That adds support to the idea that it was transported here with your forces. Or that your susceptibility and that of the male troopers is the result of the transgenic treatments."

Dredda shook her head in disbelief. "You don't have it," she said. "Everybody else has it, but you don't."

"You do understand the implications, I hope."

"What do you mean?"

"If you brought the organism along with you," Huth said, "you may well have left it behind. Given the thing's generation time, the changes probably occurred before you made your exit. The same thing that's happening here could be happening on our Earth."

Dredda's eyes opened wide. "You mean, this thing could conceivably wipe out all of humanity on our world?"

"Based on my preliminary calculations, it could have already done so."

"We solved the population problem by accident?"
He nodded.

"Too bad there's nothing there to return to," Dredda said. "A dead world full of dead people."

"I think you have to face an unpleasant choice," he said.

"And that is?"

"Having to leave this planet."

"Leave the planet? Why not just leave the area? Go to the other side of this continent? Or go to another continent?"

"Like sterilization, that is a short-term solution. This organism and its spores spread on the wind, and on other hosts who can tolerate it. Like the Deathlanders. Or the native insects. Or birds. Or wild animals. There is no end to it."

"You're saying in a month of contact we've already infected the whole damned planet?"

"No, I'm saying that in time, eventually the whole planet will be infected. There's no way to stop it. The longer you delay leaving this reality, the bigger the risk that you won't ever be able to leave it. Let me stress that death by this means will not be quick or pleasant. As the organism devours skin and flesh, there will be secondary infections of the open wounds by bacteria."

"Can't you do anything about this?" Dredda yelled at him. "Give me one reason, Dr. Genius, why I shouldn't send you back to the mines?"

"I have done something," he protested. "I have given you the information you need to survive. I have bought you a few hours with the new ointment. We can confine and successfully treat the problem prior to jumping from this reality, and eliminate it afterward. That's the best I can do under the circumstances, I'm afraid."

"A few hours?" Dredda said.

"At best."

It was all finally beginning to sink in.

"But there isn't enough energy on hand to move the entire operation! We'd have to abandon most of our equipment because we couldn't maintain the corridor long enough to get it all through. There'd be no time to send drones through first, to lay the groundwork. We'd be at the mercy of whatever reality we happened to jump to."

"The battlesuits can withstand antagonistic environments."

"Only as long as their fuel lasts."

Huth seemed alarmed at her increasing level of agitation. He glanced nervously back at the door, measuring the distance if he had to make a run for it. "Believe me, it's not as dire as it seems," he said, "if you understand the nature and depth of the parallels between realities. The conformities from one universe to the next are very close or we couldn't travel between them. The corridor wouldn't hold up. Interdimensional vibration would tear it apart. The bottom line here is, no matter where you jump using this technology, you can expect to find an oxygen atmosphere, a single sun and a class M planet of the same relative age. The details of each environment may be very different, but the general features have to be the same."

"I need a time frame," Dredda said. "How long do we have before we have to leave?"

"There is no margin for safety. And this is just an educated guess, but based on the organism's generation time, I'd say six hours, tops."

Dredda refused to sag under the weight of that terrible news.

"Mero," she said, "we have to have hard numbers on the nuke fuel we currently have on hand, and a solid estimate on how much more we can extract from Ground Zero and process in the next six hours. We need fuel to power the jump, and we need fuel to use after the jump. The amount of fuel is going to determine who and what goes with us."

"I'll get right on it," Mero said, heading for the door.

"Before you do that," Dredda said, "send the word to the troopers at the mines. There is no tomorrow. Work the slaves until they drop dead. I am authorizing the execution of slackers, at their discretion. I want every ounce of ore they can wring out of them."

Chapter Twenty

Ryan saw Jak burst out of the gloom at the end of the tunnel. The mutie albino was sprinting for all he was worth. A second later, the reason became clear. Behind Jak, at the edge of the range of the klieg lights, a trooper skidded to a stop. As he raised his pulse rifle and fired, someone deeper in the shaft let out a shout.

Jak managed to twist away from the green beam.

It didn't wink out, but like a 150-foot-long saber slashed across the width of the tunnel at belly height.

Before it could touch him, Jak dived for the floor. As it swept over his head, he rolled and came up on the balls of his feet; he came up running. The laser shot swung wide, and as the beam grazed the side of the far wall, it gouged a long, dripping channel in the glass.

As fast as and as agile as Jak was, it wasn't the kind of game he could keep on winning.

Clad in the stolen battlesuit, Ryan moved away from the interior wall, waving his arms at the kneeling trooper. He had no EM protection because the suit was out of fuel. If the guy saw through the disguise, he was a goner.

The trooper stopping firing.

Ryan grabbed Jak by the shoulder as he rushed past, using the lighter man's speed to twist him around and down. As the trooper trotted toward him, Ryan absorbed a flurry of punches and kicks from the albino. The battlesuit soaked up most, but not all of the impacts. Especially the kicks. They made Ryan feel like a pebble being shaken inside a tin can.

"It's me, dammit!" he growled, pinning Jak to the floor with a knee in the small of his back. The effort of the struggle was making him puff, which in turn was making his visor fog up. He needed more air-holes.

"You're not on-line," the trooper said as he stepped up to Ryan. His amplified voice boomed in the tunnel. "Something's wrong with your battlesuit. A malfunction in the com link."

Ryan pointed a gauntleted thumb at his crotch.

"You're out of fuel?" the trooper said.

Ryan didn't have to gesture an affirmative. J.B., Dean, Doc and Mildred rushed around the fork of the tunnel and gang-tackled the trooper, knocking him off his feet and crashing him helmet first against the wall. Before he could recover, they had hold of his arms and legs and were dragging him to the floor. Once he was facedown, they sat on him to make sure he stayed that way.

The draining of the battlesuit's fuel went even more smoothly the second time. J.B. jammed the bone blade under the armor plate and gave a savage twist. As the fuel gushed out onto the floor, Mildred unlocked the helmet and she and Doc screwed it off.

Fresh air and the reek of nuke fuel brought the trooper to his senses. He started to struggle. His cries for help echoed down the shaft.

Such cries were routine.

And they were never answered by guards.

Taking a measured swing, Doc rapped the man on the side of the head with the flat end of his ax.

The yelling and the struggling stopped.

"Come on, let's get this guy out of his armor," Ryan said, helping Jak to his feet.

They dragged the limp trooper across the floor, out of the puddle of nuke fuel, and began unbuckling his battlesuit.

"Looks like a pretty good fit for J.B.," Mildred said, holding up the front torso section.

Other slaves passing by stopped to stare at what was going on. Some of them were smiling, while others looked concerned. And with reason. There could always be mass reprisals for acts of rebellion.

The companions again used strips of the trooper's underclothes to tie and gag him.

"He's got the rash, too," Dean said. "It's all over his legs."

"Nasty looking," J.B. commented.

"See all the little pustules," Mildred said. "He's got a staph infection working."

"Perhaps the hygiene of our otherworld opponents leaves something to be desired," Doc said.

"The staph is secondary," Mildred stated. "Opportunistic. It moved into the lesions that were already there."

"What are you going to do with him?" said one of the slaves standing around. He pointed at the trooper, who was once again wide-awake, but now unable to move, and naked.

"Why?" Ryan said.

The slave glanced at the gaunt, grim-faced men beside him. "We've got something we want to show that guard. Mebbe we could borrow him for a little while?"

The trooper looked plenty scared. His mouth moved behind the gag, but no words came out.

"You can take him," Ryan told the men, "but whatever you do, don't let him get loose."

"Nah, we won't even untie him," the slave said. "You don't have to worry about that."

A couple of the slaves pushed over an empty cart and then four of them lifted the bound trooper inside. A crowd of eight or nine then shoved the sledge toward the gloom at the end of the tunnel. An equal number of slaves stayed behind, unwilling to participate in whatever demonstration the others had in mind.

"Guess that bastard is going to get what's coming to him," J.B. said.

Ryan handed the guard's laser rifle to Jak. Then he took off his helmet and used an ax point to punch out more ventilation holes. When this was done, he addressed the companions and the remaining crowd. "We're going to need a distraction up top," he said. "A major distraction. But you've got to wait until J.B. and I get close to the ore truck." Ryan looked at Mildred and Jak and said, "Don't use the pulse rifles up there, not yet. Stay inside the mine entrance and keep the weapons in reserve. The invaders might shut down the road if they see that we've armed ourselves. We can't let them do that before J.B. and I reach the camp and disable the manacles. If we're going to win this fight, we all need to be free to move."

"How are we going to know when the cuffs are turned off?" Mildred asked him.

"Chances are we aren't going to be able to signal you," Ryan said. "You're just going to have to figure it out by yourselves."

"We could always employ some of our less fortunate brethren," Doc suggested. "After all, what is a hand or a foot more or less to a dead man?"

"Plenty of recruits for that duty," J.B. said.

Jak took hold of Ryan's arm and pulled him aside. "See?" he said, indicating the foot-deep hollow the laser beam had cut in the wall and the puddle of glass drippings on the floor beneath it.

"Yeah. The melting temperature of the glass must be relatively low. It could work to our advantage against the guards."

"Indirect fire with the tribarrels?" Mildred asked.

"You got it. Don't waste your shots on the battlesuits. Their EM shields will protect them. Make the landscape work for you. After we leave, once you and Jak get started out here, the troopers are going to call for help. You can expect enemy reinforcements from Slake City."

"Road and air," Jak said.

"Afraid so. You've got to capture as many weapons as possible before that happens. Arm yourselves and the other slaves."

"Understood," Mildred said.

"Also," Jak said, bending down and picking up a baseball-sized hunk of glass. He tossed it up and caught it with the same hand. "Nonmetallic. Not bounce off EM shield."

He turned to the group of slaves and said, "Throw at battlesuits, not use axes."

"J.B. makes a striking trooper, doesn't he?" Mildred said.

The Armorer stood there, in full body armor, but still wearing his sweat-stained fedora.

Under his arm, Doc held the matching helmet, which he had already pounded holes through. From behind it looked like a monstrous cheese grater. "I know how attached you are to that well-seasoned headdress, John Barrymore," the old man said, "but it will never fit inside this bubble."

"My lucky hat."

"We know, we know," Ryan said. "Let Dean borrow it for the time being."

Reluctantly, J.B. removed it. The pressure of the sweat band had plastered his hair to his skull in a visible ring. "Take good care of it, boy," he said. "I'm going to be wanting it back in the same condition it was lent."

Dean accepted the fedora. It was too big for him. As he mashed it down on his head, Dix-style, it flattened the tops of his ears.

"Spitting image," Mildred said.

"Gimme the frigging helmet," J.B. growled.

"Your *new* lucky hat," Doc said, presenting it with a bow and a flourish.

Once the Armorer's helmet was screwed down, he and Ryan started for the mine entrance. Some of the milling slaves ran ahead of them, but most lagged behind, as if their deactivated armor still had some protective capability.

By the time they reached the top of the mine entrance's slope, the insides of their visors were fogged with the heat of their exertion. The condensation limited their vision, but it couldn't be wiped away without taking off the helmets, which wasn't an option. They stepped out into the bright glare of day.

Ground Zero's routine had resumed after last night's disturbances. A dozen guards stood around the klieg-light perimeter. Two troopers checked the loaded carts as they lined up by the ore wags. Another trooper supervised the loading of ore by hand. One guard manned the water tank, making sure the slaves got only one eight-ounce cup for their toil.

The slaves who couldn't work, who were too rad sick or who had been injured from glass falls lay curled up in the dimples. Some of them were undoubtedly already dead. Nearby, healthier slaves roasted their fresh-caught midmorning snacks over the propane burners. Bruised purple from so much kicking and bouncing, the stickie heads lay scattered around the camp.

Ryan and J.B. stayed together as they crossed the open ground, making a beeline for the ore trucks.

The other troopers didn't seem to notice them.

Ryan saw Doc and Dean working their way along the other side of the sledges lined up for unloading. They were spreading the word to the waiting slaves: throw glass, not axes.

The trooper beside the first cart in line waved his gauntlet at Ryan. He pointed at his battlesuit collar, indicating the throat mike. Ryan and J.B. kept on walking toward him.

The guard repeated the gesture.

Whatever Doc was going to do, he for nuke's sake had to do it soon, Ryan thought.

The first chunk of glass arced over from the rear of the line of sledges. With a puff of twinkling dust, it hit the trooper in the helmet. The hunk of nukeglass was big enough and it was thrown hard enough to knock him sideways a step. The missile left a whitish mark on the black armor.

Ryan and J.B. fell into a trot.

The trooper before them recovered, only to be caught in a rain of glass chunks. Many of the chunks missed their target and shattered on the ground, but the others, the ones that were thrown true, pounded the shoulders and chest of his battlesuit and slammed into his helmet.

"Stop!" he commanded the slaves, his amplifier at top volume.

There was an edge of panic in his voice.

That he was clearly in trouble only encouraged his attackers. Realizing that they could actually hurt their oppressors this way, the slaves grabbed pieces of glass from their sledges and began pelting every trooper within range. They barraged the pair at the head of the sledge line and the guard by the water tank. The trooper standing beside the ore truck retreated with his weapon raised to the front bumper as the slaves stopped throwing hunks of glass into the wag's bed and started throwing them at him.

As Ryan and J.B. came up on the side of the ore truck, they saw the trooper by the bumper take a triple hit in the helmet, which sent him toppling over backward.

From behind them came the amplified cry, "Fire!"

The air was split by a dozen whistling shrieks.

By then, Ryan was already scrambling over the top of the ore truck's cargo box. He got a glimpse of battlesuited troopers massing on the edge of the compound, unleashing a cat's cradle of green, crisscrossing beams. The guards fired a warning volley over the slaves' heads.

A moment after Ryan dropped below the rim of the box, J.B. clunked down beside him. The walls of enclosure were ten feet high on the outside. Nuke rubble filled ninety percent of the interior volume. Ryan and J.B. were riding high, so they had to flatten out and keep their heads down.

When the firing and the shouting stopped, it only took a few more minutes for the slaves to fill the wag. They tossed hunks of ore over the sides and down upon the stowaways. Ryan and J.B. lay there and took it.

The wag driver didn't look into the cargo box to see how full it was. He didn't have to. From the ground, the trooper could see the heaping mound of glass above the edge.

When he had a full load, the driver got in, started the engine and turned the ore truck around. The wag's seven-foot-diameter wheels bumped over the dimples in the glass as if they were nothing. As soon as the wag was away from the camp, Ryan and J.B. climbed out from under the blocks of glass and took off their helmets.

The air tasted sweet and the wind cooled them off. The sway and pitch of the truck on the road caused the box's razor-sharp contents to shift, forcing them to scramble to more secure ground near the cab.

"Beats walking, huh?" J.B. said.

"Yeah," Ryan replied automatically. His mind was elsewhere. He was counting the ways the whole thing could collapse. They had no weapons. Their battle-suits didn't work. They were heading into the enemy stronghold. And they were up to their eyeballs in highly radioactive ore. He stopped counting and thought about Krysty, who could already be dead. He thought about Dean, too, who was going to be dead if he didn't pull this off.

"I'm going to be damned glad to get off this fucking sea of glass," J.B. said. "I don't mind dying, you know that, but I don't want to die out here. I don't want my spirit roaming this nuked-out shithole forever."

Ryan understood what he meant. Dying here would be like dying on another planet. Or on the moon.

"We left friends behind," Ryan said.

"I'm not forgetting that. I sure as hell don't want them to die out here, either. What are we going to do when we get to Slake City?"

"What we always do," Ryan said. "Make it up as we go along."

Chapter Twenty-One

After Ryan and J.B. left Ground Zero, everything was fine for a few minutes. The camp appeared to have settled down. The slaves had resumed their dismal labor. It was as if the glass-throwing demonstration—and the guards' display of force—had never happened.

Mildred and Jak bided their time just inside the mine's entrance, holding their captured weapons well out of sight while they kept track of the troopers' movements.

About ten minutes had passed when all the guards seemed to stiffen. Mildred and Jak noticed the nearly simultaneous reaction, and arrived at the same conclusion: a new set of orders had come through their battlesuit com links.

The troopers looked at one another, then at their prisoners. Then one of them shouted to the slaves on the flatland, "Everybody up! That means everybody! You're all going down in the mines. Everybody is going to work! If you don't get up, you will be sliced and diced."

"They can't make those dying people get up," Mildred said. "The poor bastards can't walk, let alone work."

A group of troopers formed a ragged line and started advancing across the compound, driving the slaves who could move toward the mines. When they came upon those who couldn't move, those curled up in the dimples, they opened fire, point-blank. The shrieks of their energy weapons mingled with the screams of the dying.

The sick and the injured who weren't comatose or paralyzed used the last of their strength to drag themselves out of the dimples and crawl toward the mine.

"This is too much," Mildred said, dropping the trigger-block safety of her pulse rifle. "I'm not going to stand here and watch this without doing something about it."

Jak shook his head. But Mildred wasn't looking at him. She was already swinging up her tribarrel. As Jak started to speak, a naked man dashed out of the mine and rushed past him in a pale blur. It was the trooper they had turned over to the slaves. He had gotten free somehow. Battered, bleeding, with boot prints on his backside, he ran across the compound. He ran waving his arms and yelling at the top of his lungs.

Mildred swung her sights down on him. Her finger tightened on the trigger, but she held up. It was too late to stop the man. The cat was already out of the bag. And he was unarmed.

Jak fried him. He tapped the trigger of his laser rifle, firing a green beam as straight as a bowstring. The energy pulse cut the running man's spinal cord, flash-cooked his heart and made the front of his chest open up like the petals of a gory flower. The unstoppable bolt of light continued on, whistling as it slammed into the side of a sledge. The metal glowed red for an instant, then faded back to its original rust-brown color.

"One less," the albino said by way of explanation.

There was no time to discuss the matter.

The troopers by the ore truck and the water tank were returning fire. Those who had been slaughtering the helpless joined their victims, taking cover in the closest dimples.

Mildred snugged the tribarrel's butt against her shoulder and pinned the trigger. There was no recoil to the weapon. The rifle hummed softly against her cheek, fingers and arm. She painted a line of green light that sparked and smoked across the legs of the water tower. Across and through, missing the trooper stationed there by a good three feet. The tower groaned as it began to tip forward, then it came crashing down on the astonished man.

The battlesuit did him no good. Like the cave ceiling at Moonboy ville, the tank was too heavy for the EM shield to deflect. It flattened both the trooper and his armor. Water sloshed out through the tank's ruptured seams, pouring in a wild torrent over the glass.

"Look out!" Jak said, grabbing Mildred by the shoulder and giving her a hard shove. Laser beams from around the compound pinpointed their position. If he hadn't pushed her, they would have trisected her head.

"Run!" he told her.

Mildred darted from the mine entrance, angling for the closest solid cover. She ducked behind the line of loaded sledges, where other slaves kept low and out of the line of fire. As Jak joined her, energy pulses from four or five weapons skimmed the tops of the carts, passing within a few inches of them.

The companions didn't even get the chance to suck in a full breath before a beam slashed at them from the opposite, completely exposed direction, from over near the propane burners. Jak spun toward the source and touched off another pulse from a half crouch.

With a resounding wham, the propane tanks exploded, sending a ball of orange-and-yellow flame billowing into the air. The explosion lifted the shooter off his feet. He flew, arms spread wide, a black silhouette landing in a crumpled heap thirty feet from the cooking area.

Despite the impact, the trooper remained conscious. He knew he was in an exposed position. He tried to get up at once, pushing with his hands, raising his chest off the glass. Led by Doc and Dean, the slaves hiding behind the sledges, in the dimples and at the mine entrances mustered their courage and lobbed chunks of glass on him. Fist-sized hunks and bigger hammered his helmet and shoulders, driving him back to the ground.

Laser beams shrieked across compound, and the stoning ceased.

A group of guards firing from one of the mine entrances had Jak and Mildred's position zeroed in. The concentrated energy of their weapons turned the sledge the companions were hiding behind into a glowing coal on skids. Unable to stand the raging heat, Mildred and Jak advanced to the next sledge in line.

Green beams clipped the front of the cart's skis,

sending showers of fat sparks skittering over the glass.

"We're pinned down," Mildred said. "It's coming from one of the dimples. Next to the klieg light."

Jak poked his head up and immediately jerked it back down. "Two," he said, "shooting over lip of hole."

The air was torn by quavering squeals. The guards at the mine entrance had shifted their aim to the side of the new cart. After a few seconds, it, too, began to glow like an ember.

"We can't move any farther," Mildred said, wiping the sweat off her forehead with the back of her hand. "We've got to shut those guys down. Jesus, the ore in the cart is starting to melt!"

"Keep others busy," Jak said. "I'll take mine."

Mildred poked her weapon's muzzle around the front of the cart and sent beams into the centers of the helmets of the shooters hiding in the dimple. Her laser pulses struck the EM shields a foot or so in front of the guards' eyes and veered off to the right, cutting shallow trenches in the glass. Because of the intense energy flare caused by the deflection, the troopers couldn't acquire fresh targets.

Jak meanwhile had scooted between the pair of sledges. The heat waves coming off the carts made the mine entrance shimmer and dance in his tribarrel's open sights. He didn't aim for the four troopers crouched just inside the entrance's overhang. Instead, he aimed at the overhang itself. Aimed and fired, flattening the trigger. Jak swept the front edge of the tunnel roof with laser light. Like dirty green candle wax, the glass turned to liquid and poured down on the troopers.

Splashed by at least a ton of molten glass, the guards dropped, slid, fell to the ground. The liquid cascaded over their helmets, shoulders and weapons. Though their battlesuits protected them from the extreme temperature, they were coated by the molten glass. As the thin layer quickly chilled, it hardened, cementing the segmented plates together. The joints of the suits no longer bent. The arms wouldn't move, the legs wouldn't flex. The troopers turned to statues as they tried to rise.

Jak's sustained burst had evaporated the mine entrance's overhang, forming a semicircular crater on its threshold. The four frozen troopers were no longer protected by the tunnel ceiling. They fell under a hail of hurled pieces of ore.

The two guards in the dimple began picking off the stone throwers one by one.

Mildred rose up to a kneeling position and fired, sweeping her laser beam through the klieg light's tripod legs. She angled the cut so it would fall onto the men in the dimple.

The huge lens crashed into the hole. The weight of the housing pinned the troopers. A blinding arc of discharged power was followed by a cloud of oily black smoke. The arc light continued to flash, and the smoke became a plume. Inside the dimple, fire enveloped the guards.

The surviving troopers were on the move, and they moved with purpose, as a fighting unit.

Jak saw that he and Mildred were about to be

flanked. "Follow!" he said, leading Mildred around the end of the sledge line.

With energy pulses whistling at his heels, he dived behind the toppled water tank.

Mildred tried but couldn't follow because of the intensely focused fire. If she'd made for the water tank, the overlapping pulses would have chopped her into a hundred small pieces. She darted instead to the left, rounding the far side of the ore truck. As she made the turn around the back bumper, she got a look at the enemy position.

The remaining troopers had banded together. There were five of them, and they fired from the same spot. They knelt on the flat just back from the crater where the mine entrance used to be, and where their comrades still lay trapped inside their own glass-glazed battlesuits.

"Dammit to hell," Mildred muttered.

By now, the troopers had to have called for help from Slake City, which meant reinforcements were probably on their way. Which meant she and the other companions had run out of luck.

The massed fire from the top of the mine had already accomplished one thing: it had split her and Jak up, which allowed the troopers to concentrate their fire on one or the other position. They started by pouring it onto hers, on the opposite side of the half-loaded ore truck.

Everything was okay for a minute or two, then molten glass began seeping out from under the rear gate. It splashed on the ground, cutting deep pits in the surface. Mildred was forced to abandon her position and move to the front of the wag.

Across the compound, she could see Jak, dead white against the rusting steel of the water tank. He was unable to return fire because of the barrage of laser pulses striking the front of the tank. The water remaining inside the toppled cylinder had started to boil. Clouds of white steam rolled up through the splits in the tank's welded seams.

He flashed her a hand signal. Five fingers, counting down.

She nodded back.

They had no choice.

Chapter Twenty-Two

Krysty put her ear to the door of her windowless cell. Outside in the hallway, she heard the sounds of boots running and the rumble of heavy objects being rolled along the floor. She drew her head back. Something was up. Something had changed; she could sense it.

The invaders weren't just rearranging the furniture in their grim hive.

They were mobilizing for something.

An attack on some other nearby barony?

That was inevitable. As was the barony's fall. None of the self-crowned lords of Deathlands could withstand the power of the black army. And the destruction of the existing social order was just the first step in a larger plan. From what Ryan had told her, nothing was sacred to Dredda and her sisters. Everything was subject to interference, to manipulation. After the invaders had conquered and enslaved the human opposition, they would use their science to bleed the resources dry, to distort and pervert the existing lifeforms. This same philosophy had led to the destruction of their planet, but they had learned nothing from that experience. Each thoughtless, shortsighted step of theirs by default dictated the next, and the next, and the next. It was as if they were jumping from ice floe to ice floe in a partially frozen river. They deluded themselves into believing that progress was occurring, when actually the icebergs were getting smaller and smaller and farther and farther apart as the current picked up on its way to the thundering falls.

The idea that she would ever participate in the destruction of her own world, that she would become one of their sisters was absurd. That would have meant becoming a nonfemale, of discarding the elements that transferred real power, which she knew was internal, not external, a product of the intimate feminine connection with the future and the past. It was a power that Dredda and the sisters had willingly exchanged for the convenience of a bigger, more intimidating shell. Along with the male outward appearance came an acceptance of the male posture of domination through physical force. Of a right and a duty to become dominant, not just over their own species, but all species.

Krysty knew these men without balls, these women without compassion had to be stopped, and stopped now, before they bred themselves and spread like locusts over Deathlands. She had to find and smash their main comp. She had to locate Ryan's seed and destroy that, too, so they couldn't use his offspring, his genetic blueprint to accomplish their ends.

She tried the doorknob. It barely turned before coming to a hard stop. Krysty closed her eyes and concentrated, summoning the power of Gaia, the Earth Mother. Her need was real and it was pure in intent. She opened herself to receiving what she had asked for, allowing it to enter her body. The power built slowly, rising through the soles of her feet to the center of her being. It filled her like a glowing orb.

When the sensation peaked, Krysty put both hands on the knob and turned.

There was a loud metallic crack and the knob rotated freely.

Her face flushed with the exertion, Krysty pulled on the knob, and its shattered plastisteel shaft slid out of the door. She leaned against the door for a moment, light-headed from the power she had channeled and redirected. Surprisingly, the use of the power didn't drain her. Then she poked a finger into the hole in the escutcheon plate and released the locking mechanism. The door opened a crack.

And the sound of moving people and things got much louder.

Krysty waited until there was a lull in the noise, then opened the door wider. She saw the backs of a pair of troopers hurrying away from her. They were carrying armloads of small canisters. She ducked out of the cell, heading the other way.

The corridor branched in three directions before her. She took the right-hand hallway without hesitation. Because Krysty had kept track of her position from the moment she entered the domes, she knew that that route was closest to the outside of the complex. Ryan had told her that if the comp was linked to the satellite, it would need an antenna to transmit and receive signals. Which could mean that it was located in a room with an exterior wall. Even if it wasn't, she had to start somewhere and proceed methodically.

She moved along the hall, looking at the doors. From her experience exploring predark redoubts, she guessed that the comp would need a "clean room," a place free of radical changes in temperature and free of dust and other contaminants. This dictated using a different sort of gasket seal around the door. It would also dictate a self-contained ventilation system. Evidence of both could be easily seen at a glance.

Krysty found nothing in the first corridor. All the doors were alike. As she started to follow the next right-hand branch of the hallway, she heard footfalls and rumbling noises coming her way. Turning back, she tried doorknobs until she found one that was unlocked. She quickly ducked into the room and closed the door.

A second or two later, the troopers passed outside. When Krysty took a moment to look around the room, what she saw puzzled her. The place had been ransacked. Equipment and supplies had been dumped onto the floor from shelves along one wall. Whatever the invaders were doing, they were doing it in extreme haste. From the chaos, it looked as if they were preparing for an impending retreat instead of an attack.

A forced retreat.

She slipped back out into the hall and resumed her search. Before she saw the ventilation grate, she felt its warm rush of air on the tips of her hair. It was set high in the wall next to a door. And the door was unlike any other she had come across. It had a thick, pliable gasket around its entire perimeter, and a locking wheel in its center instead of a knob.

When she tried the wheel, it turned easily. The door wasn't locked. As soon as she cracked it, a chorus of chittering noises greeted her and she knew she had found what she had been looking for. The room before her was brightly lit by ceiling strips, and an entire wall was taken up by a bank of electronic instruments and LCD screens. She shut the door and moved closer to the stacked screens.

The images they contained were pictures of Earth taken from space. Not just scans of Deathlands, but the whole planet. Some of the displays used infrared to show temperature gradients of landmasses and ocean currents. Others offered analyses of current weather patterns, rock and soil types and indigenous plant and animal species. Still others pinpointed the locations of scattered human populations. On some of the screens, she could see what looked like individual people walking about between circles of huts, oblivious to the fact that they were being observed.

This unimaginable, all-encompassing view of her world made it seem small and vulnerable.

A target.

One screen in particular caught her eye. It showed clusters of bright points of blue light on a flat gridwork. There were four points to a cluster. Some were so tightly overlayed that they could only be distinguished when they moved apart. And the clusters did move, independently, as she watched. The grid squares of the overlay were either lime green or fluorescent red. The green squares formed a path that wound through a field of red; they ended, abruptly, in red. All of the blue dots were inside the green grids.

Red was dead.

The blue pinpoints were the manacles of the individual slaves at Ground Zero.

Krysty looked around for something to smash the

comp with, and, finding nothing more suitable, picked up a small chair.

As she raised it over her head, the door to the room opened, and a voice behind her said, "I wouldn't do that if I were you."

Chapter Twenty-Three

"What do you mean your troopers are unable to control the situation?" Dredda yelled in the man's face. "They have armor and weapons! The workers are defenseless!"

"It looks like the slaves got their hands on some pulse rifles," the trooper said. "They overpowered a couple of guards, then stripped them of their armor and weapons. At this point things are, well, fluid."

"'Fluid'? You mean they could go either way?"

The man nodded grimly, then braced himself for more verbal attack by his commander.

He wasn't disappointed.

Dredda put a finger in his face. "I ordered you to maximize output at the mines and instead, you have jeopardized everything. Everything! I should never have put men in charge there. But I figured that slaves—underwatered, unfed, overworked slaves—even you could handle. I underestimated them, and I overestimated you."

The trooper noncom pulled himself together and said, "To regain control of the mines, we're going to need reinforcements. We've lost men out there. They need to be replaced."

"So, I'm going to have to spend fuel and time recovering what shouldn't have been lost in the first place. The question is, should I even bother?" Dredda turned to the lanky man standing quietly to one side. "What is your analysis of the situation?"

"The cost-benefit ratio is difficult to quantify," Dr. Huth said. "There's no way of estimating the additional fuel and the time that will be required to retake the mines. Recovering the loss of time is impossible, obviously. Recovering the lost fuel depends on how quickly control is regained. If the expended fuel can't be recovered in the time remaining, with some considerable extra to boot, there's no advantage to putting down the slave rebellion. To do so would only mean less energy available before and after the jump."

"I get the feeling that everything is closing in on me," Dredda said. "Everywhere I turn I find a dead end, and I don't like it!"

"The options are definitely narrowing," Huth agreed. "I suggest an immediate, limited operation. Commit as few irreplaceable resources as possible. If during the confrontation the opposition gives any hint that it can't sustain itself, throw everything at them."

"Sounds reasonable," Dredda said. She faced the noncom and said, "I want you on the road to Ground Zero in two minutes with fifty troopers in four of the attack wags. I want that compound secured in half an hour and the ore wags rolling again. If you can't accomplish that, don't bother coming back."

The trooper started to say something, but thought better of it. He saluted, then turned stiffly and left the room.

Dredda called in the pair of sister gyro pilots who had been waiting in the corridor.

"We've got a major crisis on our hands," Dredda

told them. "There's been a slave revolt at the mines. The troopers stationed there haven't been able to get it under control. The flow of ore to the processor has been cut off, which means we can't maximize our fuel stockpile before the jump. It means we will take even less equipment with us."

"What do you want us to do?" asked the taller of the two transgenic females.

"I want you to attack Ground Zero from the air. I want you to break the back of the rebellion with a minimum loss of life and limb on the workers' side. It can't be an indiscriminate slaughter because we need the slaves to mine the ore. If you injure too many, the operation becomes pointless."

"Understood."

"Now, listen very carefully," Dredda said, "this is most important. If anything happens that eliminates the possibility of recovering more ore from the mines I want you to break off contact immediately and return here. Is that clear?"

"If the supply-line break looks permanent, we come back at once," said the taller pilot.

"That's right. If no more ore can be extracted, there's no use burning additional fuel, not to mention risking your lives and the two gyroplanes. At that point it becomes a cut-our-losses situation. We'll have to make do with what we have."

"And the troopers on the ground?" the other pilot asked. "What's going to happen to them if we withdraw?"

"I hadn't planned on taking any of the males with us, anyway," Dredda said. "There isn't enough fuel to transport both them and the gear we need. They're just extra baggage. We will jump without them.''

As the pilots hurried out of the room, Dredda felt a gnawing pain in the pit of her stomach. Other reality jumps had always been part of her master plan. Eventually, each of the original sisters would have her own Shadow World to rule. And their unique kind would disperse through the limitless, near-mirror-image parallels in time-space, proliferating themselves in each reality, using up the available resources before moving on. Always moving on. She had never considered the possibility that their first jump might end so prematurely, in such disarray, in such a nightmare of unforeseeable circumstances and inexcusable blunders.

Dredda looked over at Huth, who stood with his arms folded across his chest. ''What are you smiling at?'' she demanded.

Chapter Twenty-Four

Gradually, as Ryan and J.B. climbed away from Ground Zero and the bottom of the nuke's crater, a ribbon of the real world reappeared on the horizon on all sides. Snow-covered mountaintops peeked above the rim of glass, then familiar red mesas. The sense of oppression that both men had felt began to lift.

They had been traveling about fifteen minutes when another ore wag rounded a curve in front of them. This one was empty, and headed back to the mines. It eased over onto the right-hand side of the road so the vehicles could pass without a collision. The two men flattened themselves on the glass until after the truck went by.

"That trooper's in for the shock of his life," J.B. commented.

"Damned well better be," Ryan said.

When their wag reached the last rise leading to Slake City, the driver shifted into low gear and they crawled up the grade. Minutes later, as the wag finally cleared the top of the rise, Ryan looked down the long slope that ended in the invaders' compound. Even from a distance of fifteen hundred yards, he could see the intense activity that seemed to be concentrated in a small section of the plain. The tiny black figures were running to wags, which were parked in formation beside the cluster of domes. As he watched, a pair of gyroplanes lifted off from the landing strip and one of the wags started up and headed toward the entrance to the road.

"Sure looks like they got a bug up their butts," J.B. said. "Do you think Mildred and Jak made their play?"

"Could be this is the otherworlders' response," Ryan said. "They could be getting ready to launch an attack on Ground Zero."

"Or they could be getting ready for us," Dix said. "If they found the naked troopers, they might have guessed we're in their suits. If that's the case, that wag coming our way is big trouble. We've got no weapons and nowhere to run."

"So we'll just stay put and play it out," Ryan said. "Let's screw on our helmets and keep down."

The first assault wag zoomed up the track toward them, but it didn't slow down and it didn't stop. Ryan watched it go by through the crack between the wag's rear gate and side frame. J.B. gave Ryan a thumbs-up sign.

So far so good.

Their ore wag continued down the road. When it reached the edge of the glass and rumbled onto the dirt, three more assault wags roared around it and shot up the road toward Ground Zero. The ore wag circled the domes and stopped beside the processing trailer, where another truck was in the middle of being unloaded.

Ryan tapped J.B. on the helmet and they bailed out of the back of the wag. Vaulting the far side of the bed, they scrambled to the ground. Then they moved quickly around the front of the wag and along the side of the trailer.

The compound was in chaos. And it wasn't just men readying themselves for battle. Troopers were pounding fluorescent-pink perimeter markers into the dirt, creating a roughly elliptical shape around a lineup of their mobile gear. At either end of the row were big black trailers. Not ore processors. These had no hoppers for dumping in nukeglass. And they were connected to the fuel trailer by long, thick, black hoses. They were the only machines connected to the fuel trailer, which stood in the middle and to one side of the ellipse.

Around the processor there was a frantic jockeying of other gear. Troopers were using wags to tow gyros into the line. The aircrafts' rotors were secured for transport, folded up into points above their fuselages. Other equipment was stacked on pallets, covered with plastic webbing. Ryan could see battlesuited troopers carrying stuff out of the cluster of domes, moving it inside the marked perimeter.

"What the blazes is all this about?" J.B. asked, his voice muffled by the helmet.

"Looks like moving day," Ryan said. "Except for that." He pointed up the road at the last of the four wags as it disappeared over the summit of the rise. The two gyros were long gone. "They are definitely sending troops to Ground Zero," he said. "The assault wags will take some time to get there. But not the gyros. They'll be within striking distance in a few minutes. We've got to find the main comp and disable the cuffs."

"What about Krysty?" J.B. asked.

"The cuffs first, then Krysty," Ryan said. He took Dean's bone blade out of the top of his boot and palmed it. "Let's go."

They started walking for the entrance to the domes. Because everyone else in the compound was running, Ryan broke into a trot. He and J.B. blended right in. No one paid them any mind. The other troopers were too preoccupied with their own duties to notice the unusual condensation on the inside of their visors, or the crude puncture holes in the backs of their helmets. Ryan knew the possibility that the naked troopers had been discovered and that they were heading into a trap was growing less and less likely. Which was a break since their only chance if a firefight broke out was to be inside the structures.

As they entered the doorway, a pair of troopers exited carrying armfuls of green canisters.

The doors along the hallway were all ajar. Ryan slowed his pace so he could look into each of them as he passed by. J.B. followed closely behind him. The rooms looked ransacked, and there were no comps in evidence. More troopers came their way, pushing dollies stacked with heavy crates. They passed in the corridor without incident.

Then Ryan looked into a room on the right and saw a trooper bent over something that might have been a comp. When he stopped in the doorway, the trooper looked back through a cleared visor. He was bent over a black cube on little wheels. Not a comp. The trooper stared at the dewdrops on Ryan's visor, puzzled for a second.

Ryan could see the guy put two and two together.

His expression changed. His hand reached up for his throat mike.

The one-eyed man launched himself through the doorway. He hit the trooper with his shoulder as the guy rose from the crouch. Ryan bowled him over the cube backward, and they both crashed against the wall.

J.B. was right on their heels. He pulled the door shut behind him.

"Get his hands!" Ryan said.

J.B. caught the gauntlets by the wrists and the two of them controlled the guy with brute force, making him fight their combined body weight until he had exhausted himself, which didn't take long. When J.B. screwed off the guy's helmet, the trooper's eyes got big with fear. He had an angry rash across the top of his nearly shaved head. It was peppered with sores that oozed pus. The ochre-colored discharge smelled sweet and rank.

"Who are—?" the trooper started to say.

Before he could finish, Ryan slapped him across the face. "I'll ask the questions." Then he showed the trooper the bone blade. "Where's the comp that controls the cuffs?"

When the soldier didn't answer, he held the serrated edge of the bone blade up under his chin. "Did you say something? I didn't hear it."

"Down this hall," the trooper told him, "take the first fork to the left, stay left."

"Do you think he's telling us the truth?" J.B. asked. "Came back kind of quick with the info if you ask me."

"I'm going to give you a chance to change your

story,'' Ryan said. ''If it turns out you're lying, we're coming back to finish you.''

''I'm not lying.''

Ryan punched him hard on the point of the chin. The back of his head hit the wall with a thud, then his eyes fluttered shut.

The door to the room opened as J.B. straightened. Two troopers, one armed with a laser rifle, stepped in. The newcomers were clearly stunned to see an unconscious man in battlesuit and two guys with air holes punched in the backs of their helmets leaning over him.

Before either of the troopers could react, J.B. grabbed hold of the tribarrel's flash-hider and used the rifle like a lever across the man's chest, forcing him from the doorway and into the corner. The trooper couldn't let go of his weapon to go for the com link.

The other trooper jumped on J.B.'s back to try to pull him off.

That was a mistake.

Ryan lunged up from the floor, throwing an arm around the second guy's helmet from behind, blocking his access to the throat mike. With his other hand, Ryan slipped the point of the bone blade under the armor just below the man's right shoulder blade. Feeling the angle of the slot between the overlapping plates, he pushed the dagger home.

It sank in to the hilt.

The trooper went rigid against him as the blade skewered his lung and heart. Then the man sagged, his legs buckling. Ryan let him topple over onto his side.

J.B. in the meantime had his hands full. He see-sawed back and forth with the pulse rifle, trying to get the advantage on his adversary. He managed to work the guy's back against the wall, but they were too evenly matched strengthwise; he couldn't get control of the weapon. The Armorer timed the flip perfectly. He caught the trooper off balance, pulling as the man pushed. He let himself fall to his butt on the floor and, using the guy's forward momentum, sent him whipping over onto his back across the top of the cube.

As the trooper crashed down, he let go of the pulse rifle.

Ryan hit the helmet release and, fighting off the trooper's hands, unscrewed it.

J.B. put the muzzle of the tribarrel against the guy's forehead and dropped the safety.

"Dark night, look at his face!"

That was exactly what Ryan was doing. He couldn't help himself.

The trooper's face was covered with a hideous, weeping red patch. His nostrils were crusted over with scabs, and his left eye was cemented shut. On his cheeks, striated flesh was exposed; it looked like naked muscle.

The guy's hand shot up to his throat mike. His mouth opened.

"Stop him," Ryan said.

J.B. pulled the trigger. The pulse rifle hummed, and a fraction of an instant later a smoking slot appeared in the middle of the man's forehead. His jaws slammed shut and he grimaced, showing all his teeth. Then the trooper's hand slowly fell away from his throat and his eyes glazed over. The wound was through and through. Through the backside of his skull and into the floor. The smell of flash-cooked brains and melted plastic filled the room.

"Damn, that's nasty!" J.B. said as he stepped back.

Ryan knelt down and checked the cube. Whatever it was, it wasn't a comp. "Come on, we're wasting time here," he said.

Taking the laser rifle with them, they exited the room and moved down the tubular hallway, following the directions of the first trooper.

After taking the left-hand fork, they heard the tramping of many pairs of boots. A squad of troopers appeared around a turn ahead. Ryan and J.B. ducked into an open room to avoid them.

They surprised four men who were working over a long table. They were dressed in charcoal-gray fatigues, splattered with blood and bodily fluids. One of them was cramming what looked like a deer haunch into a monstrous pulverizing or liquefying machine. The whirring blades turned the red meat into red paste. The blades stopped whirring. The other men held cleavers and long knives. They stopped what they were doing, too.

Ryan and J.B. had stumbled into the invaders' kitchen. It was impossible to tell from the butchers' faces if they realized the intruders were impostors. With armed men bearing down on them, there was no room for error.

J.B. shot one of them immediately, pinning the trigger and slashing the light beam across the man's head. Due to the steeply angled cut, the top of the man's skull slid off, along with most of his right ear. The butcher fell to the floor behind the table with a loud thud.

"Don't move!" Ryan told the others as the tramp of boot falls in the hall grew louder. "Don't make a sound!"

The butchers obeyed and the squad of troopers passed the doorway without looking in or stopping.

"Dark night, what's that stink?" J.B. asked.

Ryan could smell it, too, right through his helmet.

Because they had come from a world stripped of its native species, protein on the hoof was a new territory for them. The table in front of the butchers was heaped with animal carcasses and offal. All of them had been killed with lasers; most were missing one or more essential parts. Plucked songbirds sat pink and naked in a big pile of feathers. A pair of buzzards lay likewise stripped and gutted. There were lizards of all sizes, some in their skins and some without.

Ryan recognized the jumbled parts of gophers, prairie dogs, jackrabbits and antelope.

There were bugs, too. Honking big Deathlands bugs. Eight-inch-long cockroaches. Scorpions as big as Chihuahuas. Spiders the size of basketballs. One of the butchers had been feeding shovelfuls of these insects into a huge pulverizing unit, along with leaves and branches of shrubs and bushes.

The contents of the pulverizers went directly into a row of twenty-gallon pots that sat on propane burners.

It wasn't the animal carcasses that stank so badly. It was the beige, glutinous slop simmering in the pots.

"What we had to eat at Ground Zero suddenly doesn't seem quite so bad," J.B. commented.

"Looks to me like these guys are packing themselves a big picnic lunch," Ryan said. He pointed at the ten-gallon plastic jugs lined up along the wall. Some were already sealed with lids; others had funnels poked down their mouths. There was beige slop inside all of them, and it was spilled down their sides and onto the floor.

"Where are you going?" J.B. asked them.

"How are you getting there?" Ryan said.

One of the butchers answered by throwing his meat cleaver. His right hand moved in a blur. Before Ryan could dodge or duck, the cleaver struck him in the middle of the visor. The point of the blade penetrated the armor by about half an inch.

J.B. cut loose on the guy at once, drawing a smoking line from his chin to his crotch. The bloodless wound gaped so wide that J.B. could see the wall on the other side through it. With his innards neatly divided, and ninety-five percent of his spine vaporized, the butcher slumped across the table, then slowly melted to the floor.

The other butchers were moving, in opposite directions, at high speed behind the cover of the table. J.B. sawed the legs out from under one side of it, dropping the top, and dumping the collection of dead things onto the floor. Then he sliced the overturned tabletop in half lengthwise. Behind it, one of the surviving men was also cut in two.

The third ran for the open door, screaming.

J.B. kept the trigger pinned and swung the muzzle up his track, in the process cutting through the bubbling pots, spilling seventy gallons of slop, shattering the assembled beakers and electronic toxicity analyzers and chopping machines. The laser crossed the man's midsection, and he stopped screaming. The top half of his body fell backward as his legs fell forward; both sections crashed to the floor.

"Let's get out of here quick," Ryan said, heading for the door.

Outside, the hallway was clear. They left the kitchen and continued on until J.B. noticed the gasketed door, which was shut. "This could be it, Ryan," he said.

As the one-eyed man reached for the door's locking wheel, he heard the sounds of violent struggle on the other side. Landed blows. Scuffling feet. Then a woman's voice, howling a curse.

A familiar voice. And a familiar curse.

Chapter Twenty-Five

In the lee of the boiling water tank, Jak held up his fingers for Mildred to see and counted them down to zero. Words weren't necessary between the teenaged albino and the cryogenically preserved black woman. Based on the situation, based on their past experience, they knew exactly what had to be done.

Jak coiled himself and sprang for the water tank's twisted ladder. Though the tank was tipped over, the ladder offered a protected route to the top side. The rear of the crumpled cylinder was hidden from the view of the troopers massed on the flatland, but not from the heat of their concentrated laser fire. Showers of white-hot sparks rained on him, and the ladder rungs scalded his hands as he climbed.

On the other side of the compound, Mildred was likewise trying to gain some elevation on their targets. Avoiding the puddles of molten glass around the wheels, she climbed the side of the ore truck's cab.

As Jak reached the top side of the tank, the steam billowing up from its ruptured belly partially hid him from the enemy. Standing on the side of the cork-screwed ladder, Jak raised himself up, shouldered his pulse rifle and sent a green beam screaming across the compound. He didn't aim at the kneeling black figures. He aimed instead at the glass beneath and around them.

He only got off a short blast of energy before the answering fire ripped back at him. He ducked as a fountain of sparks erupted from the shoulder of the tank and a stunning wall of heat hit him.

By then, Mildred was on the roof of the wag, firing at the battlesuited troopers. And drawing fire in return.

As soon as the energy blasts from the flatland shifted her way, Jak popped up again and poured more green light onto the glass. It didn't take much to soften the material. A few seconds and the surface turned wet and shiny.

As the five troopers began to shift their aim points again, chunks of glass started arcing down onto them. The slaves had picked up the fight, which made the troopers shift their aim points yet again.

There were too many threats to deal with at once.

While the troopers were trying to keep Doc and Dean and the others from stoning them to death, Jak's and Mildred's laser beams turned the glass under their boots to gel. Whether they could sense the heat through their battlesuits or not, the troopers didn't move.

It was a mistake.

The entire section of glass, which was a continuation of the already partially collapsed roof of the tunnel, caved in on itself, dropping four of the five troopers twenty-five feet to the mine floor. The fifth trooper sank to his armpits in a much smaller hole in the glass, but stopped himself from falling through by extending his arms. To do this, he had to drop his weapon.

Another mistake.

Before he could drag himself out of the hole, the molten glass cooled and resolidified around him, sealing him in place like a cork in a bottle.

By the time Jak and Mildred jumped from their shooting platforms and crossed the compound, the slaves had closed in on the hapless trooper. They had taken off the guy's helmet and were using his head as a kicking-punching bag. Because he couldn't twist or turn his torso, he couldn't use his arms to block or defend himself from blows from behind. He couldn't fall over, either, because the battlesuit was holding him up. A stationary target.

Jak stepped to the larger hole he and Mildred had cut and looked over the edge. The other troopers lay on the ground below. It was impossible to tell whether they had broken limbs as a result of the fall or whether the melted glass had hardened; either way, they weren't getting up under their own power. Some of the slaves started tumbling big glass blocks on top of them, but they were called off by their comrades, who had other ideas about vengeance.

Most of the slaves rushed down to the ruined mine entrance and swarmed onto the fallen troopers. They took away their weapons, then removed their helmets so their heads could be summarily bashed in. The slaves used the butts of the captured pulse rifles, as well as chunks of rock to accomplish these feats.

It was ugly work, but in Jak's opinion it needed doing. No reason to be squeamish over the fates of coldheart chillers. While the companions didn't take part in the animalistic bloodletting, they didn't try to stop it, either.

When it was over, Jak walked over to the water

tank and clanged on its side with his rifle butt to attract the mob's attention.

"Everyone with laser rifle, come," he said. He waved the armed slaves after him to the mine entrances. "Seal up," he told them. "Nobody down there again."

They formed into a firing line. The crisscrossing green beams collapsed the entrances, turning them into waterfalls of molten glass, which buried the battered remains of the troopers.

When this was done to his satisfaction, Jak said, "Everybody in the back truck. Take wounded."

The slaves did a dimple-by-dimple search. They carried the injured to the truck. Only about fifty were left alive.

Mildred, Dean, Doc and Jak piled into the bench seat in the ore wag's cab. The front and side windshields were blacked out. There was a dashboard, but no driver controls, no features at all except for a series of buttons arranged in a geometric shape. The only light came from a red bulb in the middle of the headliner.

"Maybe this thing has to be driven from a battlesuit," Mildred said. "That plug there could be some kind of coupling."

"May I suggest that you try that red button in the center?" Doc said. "Red usually indicates something important."

Mildred pushed it.

Instantly, the wag's nuke-fueled turbine howled to life. And as that happened, a compartment opened up in front of Mildred's seat and a joystick popped out.

"That's great," Mildred said, "but we're still driving blind. Looks like the inside of a steel-belted radial in here.''

''Move the stick a little,'' Dean suggested.

Mildred reached out for it. As soon as her fingers closed on the knurled plastisteel lever, the windshields cleared. She figured the rest out in a hurry. The button on top of the stick was the engine-speed control. Push the stick left or right for steering. Pull it back for reverse. Push the stick straight forward for brakes.

''We're outta here,'' Mildred said. With a jolt, she pulled away from the ruin of Ground Zero to cheers and whistles from the cargo box.

''Back across the River Styx, back to the world of the living,'' Doc said. ''A miracle of resurrection. We who are about to be reborn, salute you, Dear ferryperson.''

''Shut up, Doc,'' Mildred said, ''I'm trying to keep this lurching death trap on the road.''

Even though she had the whole road to herself, it wasn't easy. It was difficult to pick out the shoulders what with the glare from the glass. Mildred showed a definite tendency to bounce off one side of the road and veer to the other. A case of overcompensation multiplied. Before things got completely out of control, she had to take her thumb off the speed button and let the uphill grade slow the wag.

The consequences of any error on her part would have been grave. If the wag left the road proper, it would cost everyone on board their hands and feet. And that didn't take into account the whirlpools of frozen glass that loomed just off the shoulders. These whirlpools were fifty yards across with spiraling black centers that dropped thousands of feet into emptiness. If she tipped over into one of those great, slick funnels, it would have meant a much more complete disaster. The kind no one survived.

As Mildred rounded the edge of a particularly scary pinwheel of a chasm, she and the others saw something stopped on the road dead ahead.

Something big and black.

"It's another ore wag," Dean said.

"Why is it stopped like that, do you suppose?" Doc said.

"It mebbe wait," Jak replied. "Block the road so we not get past."

"I don't see anybody around it," Mildred said, reducing her speed to a crawl.

"Mebbe ambush," Jak said, scanning the surrounding glass with his keen red eyes.

A pencil-thin green beam squealed over the wasteland, hitting the wag's cargo box. The slaves back there started yelling their heads off. They yelled louder still when a second beam from the other side of the road zeroed in on them.

One of the shooters was firing from behind a jumbled row of ten-foot-high glass spikes. The other lay atop a small knoll above a gigantic whirlpool. Triangulated fire.

"They've got us pinned," Mildred said.

Some of the slaves in the cargo box attempted to return fire. To do that they had to stick their heads up. Two of the captured rifles fell from the top of the box, followed by arms and heads of the men who'd tried to use them.

"They want to hold us here until reinforcements arrive," Jak said.

"They happen to be doing an excellent job of it, too," Doc stated.

"Not let do that," Jak finished.

"It's gonna be tough taking them out," Mildred said. "We can't leave the road because of the manacles. We can't go forward because of the other wag. And they've got the high ground."

"Why didn't they just cut the road if they wanted to trap us?" Dean said. "Wouldn't that have been the easiest thing?"

"I think Dean has something there," Mildred said. "All their shots have been at the top of the cargo box. They don't want to risk melting the road. Especially not here where it slides off so steeply. They want to keep the road to the mine open. We can use that."

"How, pray tell?" Doc said.

"It means they're not going to fire at the wheels," Mildred said.

"Hide behind wheels," Jak said, snatching up his laser rifle from the floorboards.

"And fire as I creep this wag forward," Mildred said. "When they see that I intend to push their truck off the frigging road, you and Doc might get clear shots."

"What about me?" Dean asked.

"I'm holding you in reserve," Mildred said. "In case I need you when we get to the other wag."

"Move fast, Doc," Jak said. "Under wag quick."

"I understand the strategy, dear lad," Doc said. "Lead the way."

Jak popped open the passenger-side door and hit the road running. He took five steps, then dived beneath the undercarriage, thrusting the laser rifle out in front of him. Doc followed a second later.

"Mildred right," Jak said. "Drew no fire. Not want to hit the road."

"Insightful woman, our Dr. Wyeth," Doc said. "I shall take the left side, if you do not mind."

Jak nodded and moved to the inside of the opposite wheel.

With Mildred at the controls, the wag began to inch forward on its seven-foot-wide tires.

Jak and Doc watched their targets, holding their fire. They crawled along with the wag, keeping hidden behind the wheels. The shooters angled downward fire without changing their positions, zapping the sides of the cargo box again and again, but they could only do so up to a point. Once the rebel ore wag had moved far enough up the road, their only target was the wag's rear gate. As the slaves were now staying well down, out of their line of fire, hitting the gate served no purpose.

When Mildred was within thirty feet of the other wag, her intentions were obvious. As were the shortcomings of the troopers' ambush plan.

"Mine's moving," Doc said, swinging the alien weapon to his shoulder and lining up the sights.

The trooper on top of the knoll scrambled to his feet and started running downhill.

Doc led him and squeezed the trigger. The resulting hum surprised him. As did the lack of any recoil. His first shot went low and wide. Pinning the trigger, he painted the slope with the laser beam.

Doc's blast cut the glass out from under the man's feet. He lost his balance and slid facefirst, leaving his rifle behind. The old man watched over his sights as the trooper tried to slow or stop himself by putting out both gauntleted hands, palms forward, and digging in the toes of his boots. But the incline was too steep and the glass too slick.

The figure in black shot over the lip of the whirlpool and vanished into its yawning maw.

Jak's target didn't make a break for it until Mildred actually nudged the other wag. She put her front bumper against its front bumper and began to push, feathering her speed to keep her wheels from spinning and losing traction. She found the wag's gearshift and dropped the transmission into low to get more torque.

The other wag was lighter, since it was unloaded, and even though its parking brake was on, it started to move in reverse. Slowly at first, as Mildred got a feel for how much pressure she could apply.

Seeing the roadblock being pushed out of the way, being pushed toward a bend in the road that emptied onto a deep divide, the trooper behind the glass fence fired a last, futile shot, then broke from cover. He had fifty feet of open ground before he reached the next safe spot.

From under the wag, Jak took a swinging lead on him and touched off a quick shot. The trooper went down flat on his belly, but he wasn't hit. He squirmed into a prone position and returned fire, trying to keep Jak pinned by hitting the cargo box on that side.

Doc moved under the truck and added his weapon's shrill squeal to the mix.

The trooper rolled away, unable to maintain his position in the cross fire.

The other ore wag was moving nicely now, even though the brakes were locked. Its rear wheels bumped up and over the shoulder. Mildred kept pushing. Its middle wheels hopped the shoulder, and she gave a final shove.

As the front wheels popped off the road, the rear wheels hung in space. The balance point was on the middle wheels, and they were sliding. With a tremendous groan, the ore wag tumbled into the chasm beyond. A second later there came a loud crash.

"We've got a clear road ahead," Doc said. "We can leave our battlesuited friend right where he is. No need to spend another moment in his dubious company."

Jak and Doc scrambled out from under the far side of the wag and climbed up onto the side of the box.

"Go, Mildred!" Jak said, pounding on the cab roof.

She accelerated up the grade, away from the ambush site. Around the next bend, out of range of the trooper, Mildred stopped and got out.

She and Dean joined Doc and Jak as they looked into the cargo box. More slaves were dead, hit by the beams directly, or horribly burned alive when the sides of the box heated up. Those who survived were badly shaken.

"Look!" Dean cried, pointing at the pair of black gyroplanes sweeping down on them.

The companions dropped from the cargo box and jumped into the cab. Laser cannons flashed from the noses of the aircraft. The streaming energy pulses hit the ore wag's EM shield directly in front of the driver seat and sheered off to either side.

It was a wake-up call.

The gyros hovered, holding their fire as Mildred got the wag moving again.

"The cargo box doesn't have an EM shield," she said. "If those pilots wanted to, they could hang right over it and chill all of the slaves. Maybe they're as valuable as the road."

"Difficult to run a mine without workers," Doc said. "As difficult as it is to move ore without a road."

As Mildred continued to climb out of the bowels of the crater, the gyros retreated along with her, maintaining position and distance.

Then, without warning, the cannons fired again, simultaneously. The two pulses hit the same spot, and the energy flare off the cab's shield was ten times brighter than before.

"Damn!" Mildred said, rubbing her eyes.

"They can't hurt us," Dean said.

"Or they don't want to yet," Doc told him. "They could have something up their sleeves, just biding their time until the proper moment."

As it turned out, they had nothing up their sleeves.

The gyroplanes suddenly rose in the air, wheeled around and sped back toward Slake City.

"I'm sure glad to see their backsides," Mildred said.

"Did we win already?" Dean said. "Is it over?"

"I am sorry to say that it has not yet begun," Doc replied.

More black wags appeared on the road above them. These weren't ore trucks; they were attack wags and they were closing fast.

Chapter Twenty-Six

"I wouldn't do that if I were you."

Krysty looked over her shoulder as the speaker entered the room. The she-he had close-cropped blond curls and pale blue eyes. The charcoal-gray T-shirt the creature wore was skintight over a wide, muscular chest. What startled Krysty the most was the width of its neck. The trapezius muscles formed a broad triangle from below the ears to the rounded domes of its shoulders.

Instead of swinging the chair down on the comp, Krysty pivoted her hips and brought it crashing against the she-he, who raised both forearms to block the attack. Although the blow forced the she-he to take a step back, the chair bounced off.

Bounced off and flew across the room as if it had rocket-assist.

"Not nice," the she-he said.

Krysty winced. Apparently, she had done herself more damage than her intended target. Her hands had gone numb to the wrists from the shock of the impact.

"Come here," the creature said playfully, crinkling an index finger toward herself, "come to Mero. We'll take you back to your cell."

As Krysty retreated and the she-he turned, Krysty got a look at the mass of weeping sores on the side of Mero's neck. "What's that you've got there?" she asked. "It looks plenty bad. Probably hurts like hell. Did you spill a bucket of battery acid on yourself?"

"Don't worry about that," Mero replied. "Just get your butt over here. Don't make me chase you around the room."

"Not up to it, huh?"

Mero lunged for her. Krysty easily moved out of the way, sidestepping the outstretched hand. As she came around on the balls of her feet, Krysty launched a side-kick into the back of the she-he's weight-bearing leg. Mero staggered forward, throwing both arms in the air to keep from falling. Krysty spun 360 degrees and power-kicked the she-he in the throat. The toe of her boot bored deep into the soft tissue.

For anyone else, it would have been a killshot.

Mero lurched backward, but in so doing managed to grab hold of Krysty's ankle. With one hand, the she-he almost casually flipped the redhead onto her back.

Krysty landed on her kidneys. The impact with the floor knocked the wind out of her for a second. Long enough for the she-he to get a better grip on her left foot, wrapping fingers of steel around her instep.

The redhead reared back and kicked Mero in the face with her free leg. Her heel made a satisfying crunch as it crushed and spread the fragile cartilage.

As Mero's head flew back, bright blood squirted from both nostrils. The she-he coughed, spraying blood mist. Staring down at the red streaming through her fingers, Mero withdrew.

"You shouldn't have done that," the she-he said. "You really, really shouldn't have done that."

Krysty was already on her feet, and moving towards the wall of electronic equipment. She couldn't reach the monitor with the manacles on it without coming into Mero's range, but she could reach the one with the infrared scan of the oceans. She tipped the screen to the floor, and it landed with a crash, hissing, sputtering and arcing power. "I probably shouldn't have done that, either," she said.

Mero hooked the fallen chair with her foot and kicked up from the floor, at Krysty's head. As the redhead ducked and turned, the she-he closed on her. The fingers of steel caught her wrist and twisted it behind her back. With the other hand, Mero grabbed the back of Krysty's head, digging fingers into the mass of her hair, which separated into tendrils and coiled around the she-he's thick wrist like miniature pythons.

"My, my, what do we have here?" Mero said.

Krysty said nothing and she didn't struggle. The she-he held her arm at the dislocate point. Another ounce or two of pressure and it would have popped out of the shoulder socket.

Mero played with the mobile strands. "Does it do any other tricks?"

"Let me go and I'll show you."

"No, I don't think so. I think we're going to go back to your cell. Don't worry, you won't be there long. We sisters have all agreed that you're coming with us when we make the next jump, which should be any minute now. We think you'll make a fine incubator for our offspring. Actually, you're going to be the only incubator for the foreseeable future. We had planned to recruit many dozens of Shadow World females for the job, but under the circumstances there isn't time.''

Krysty tried to twist away, but Mero tightened the hammerlock. The pain shooting through her shoulder made her groan.

"When you're nine months heavy with my baby, mine and Shadow Man's,'' Mero said, "you're going to be a lot less troublesome. Less likely to spin-kick, that's for sure. I know you're going to make a good mommy for my baby. For all our babies.''

Krysty growled a curse, then tried to crush the she-he's toes with the heel of her boot. The two of them danced around for a minute before Mero once again got the upper hand.

As the she-he pinned her face against the wall, the door to the room opened and two troopers entered.

"Good,'' Mero said, hardly glancing at them. "You can help me with this hellcat. Get hold of her legs.''

The taller of the two troopers stepped closer. When Mero turned again, he used his helmet like a cudgel, headbutting the surprised she-he in the middle of forehead.

Knees buckling, eyelids fluttering shut, Mero dropped like a stone.

"Krysty, it's us!'' J.B. said, using his hands to block her flurry of full power punches to his chest.

She stopped fighting. "Ryan?'' she said to the taller trooper. "Is that you?''

"Of course,'' he said. The one-eyed man unscrewed his helmet and took a breath. His long, black hair was damp with sweat. "Where's the comp?''

"Over here, I think,'' Krysty said. She pointed to

one of the monitors. "That shows all the slaves. Green zone is safe. Red zone isn't."

"This must be the CPU," J.B. said after taking off his helmet, too. He indicated a cube from which all the monitor cables emerged. "Should we just unplug it from its power source?"

"No, I've got a better idea," Krysty said. She picked up the chair and smashed its legs down on the CPU. The first blow made the images on the bank of screens quiver wildly. It took two more blows to crack the comp's plastisteel housing, but on the second one, all the screens went dark.

For good measure, Krysty hit the thing a few more times, breaking the internal contents into numerous small pieces.

While she was doing this, Ryan and J.B. booted the monitors into similar fragments, turning them into heaps of electronic rubbish.

"We've got to see if we're safe," Krysty said. "Let's get one of these manacles off. We can cut it with that tribarrel of yours, J.B. Do mine first."

"Wait a minute," Ryan said. "Something just occurred to me. There could be a backup system for the cuffs somewhere else in the compound. We haven't searched the whole place yet."

"Well, we can't just stand here," Krysty said.

"J.B.," Ryan said, "cut one of mine first."

"No, Ryan."

"Do my left hand." Ryan took off his gauntlet, exposing the dull silver band.

J.B. didn't hesitate. It wasn't the kind of decision made easier by a pause to reflect. He angled the muzzle under the manacle. When he pressed the trigger, the green beam sawed through the cuff, cutting a neat slot across it about an inch wide.

"Guess we chilled the bastard," Ryan said as he twisted the smoking thing off his wrist.

"Which means we can help free Mildred and the others," J.B. replied.

"There's something else we've got to see to first," Krysty told them. She quickly explained what had happened to her, why she had been kidnapped and what Dredda and the she-hes intended to do with what they had stolen from her, and from Ryan.

Krysty pointed at the she-he on the floor, who was just beginning to stir, and said, "That one told me they were getting ready to make another jump."

"From what's going on outside, that sounds about right," J.B. said.

"No way am I going to father an army of these hell bitches," Ryan told them angrily. "Before they jump, we'd better find that damned stuff and destroy it."

Chapter Twenty-Seven

Four black wags skidded to a stop on the long straightaway above Mildred. There was nowhere for her to go. She couldn't back up and she couldn't proceed. As she braked the ore truck, the first two attack wags pulled side to side, so both could bring their forward weapons pods to bear. The cannons locked on target. The range was 150 feet.

"Oh, man," she groaned, anticipating annihilation.

When the cannons fired, they did so simultaneously. The double flash exploded into a blinding wall of green as the pulses slammed the ore wag's EM shield.

This was serious weaponry.

The impact of the cannon beams against the shield made the ore wag jolt backward, despite the fact that Mildred was holding down the brake. The six locked wheels slipped in reverse a good twenty feet, making a grinding noise on the road as the truck slewed slightly sideways.

"I hesitate to bring up the matter," Doc said, "but there's a bit of a drop-off on this side."

Mildred glanced over his shoulder and got a powerful adrenaline rush. "A bit of a drop-off!" she exclaimed.

What loomed just off the shoulder of the road was a yawning crevasse. It looked bottomless. If they tipped over into it, they weren't coming out again. Ever. Craning her head around to look behind them, Mildred saw that the chasm necked down at its Ground Zero end, its ragged lips coming together, melding into a flat, glassy field. Even from where she sat, she could see the field was split by wide surface cracks.

The assault wags sent a second dual blast their way. It had the same effect.

The huge wheels, though locked, and the cargo box, though loaded with people and ore, were insufficient to anchor the wag where it was. Like an invisible hand, the blowback from the EM shield pushed the truck farther down the road, increasing the sideways cant, bringing the back wheels closer to the edge of nothingness.

"Another shot we go over," Jak said.

"Fuck this," Mildred cursed. At the same instant the assault wags fired, she mashed down the joystick's speed button, plowing the nose of the ore truck into the next shot.

The jolt sent the companions bouncing off the dashboard, but they lost no ground. Mildred crept the wag back into its original position. When the enemy tried another blast, she did the same thing, powering into the pulses. Again, she, Doc, Dean and Jak were thrown into the dash. Again, they maintained their position.

"You know I can't keep this up," she said. "If I screw up the timing just once, we're in deep trouble."

"Got get out," Jak said.

"And do what?" Mildred asked him.

"Drop road with them on," Jak told her.

"That would certainly solve our problem," Doc said. "How do you intend to manage it?"

"With these," Jak said, slapping the side plate of the pulse rifle he had picked up from the floorboards. "Undercut road with these. Make it slide into big hole."

"I think our lad has something there, Mildred," Doc said. "The captured longblasters will cut through the supporting strata like hot knives through butter."

"I'll take slaves from cargo box," Jak said. "Go around big hole. Hit road from other side."

"What are the rest of us supposed to do while you're circling?" Mildred said.

"Keep troopers in wags," Jak said. "All go down at once."

With that, the albino teen popped open the passenger door and slipped out. Without a word, Dean, who was sitting beside him, grabbed a pulse rifle from the floor and ducked out behind him.

"Dean! No!" Mildred cried. "Come back!"

The boy either ignored her or couldn't hear her for the scream of the laser cannons that once again pounded the truck's EM shield. As the wag slid backward out of control, Dean ran past the cargo box on Jak's heels. Not only was the boy lightfooted, but he was also frisky and wild with excitement, like a pup who had just evaded righteous punishment.

Jak shouted for the armed slaves to follow them. As six of the former residents of Ground Zero piled over the rear gate of the cargo box, he and Dean sprinted down the road, keeping the wag and its cab's EM shield between them and the enemy cannons. When they reached the point where the sides of the crevasse came together, Jak didn't stop but turned for the shoulder.

"Jak, the cuffs!" Dean shouted.

The albino didn't answer, and he didn't stop.

There was no time to check whether Ryan and J.B. had succeeded in disabling the manacles. No time to drag out a dead body and throw it off the road. To reach the firing location Jak had in mind meant taking a treacherous route over glass. If they didn't reach it as quickly as possible, their effort would have been in vain.

Jak took the offroad plunge in a mad leap, his eyes shut tight.

"Jak!" Dean cried.

Nothing happened.

The teenager landed on the balls of his feet, and his feet remained attached to his ankles. His hands stayed stuck to his wrists. "Ha!" he shouted triumphantly, waving the others on.

Dean jumped off the road, and the armed slaves followed him. Jak took them on an erratic route across the field of glass, dodging the branching surface cracks whenever he could, vaulting over them when he couldn't. The splits were only six feet wide, but they opened onto nothing. One look down told Dean that the chasm continued beneath their feet, that only thin bridges of glass separated them from the abyss.

As they worked their way toward a ridge of rotten glass, its wafer-thin summit like the back fin of some gigantic sailfish, shot through with thousands of holes from a century of windblown grit, they got their first side view of the straightaway. It hung precipitously over the drop-off, sitting atop a two-hundred-foot-long mass of deeply undercut glass.

Looking in that direction was painful.

Mildred, Doc and the slaves in the ore truck were taking hit after hit from the first two assault wags. The green glare of deflected laser pulses was tremendous.

Once Jak, Dean and the slaves moved onto the flat, they came under the cannons of the back pair of assault wags.

The tortured squeals of air ripped asunder arrived a half second after the energy pulses impacted. Even though Jak anticipated the barrage and guided the men around the back side of the ridge, it offered no real cover. The blasts of big-bore laser light burned four-foot-diameter holes through the glass, sending sprays of molten droplets flying. The beams continued on, flat and straight, through the next ridge, seventy-five yards away.

Dean managed to avert his face from the mist of liquefied glass. It sizzled against the back of his coat. Two of the former slaves weren't so lucky. They turned to look at the explosion above them, and the fall of scorching droplets burned through their eyelids and into their eyes. Screaming, hands over their faces, they staggered back the way they had come.

"Stop them!" Dean cried. "Somebody stop them!" When no one moved to help, the boy scrambled up from the glass.

Jak grabbed him by the collar and pulled him back. "No," he said, "can't save."

They watched from the ridge as the blinded, pain-mad men blundered, stumbling into the maze of cracks. First one, then the other was swallowed up by the glass.

"THE BOY WILL BE all right," Doc told Mildred. "What is done is done. Jak will watch over him."

"I'd feel better if he was with us."

The cannons hit the ore wag's EM shield again. Mildred reacted by thumbing the speed button.

"We are going to have to get out," Doc said after their truck had recovered from the impact.

"If we get out," Mildred countered, "they'll push the wag off the road. And we need it for cover."

"May I suggest that you advance up the grade. Halve the distance between ourselves and our enemies. If they persist in firing upon us, that will buy us precious minutes before our chariot is overthrown."

Mildred drove the wag forward seventy-five feet.

"Let's move," she said as she set the brakes, "quick, before they blast us again."

The two of them each seized a pulse rifle from the floor and jumped out of the driver's side of the wag's cab. It was also the cliff side. As they raced to the rear, Mildred glanced into the void. She saw sheer, striated walls angling together five hundred feet down. They met in a bulge of glass that wasn't the bottom of the crevasse, but a second, narrower opening to a much deeper chamber.

As she and Doc climbed up the sides of the cargo box, the wag took another double laser blast. They hung on as the truck slid backward, wheels crunching on the glass. Accompanying the flare of brilliant green light was a wave of withering heat. Something they had not felt inside the protection of the cab.

To the five armed slaves who greeted them in the box, Mildred said, "Use your pulse rifles. We've got to try to keep the troopers in their wags."

As they lined up along the front edge of the box, just above the cab's roof, she knew they had their work cut out for them. The assault wags' EM shields and the soldiers' battlesuits would deflect their laser blasts.

"Shoot at their feet," she told the others. "If they come out, shoot at their feet."

Another blaze of green followed by a blast of heat made them duck back behind the cover of the box. The wag skidded down the road, its rear end twisting closer to the edge.

Then the rear pair of enemy wags opened fire. Not on them, but on Jak and the others, who were sprinting around the end of the chasm. The beams screamed across the road and slammed into the ridge top opposite.

"Bastards!" Mildred said. She popped back up and fired, using a sustained beam to define the limits of the forward wags' EM shields. She had found it, some fifteen feet in front of their bumpers, when a pod on the roof of the left-hand wag opened and a barrel emerged.

"What now?" Doc said.

There was a loud bang and a projectile shot out. It flew almost straight up. It was very slow moving; they could track it easily with their eyes. It arced high over the cab's EM shield, before dropping toward the cargo box.

"Oh, shit," Mildred said, covering her head with her arms.

Then the projectile banged again, disintegrating in midair. As it did, it send a volley of smaller projectiles raining on them. The fléchettes hissed like angry insects, their needlepoints plinking off the blocks of glass, off the rim of the cargo box, and slapping into flesh and bone.

The wounded, Mildred included, cried out in pain. Wincing, she looked at the plastisteel missile embedded in her forearm. It had a fringe of black synthetic feather to make it spin as it fell. The long, thin point was stuck in her flesh only half an inch. She pulled it out and threw it away.

The other slaves who could, did likewise, either yanking the fléchettes out themselves, or if they had been hit in an awkward spot, allowing someone else to remove them. Those already grievously wounded or comatose or dead just lay there like human pincushions.

As the rear wags continued to pound Jak and Dean's position, a loudhailer from one of the lead wags bellowed at them, "Surrender now, throw out your weapons, or you'll get another dose of darts. And they'll be full power next time."

Mildred shouted back a twentieth-century profanity.

She wasn't sure they'd understand it because she didn't know if they had mothers, but they had to have gotten the gist because almost at once another of the slow-flying warheads came arcing their way.

Doc used his pulse rifle to pick it off like a clay pigeon. As it crossed the path of the emerald-green beam, the warhead exploded, sending its deadly fléchettes spraying in all directions but theirs.

When the assault wag tried the same trick again a third time, the warhead had seven green beams to contend with. It blew up at the top of its arc.

"Look!" Doc said. "The wags in back!"

Troopers in black were piling out of the rear doors of both of the wags, clearly heading around the upper end of the crevasse to intercept Jak and Dean and the others.

"Shoot them!" Mildred cried as she sighted down on the running men.

The concentrated fire of seven laser rifles did no good. Their initial shots veered off the EM shields of their targets' battlesuits. The troopers were moving too fast to aim for their feet.

Then the forward wags fired their cannons again.

At the energy flare, the ore wag lurched backward violently, throwing Mildred and Doc onto their butts onto the heap of glass blocks. The wag continued to slide this time, and as it did it twisted sickeningly, turning the unprotected side of the cargo box toward the pair of cannons.

CANNON FIRE FROM the other side of the chasm drove Jak and Dean from the ridge top. Joining up with the four surviving slaves on the back side, the mutie albino said, "Another hundred yards, then we cut away the road."

With Jak in the lead, they ran along the side of the slope, harassing fire from the cannons sending chunks of the ridge avalanching around them. The distance as the buzzard flew was closer to sixty yards, but the ridgeline didn't run straight. It wound back and forth in a serpentine of glassy talus, gaping splits and sheer drop-offs.

Because of the twists and turns, because they were out of sight of the road, they didn't see the troopers coming at them until it was too late.

Jak reacted to a glimpse of black moving among the green-gray blocks of glass on the slope ahead. He jumped aside, taking Dean with him. A flurry of laser beams sliced through the space where the two had just been. They sliced through the man following behind. He toppled, suddenly in five large pieces, arms, legs, head bouncing in different trajectories down the side of the ridge.

The slaves in back of the dead guy dived away and were missed by the through and throughs.

"Aim for ridge above them," Jak shouted to the others. "Drive them back."

It was a stalling action, at best.

They sent energy pulses hammering into the ridge, which melted the glass, and sent it rushing downhill in a torrent. The troopers were unable to fire back because they were too busy retreating from the glass flow. They moved up the side of the slope, trying to get as high as possible to keep the same thing from happening again. They scurried up until their backs were against the brittle fin of eroded glass.

The increased altitude exposed the troopers to the slaves' fire, but they were relying on their battlesuits' EM shields to protect them. The higher elevation gave them much better positions to shoot from. And they put them to use immediately.

Screaming beams bracketed the slave who was farthest down the slope. They melted the glass around him as they sawed through his body. The first slash bisected his torso from right shoulder to left hip. The others chopped him into much smaller pieces. His remains sizzled and smoked along with the bubbling puddle of glass.

"Over the top!" Jak cried. "Everybody goes! Mass your fire, drop the road! I'll cover!"

Dean scrambled up the slope along with the others. Every step they took reduced the angle of advantage the troopers had. Behind him, Dean heard the squeal of Jak's laser rifle returning fire. There was no time to look. He picked his way over the glass rubble near the summit, found a gap in the ridge's fan and threw himself belly down.

Before him, the road stretched out straight. The forward wags were punishing the ore truck, driving it backward toward the abyss with double pulse after double pulse. He could see the people in the cargo box. They fell each time the EM shield was hit. As he shouldered the laser rifle and dropped the safety, the ore wag was hit again and the impact turned it sideways in the road, offering its unprotected flank to direct fire.

Dean pressed the trigger, holding it down as he fanned the point of the green beam over the fattest part of the road's supporting glass. The other slaves opened fire at almost the same instant. Their combined beams melted back the layers of glass, in seconds creating a roaring waterfall more than a hundred feet wide. The entire section of road shifted with a short, shrill shriek that could be heard over the lasers' whine.

Its facing edge dropped down a foot.

Then another, as Dean and the slaves burned back the top of the undercut ledge.

The resulting shriek was lost in a tremendous, ear-splitting crack as the road gave away. In slow motion, the four black wags slipped downward, along with a hundred feet of road and ten thousand tons of nuke-glass rubble. The wags tumbled, crashing against the sides of the chasm.

Dean looked over at the only vehicle remaining on the road, their ore wag. People were standing up in the cargo box, waving their arms excitedly. What they couldn't see, or hadn't noticed was how close they were to the edge of the cave-in.

As he opened his mouth to yell a warning, the road under the uphill side of the wag began to slough off, tipping the box toward the abyss. As the box tilted over, it spilled bodies and ore down into the crevasse. Then, with a groan, it slid off the edge of the road.

"Jak!" Dean howled, looking behind him for the albino.

The albino teen wasn't there. He was hurriedly mopping up the troopers near the ridge. Having dropped big sections of the fan of glass on top of them, he walked among their trapped bodies, removing helmets one by one, and cooking their brains with short, single pulses of his energy weapon. At Dean's shout, he looked over from his grim duty.

"Mildred and Doc!" the boy cried. "What about Mildred and Doc!"

MILDRED AND DOC WATCHED with delight as the road gave way and the attack wags dropped from view.

They were celebrating along with the other slaves as the cargo box began to tip.

"Jump!" she shouted to the others.

Over the grinding roar of the collapsing roadway, no one heard her.

As she jumped to the rim of the box, Doc launched himself ahead of her, stretching to the utmost, his skinny legs churning to reach the lip of solid ground that remained downslope. Mildred landed half on, half off the ledge. Doc turned and pulled her up by her armpits.

Their toes inches from the edge, they looked down into the chasm. Clouds of dust rose up as the ground rumbled underfoot. Like sand through an hourglass, big chunks of glass slipped through the dark slot below them. Bodies slipped through them, too, limp bodies cartwheeling into the void. The wags themselves were too big to fall through. They lay wedged between the edges of the second crevasse.

The ore wag was upside down. Three of its wheels had been broken off by the fall.

Everyone in the cargo box was gone.

As Doc and Mildred watched, a side door to one of the assault wags opened and three tiny human figures crawled out. Some of the troopers had survived, but there was nowhere safe for them to stand outside their crumpled wag. Their weight caused the precariously balanced jumble of blocks to move. And when the blocks shifted, they opened new routes to the yawning emptiness below.

With a grinding roar, the three troopers and a wide section of rubble vanished.

If more of the enemy were alive, they didn't show themselves.

From the opposite side of the chasm came a shout. Jak's white mane of hair was unmistakable. He waved them around the lower end of the crevasse, then pointed to the upper end.

"It appears that we are to rejoin the road above the slide," Doc said.

"We'd better get a move on," Mildred stated. "We've got a long, hot walk ahead of us."

Chapter Twenty-Eight

Dredda herself supervised the towing of the last two gyroplanes into position inside the pink-flagged transport field. Between the twin fifty-foot-long trailers that housed the trans-reality units was an ellipse of vital gear, most of it self-propelled or at least mobile. When the gyros were parked in their assigned places, she gestured impatiently for the wag drivers to exit their vehicles.

The drivers were men, and they weren't coming along.

She ordered her sisters to start up the reality-field generators. When the switches were pulled, a low hum emanated from both of the trailers, and the air just in front of and between them seemed to shimmer and blur.

That's when the trouble started.

The troopers stood anxiously outside the perimeter of pink flags. The she-hes stood inside it, resolute, with gauntleted hands on their genetically engineered hips. Until that moment, it hadn't occurred to the troopers that they weren't invited to the next party.

As Dredda locked down her helmet, Mero burst from the doorway of the big dome. She had her battlesuit on and carried her helmet under her arm. Mero rushed up and said, "Shadow Man is here. He freed the red-haired bitch. They're loose in the compound."

None of that mattered anymore. They were in countdown mode.

"Put on your helmet," Dredda told her. "We're about to make the jump."

"What about us?" one of the troopers demanded, his voice painfully loud inside her helmet.

She turned down the volume.

"You're not leaving us here!" the man insisted. "We'll all die from the bacteria!"

The other troopers shouted their agreement.

Dredda keyed her com link to her sisters. "Be ready for them when they charge," she said. "We don't have time to play, now. We must finish the job quickly."

As the men rushed forward, the sisters stepped through the shimmering curtain to meet them.

The job in question was hand to hand because the EM shields of both sides' battlesuits rendered lasers useless, even at close quarters. The men were no match for the she-hes in either physical strength or in stamina. The disease the invaders had brought with them had affected all of them more or less equally. If the sisters were weakened, so were the men. And it didn't matter that the troopers outnumbered their opponents more than two to one.

Dredda joined her sisters in the fight. She couldn't have stopped herself even if she'd wanted to. Through the cleared visors of their helmets, Dredda could see the rage on the faces of the two troopers who attacked her, the rage and the blood lust. They wanted more than a free ride, more than to merely save their lives. They wanted to reassert their masculinity.

It was a sad commentary.

Dredda short-punched the first trooper, ending the blow with a savage twist of the wrist. The breastplate of his armor buckled inward, and there was a loud snapping sound. Her fist had shattered his breastbone, and from the way he dropped, as if all his strings had been cut, the sharp ends of imploding bone had torn his heart to shreds.

The second trooper wheeled around the body of the first, trying to come at her from the side. Dredda let him come, offering him an undefended right hip. The trooper swung a kick into the small of her back. From his expression and the loud grunt he made, it had everything he could put behind it. She absorbed the blow easily, letting it drive her a half step forward, then shifted her weight and kicked, herself. Her heel came down in a slashing arc against the side of his helmet. The helmet cracked.

It cracked in a circle of spider-shattered plastisteel. The shock of the impact killed the man, like a sledgehammer to the side of the head.

Dredda took a moment to look around the field of battle. Her sisters were acquitting themselves splendidly. Jann held a trooper overhead, a hand on his suit collar and a hand on his crotch, then dropped his back onto her upraised knee. His battlesuit didn't protect him. The cracking of his spine resounded like a gunshot across the compound. Other sisters pounded their opponents into the beige dust, snapped their arm and leg bones and then finished them off with elbow strikes to the heart.

Only Mero seemed to be having trouble. Three troopers surrounded her, and although they couldn't bring her down, Mero couldn't defeat any of them, either.

It was the disease, Dredda thought as she closed the distance between them. It had to be the disease. Poor Mero had a more advanced stage.

One of the troopers turned away from the three-on-one attack in time to glimpse the battlesuited figure bearing down on him. He didn't have time to get out of the way, or to avoid the hands that gripped his helmet. Dredda used both arms and the power in her legs to crank him off his feet, sending him spiraling sideways across the compound. His windmill flight ended at the feet of two other sisters, who immediately took charge of him.

Dredda stomped the nearest trooper's kneecap, and despite the overlapping plates of his battlesuit, the knee crunched and bent inward in a way it was never intended to bend. The trooper fell, screaming to the dirt, and Dredda fell upon him, launching a snap-kick to the middle of his visor. Again, the helmet cracked like an eggshell thumped by the back of a spoon. Gore spewed over the inside of the visor, but not before Dredda got a good look at the dead man's face. One eye stared up; the other stared toward the flattened ruin of his nose.

Mero caught hold of the last trooper and, as they tussled, face-to-face, knocked him down with a leg sweep. Before he could roll away from her, she jumped in the air and came down on her right knee, which landed in the middle of his chest. The battlesuit torso plates buckled with a crunch, and her knee drove deep into his chest cavity, taking with it the splintered remains of his sternum and rib cage. The trooper struggled for a moment more, then became still.

Dredda reached out a hand and helped Mero up. The compound had one-third as many standing figures as it had a few seconds before. All but one of them were sisters.

Dr. Huth, also in a battlesuit, hurriedly crossed the open space as Dredda and the others moved back into the trans-reality field. He pushed a tall, silver cylinder on wheels before him. Of all the males, Dr. Huth was the only one of any use to them; the only one worth the fuel to bring along.

Huth wheeled the tank through the shimmering curtain and set it down beside Dredda, who stood at the head of the line of sisters.

As the field built in power, a whirlwind whipped the dirt inside the marker stakes and the air was choked with a nauseating petrochemical stench. The lips of reality appeared, a seam in space and time that gaped around them like a giant, hungry mouth. Dredda took a last look around. They were leaving so much behind, so much wrecked gear, so much potential. But there were still ten sisters and they had the keys to a million other worlds.

A fraction of a second before the thundercrack that announced their departure, through the swirling eddies of space-time, Dredda saw Ryan Cawdor emerge from the big dome. He wore a battlesuit without a helmet, and next to him was his red-haired lover. Her last image of this reality was his fierce and confident smile.

Shadow Man had won.

Deathlands had won.

But Dredda was taking part of both with her. The silver cylinder by her side held Ryan's potent seed.

Let the futures tremble.

Chapter Twenty-Nine

Ryan, Krysty and J.B. climbed up from the Slake City encampment, up the long grade to the end of the road's first rise. Though they had defeated the enemy, driven them from their world, this was a journey of dread. Not only because they were once again forced to venture into the nukeglass sea, but because they didn't know which, if any, of their loved ones they would find alive at their journey's end. They might walk all the way to Ground Zero just to dig a mass grave.

When they reached the top of the rise, the dread vanished. It disappeared when they saw a row of figures climbing toward them, out of the nuke's crater.

Recognizing his father, Dean broke away from the file and ran up the hill. Tossing down his laser rifle, the boy threw his arms around Ryan and hugged him hard.

"It's okay, son," Ryan said, mussing the boy's hair. "Everything's okay now."

When the rest of the former slaves came close enough for Ryan to do a head count, his expression of joy faded. As Mildred, Jak and Doc joined them, he said, "This is all that's left?"

"All that survived the trip from Ground Zero," Mildred said. She looked exhausted. "There's just the eight of us. We got hit hard, but we returned the favor. None of the troopers they sent out are ever coming back.''

"We heard big bang," Jak said.

"That was the she-hes saying bye-bye," J.B. told him. "They cranked up their trans-reality gear and disappeared into thin air. They left a lot of dead troopers behind, though.''

"Will they be back?" Dean said.

"Let's hope not," Krysty replied.

Doc looked down the slope. "It appears the she-hes have abandoned their domes, as well. Perhaps in their haste they left some food behind? I am ravenous.''

"There's food down there," J.B. said, "but I guarantee you won't want to eat most of it. Strangest radblasted mixtures you ever saw. The stuff needs to be buried in a deep hole.''

The companions and the four former slaves started down the slope to the encampment. They were about halfway there, when Jak said, "Somebody coming.''

He pointed at a dust cloud whirling its way across the plain, over the rough track in the direction of the Slake City compound. The companions watched it approach in silence for a moment. As the vehicle drew closer, through the haze of swirling dust it raised, they could make out the gaudy neon colors of the magic bus.

"I'll bet the bastard's got himself another load of doped-up slaves for Ground Zero," Krysty said.

"I guess this means we're not quite done here, yet," Ryan said.

"That bastard's in for a big surprise when he pulls

up and finds the she-hes long gone and us in their place,'' J.B. added.

"I foresee a most delightful and well-deserved welcoming party," Doc said. "If you will excuse my rudeness, dear friends, I must hurry ahead to the camp. I need to locate my swordstick. I intend to put it to excellent use momentarily.''

TAKE 'EM FREE

2 action-packed novels plus a mystery bonus

NO RISK
NO OBLIGATION TO BUY